ALSO BY STEPHANIE DIAZ

*Extraction*
*Rebellion*

# EVOLUTION

## STEPHANIE DIAZ

St. Martin's Griffin
New York

This is a work of fiction. All of the characters, organizations, and events portrayed in this novel are either products of the author's imagination or are used fictitiously.

The Library of Congress Cataloging-in-Publication Data is available upon request.

ISBN 978-1-250-04126-5 (hardcover)
ISBN 978-1-4668-3737-9 (e-book)

Our books may be purchased in bulk for promotional, educational, or business use.
Please contact your local bookseller or the Macmillan Corporate and
Premium Sales Department at (800) 221-7945, extension 5442, or by
e-mail at MacmillanSpecialMarkets@macmillan.com.

First Edition: September 2015

10  9  8  7  6  5  4  3  2  1

*For Matthew,*
*because you were right*

# EVOLUTION

# 1

Marden's warships drop from the sky like falling stars.

My view of them is partially obstructed by the snow-peaked mountains looming over the valley where I came against my will with Sam and his men to destroy the Alliance compound. Mere minutes ago we were escaping the compound as the tunnels blew apart behind us. We barely made it out in time, only to find the dots of warships up among the stars, descending from the fleet of battle stations settling into orbit just beyond Kiel's atmosphere.

The warships are so small from far away, I can almost trick myself into believing they're nothing more than a swarm of buzzards. Harmless.

If only that were true. The fleet carries passengers aboard, aliens from the planet Marden. Enemies that were thought to be long gone, who've crossed the universe to restart the old war between our races. Judging by the size of their fleet, they've brought a formidable army.

Not long ago, when I was still under the influence of Commander Charlie's serum, trapped in my own body and unable to disobey his orders, part of me prayed the Mardenites would arrive early. That part wanted them to put an end to my fight against Charlie and the other leaders of the planet, because I've been fighting and losing for too long.

At least if Marden's warriors wiped us out, the Developers who rule Kiel would finally be defeated. The suffering I've known since the day I was born in an internment camp would end. All of this would be over.

But as I watch the Mardenites invade the acid sky from their battle stations, I feel no relief. All I feel is terror.

After I was Extracted from an internment camp on the Surface and told I would live a safe life in the Core, I was naïve enough to believe Commander Charlie was my salvation. But the Core wasn't what it appeared to be and Charlie had terrifying ulterior motives. He tried to use me to betray my friends, but I fought back. He became my worst enemy, the reason I was fighting for my life and lost so much.

Just as he was beginning to show weakness the Mardenites reappeared, and they are a much bigger threat. The last time humans fought them, our army attempted to steal their home and enslave their people. Marden's warriors struck back by planting a machine on the moon that bled acid into our atmosphere. We survived by building cities underground and a force field in the sky to deflect the moon's acid, but we only just managed to destroy the machine on the moon.

With the Mardenites' life span lasting hundreds of years, they've had time to wait, plan, and design powerful weapons. And now when Kiel is at its weakest they have come to attack. Not only to ensure humans can no longer threaten their kind, but also because we took something from them during the last war, something that Charlie has kept secret. The Mardenites believe we murdered their old leader, a being they considered the god of their people, and for that they won't stop until they've destroyed every last citizen.

Even if Commander Charlie finds a way to save himself and his precious citizens in the Core, I don't know how my friends and I will survive a war. The Alliance is weak and scattered throughout the sectors. The old military compound that was the headquarters of our rebellion is in ruins, and those of us who escaped its demolition have nowhere safe to run. The Developers rule the cities belowground and a new enemy descends from the sky. Anywhere we go we'll stumble straight into the path of destruction.

Despite this, every cell in my body rages, screams the same thing: *I can't give up. I need to keep fighting.*

I need to find a way to survive.

Beechy lands our X-wing in a forest clearing close to the river. The trees around the clearing grow dense and gnarled, nearly as tall as buildings, blocking out much of the moonlight. Hopefully they'll also block us from the view of enemy ships passing overhead.

The cover of the X-wing opens and freezing wind rushes inside, making me shiver in my safety suit. I'd give anything to be back in the Alliance compound, tucked into a warm bed in one of the bunkrooms with Logan beside me under the covers. My head would rest against his shoulder and he would hold me close as we slept, guarding me from the people who would harm us. The invasion by Marden's army would seem like just a bad dream.

But I can't go back there. The cots, showers, and training rooms were blasted apart and buried beneath the mountain by Sam and his troops. The one place I felt truly safe in the world is gone.

In the seat behind me, Lieutenant Dean unbuckles his seat belt and gets to his feet. "The Mardenite raiders look like they're headed for these mountains," he says.

I follow his gaze beyond the treetops. Before we landed, the smaller Mardenite warships were splitting up into groups, probably to target different locations on the Surface at once. I'm sure many of them will target the city on the other side of the Surface. The city where thousands of innocent child workers, including my friend Nellie, are trapped as bait with bombs implanted in their bodies. Commander Charlie plans to detonate the bombs in the hope of crippling Marden's army. I thought I still had time to convince him his plan wouldn't work and make him pull the child workers out of the city. But Marden's army arrived two days early, and now there's nothing I can do to save them.

Now, the survival of the Alliance rebels and myself takes priority. Most of the groups of Mardenite raiders have passed out of sight, but one is still visible high above the mountain peaks, tiny warships descending through the clouds. At least twenty, thirty in this swarm. They're still far away, but they already look closer than they did a few minutes ago. They must be moving fast.

As long as we keep our X-wing powered down with the lights off, the forest should conceal us if any raiders fly over the valley. But we can't stay here long. With the Alliance base destroyed, we have hardly any supplies and no fortified hideout. We wouldn't last more than a few days exposed out here in the mountains, and it's likely the raiders would discover us sooner than that. We need to get ourselves off the Surface as quickly as possible.

"How far is Sam's hovercraft?" I ask.

"Just through those trees." Beechy's voice sounds muffled through his helmet. It doesn't help that my left ear is still plugged up after my eardrum ruptured during explosions in the Crust camp; it could take months to heal, months for me to hear clearly again. Beechy points to the east, in the opposite direction of the river. "Maybe fifty yards."

That's where Sam and his troops were headed after they fled Alliance headquarters. The hovercraft is their passage back to the Core, though the invasion of Marden's army will slow down their departure.

The Core is the farthest sector from the Surface. It's where we'll all be safest from the fleet and where we can organize ourselves against Marden's army. It's where I need to go in order to convince Commander Charlie to let Logan and the rest of the Alliance prisoners go.

Sam is the last person I want to rely on for help. He targeted me and tried to take advantage of me because I outperformed him in soldier training exercises in the Core. His hatred for me has only grown stronger since then, and now I've gone and shot him. But his hovercraft has a medical facility to treat our wounded, and more supplies than we have aboard the X-wing. If we end up trapped out here for more than a night, or if bombs start raining down, we'll have the best chance of surviving aboard Sam's hovercraft.

We must survive, even if it means allying with the person I'd very much like to kill.

"Then let's get moving," I say.

I swing my legs over the side of the X-wing and hop down into the grass. The jolt of landing worsens the throbbing in my arm where I was struck with a laser by one of Sam's soldiers. Wincing, I press my hand against the wetness of blood on my sleeve. I feel a bit faint, and my heartbeat seems irregular. Signs my body is experiencing mild shock from the injury. But I can't let it slow me down. I can't rest until we reach the hovercraft.

"You all right?" Dean asks, his boots squelching in the mud as he joins me on the ground.

He touches my shoulder to steady me, and I stiffen. He might've assisted Beechy and me in our escape from the Alliance compound, but that doesn't mean I trust him. I haven't forgotten how he knocked me unconscious when I was undercover in the Crust camp a few days ago. How he stood by and watched while Commander Charlie injected me with a serum that took away my free will and turned me into a mindless, obedient soldier, and did nothing.

"I'm fine," I say, pulling away from him. Immediately I regret it, as the movement worsens the pain in my arm.

Dean's gaze becomes stony, but he doesn't argue. He tramps a few feet away from me, toward the back end of the X-wing, pulling a small device out of his pocket. It looks like a computer chip.

"What are you doing?" I ask, still clutching my arm.

"Putting a disabling device on the X-wing's transmitter, so it can't release any signal that could give away our location." He disappears around the backside of the ship.

I turn to Beechy, who's climbing out of the pilot seat. "Could the Mardenites have picked up our signal before we landed?"

"It's not likely, since they're still far away," he says. "But we'll know soon enough."

Beechy pauses to catch his bearings on the ground. His eyes

slide to mine and stay there, emotions flickering through them. Words we haven't had time to say. We haven't had a real conversation for days, not since before the Alliance infiltrated the lower sectors and he and I were separated. He was captured before I was, and I spent two days in the Crust camp wondering if he was dead or alive. After I was caught and taken to the Core, I found out he was alive but no longer himself. We were both injected with Commander Charlie's serum and sent on this mission against our will.

We have a lot to catch up on, but not until we're somewhere safer than out here.

Beechy turns back to the transport. Uma, the nurse who was stationed in the Alliance compound, is sitting up in the copilot seat. Her shaky arms prop up the limp body of Sandy—Beechy's wife, one of the Alliance leaders.

It's too dark for me to see Sandy well, but I can hear the weakness of her breath as she tries to suck in air. The last time I got a good look at her, the blood seeping from her pregnant belly had already soaked through the cloth Uma was using to keep pressure on her wound.

Sandy took a bad hit back at the compound. I saw her moving into the path of the fire, and I tried to stop her. I wasn't fast enough.

"How's she doing?" Beechy's voice is uneven. I'm amazed how well he's keeping it together, given how badly his wife was hurt.

"She's hanging in there," Uma says, sounding anxious too, "but she's lost a lot of blood. There's not much I can do for her without any supplies."

There wasn't time for any of us to grab anything from the compound, not even a medi-kit. I was lucky I still had my gun in my hand, or Dean would've been the only one of us with a weapon.

One of Dean's boots snaps a stick in the grass as he returns from the backside of the X-wing. "There's an infirmary aboard Sam's hovercraft. His medic should be able to stabilize Sandy until we get her to a surgeon in the Core."

Beechy's body is rigid with worry, and I can tell he's struggling to keep it together. I bet he's thinking the same thing I am: Who knows how long it will be until we reach the Core? If the Mardenites bomb the valley, we might not make it back at all.

But there's nothing we can do except take things one step at a time. First we get to the hovercraft. Then we'll worry about getting off the Surface.

Clenching his fists, Beechy moves closer to the side of the X-wing. "Here, hand her down to me."

Uma carefully lowers Sandy's half-unconscious form into his arms. She stirs a little, a soft moan escaping her lips, her eyes fluttering open. She looks like she's trying to say Beechy's name, but her lips are having difficulty forming the word.

"You're gonna be okay," Beechy says, his voice so soft, so fragile, I feel like I'm intruding on a private moment between the two of them. "I've got you."

Sandy's eyes slowly close again, and her head flops against his chest.

I remember the first time I saw them together, before I knew Sandy was Commander Charlie's daughter, or that she and Beechy were secretly plotting an insurrection. We were in a hallway in the Core maternity ward, and they'd just found out Sandy was pregnant. I'd never seen two people so happy before. They couldn't stop smiling and hugging each other.

Nothing in the Core had turned out the way I'd expected before I was picked for Extraction. The freedom I thought I'd won had turned out to be another series of tests to prove I was strong, intelligent, and obedient enough to be kept alive. I was terrified I wasn't going to pass. But Beechy and Sandy gave me hope things could get better. They've given me hope time and time again, and saved me more times than I can count. I owe it to them to return the favor.

"Clementine, take this," Uma says from her seat in the X-wing. She's holding out the bloody rag.

Swallowing hard, I hurry forward and take it from her. "What do I do?"

"Put pressure on her wound until I get down."

I quickly press the rag against Sandy's stomach. But there's so much blood seeping through Sandy's uniform, my slippery hands can barely hold the rag steady. The baby growing inside her . . . how can it still be alive after an injury like this?

For Beechy's sake, I hope we'll make it to the medic in time to save both of them.

Once Uma climbs down from the X-wing, she grabs the rag from me and takes over. I'm grateful; the stench of blood is making my stomach uneasy. I step back a few feet and inhale fresher air through my nose. But the nausea doesn't go away. My light-headedness is also getting worse.

"Everyone ready?" Dean asks behind me.

"As ready as we'll ever be," Beechy says. "Let's get this over with."

Dean draws his weapon, so I pull my copper out of its holster. It's not like a laser gun will do any significant damage in the face of a raider attack, but holding the weapon makes me feel stronger. It reminds me I'm in control of my hands again, no longer a slave to Commander Charlie's orders. Capable of fighting to save the people I care about.

"This way," Dean says, turning and tramping toward the eastern side of the forest.

Before the rest of us can follow him, there's a *whirring* sound overhead, somewhere in the sky behind us. Panic rushes through my veins like a stream of icy fire.

*Raiders.*

I whip around, raising my gun. It can't be them. They can't be here already.

A flight pod hovers into view above the trees. Floodlights beam down on us, blinding me.

"It's the others!" Uma says. "The Alliance survivors."

It takes me a minute to realize who she means: Darren and Fiona. The other rebels who escaped from the Alliance compound. We lost contact with them after the transmitters aboard the Mardenite ships interfered with our comm system. But they shouldn't have been far behind us. They could've seen us land.

Still, I hold my gun steady as the flight pod lowers onto the grass. We need to be sure it's them.

The engine sputters and dies. A few moments later, the side door opens and two figures stagger out: Fiona, one of my old roommates when I stayed in the compound, and Darren, an Alliance pilot. The two of them slowly make their way toward us, Darren leaning on Fiona for support. His pant leg is bloodied and he struggles to keep his composure with every step.

"Don't shoot," Darren says. "It's us."

I lower my gun. "Are you okay?"

"We're alive," Fiona says. Through her helmet visor, her tan cheeks are flushed and strands of her black hair stick to her sweaty forehead. "So I guess we're lucky."

Their flight pod was nearly out of fuel. We weren't sure they were going to make it out of the compound at all.

Beechy looks past them to the pod. A third rebel was supposed to be with them. "Where's James?"

"We lost him back at headquarters," says Fiona. "We hoped he was with you."

Heavy silence fills the air. He's not with us. Unless he somehow made it onto one of the other ships, he went down with the facility.

I hardly knew James, but I was aware of him because he was one of the rebels Beechy and Sandy sprung from Karum prison when they rescued me. I was only locked away there for a few weeks, but James had been there for too many years to count. He'd lost sight in one of his eyes due to the experiments the prison doctors had performed on him. He joined the Alliance to fight the people who'd sent him to Karum—Commander Charlie and the other Developers.

"I'm sorry about your friend," Dean says. "But the raiders are coming in fast. We need to move."

The heaviness lingers for another moment. But Dean's right. There will be time to mourn the people we lost, but not until we've escaped Marden's army.

As Dean leads the way into the forest, thunder rolls in the distance. I lift my eyes to the sky. The clouds are moving in steadily over the mountains in thick clusters that can only mean a storm. The dots of Mardenite raiders are growing bigger by the second, still on a course that could bring them close to the valley. The question is whether they'll notice we're here, or whether they'll pass by overhead.

We're dealing with a new enemy, an alien no human has dealt with in combat for hundreds of years. We can't predict their moves, or know exactly what they want from us.

All we can do is try to be ready.

# 2

Light raindrops are pattering on my helmet by the time we spot Sam's hovercraft through the trees. The massive transport looms a few yards ahead of us in the darkness, its curved roof nearly level with the treetops. The shapes of the X-wings Sam and his troops used to invade Alliance headquarters are visible to the left of the hovercraft.

Blood is still flowing from the wound in my arm; the laser must've struck an artery. I touch the tree branches for support, still breathing through my nose to combat my light-headedness and uneasy stomach. We're almost to an infirmary with emergency supplies to treat shock from blood loss. I just need to make it a little farther.

As we near the hovercraft, I make out figures in the rain. Soldiers march between the X-wings and the hovercraft in both directions, some of them lugging cargo, others wielding pulse rifles.

"What's the plan?" Fiona asks, helping Darren limp-walk ahead of me. "We can't exactly fight our way aboard the hovercraft."

"We're not fighting them," Beechy says, a bit breathless from carrying Sandy all this way. But his jaw is hardened and his voice is steadier now; he sounds more like the man who broke me out of prison and led the Alliance into battle. A man determined to get what he wants. "We're going to make a bargain. We'll help Sam and his troops evade the raiders in exchange for him treating our wounded."

"A truce," Darren says. He accidentally puts too much weight on his hurt leg, and winces. "For how long?"

"Until we're safely in the Core."

"And then what?" Fiona asks. "We'll be prisoners, won't we?"

"We'll deal with that after we escape the Mardenites," Beechy says stiffly.

I have no intention of letting Commander Charlie throw us in prison cells upon our arrival. I'll convince him he needs our help to defeat Marden's army. I'll make him release Logan and pardon the other rebels. I'll do whatever it takes.

But Beechy's right—there's no use worrying until we've evaded the Mardenite raiders and made it off the Surface. One enemy at a time.

"And if Sam doesn't agree to a truce?" Fiona asks, holding a hand up to shield her helmet visor from the rain. It's coming down harder now.

"He will," Lieutenant Dean says, knocking branches out of his way at the front of our group. "He can't let Commander Charlie's daughter go untreated when she's dying. And with the raiders coming, he'll need Beechy's help piloting the hovercraft. Sam will see reason. Trust me."

I press my lips together, watching Dean tramp through the trees ahead of us. The trouble is, I don't trust him. He hasn't denied that he's on Commander Charlie's side, and he hasn't told us why he's helping us stay alive. There's a good chance he's still following Charlie's orders, working toward some end goal I can't see.

Right now it doesn't matter, though. Trusting him is our only choice.

"Stay close," Dean says when we reach the edge of the forest. "Put your weapons away and let me do the talking."

I slip my copper into my holster so it won't be visible. But I keep my hand close in case I need to quickly pull it out. I've dealt with Sam enough times to know there's a good chance this won't go according to plan.

One by one, Beechy and the others step out into the clearing. A fierce wave of dizziness washes over me as I follow them. I stumble a little, grabbing on to the last tree in my path to steady myself. *You're okay. Just breathe.*

We're almost to the hovercraft. The boarding ramp is straight ahead, only there are soldiers in our path. Three of them are already running toward us, hoisting their guns to eye level. They must've been expecting us.

"Alliance rebels," a soldier says. "Halt right there."

"Stand down," Dean says. "That's not how you address a commanding officer."

The soldier's eyes flit to the golden moon pinned to the chest of Dean's armor, and he falters. But he doesn't lower his weapon. "Lieutenant Dean. We didn't know if you made it out of the compound."

"Take the rebels aboard the ship," Dean says. "Get the commander's daughter in the sick bay. That's an order."

"We were given orders to take them to Lieutenant Sam if they arrived, sir."

"Lieutenant Sam is aboard the hovercraft, correct?"

"That's correct."

Dean steps forward. He looks menacing in all his armor. "So take them aboard the ship. I'll speak with the lieutenant myself."

After a long moment, the second soldier nods to the first, and both of them lower their weapons. They move to either side of our group, herding us after Dean toward the boarding ramp.

My vision's blurring around the edges, and I can barely stand up straight anymore. *Just a few more steps.*

Someone's coming down the ramp. His lankiness and the golden moon pinned to his armor, displaying his lieutenant rank, tell me immediately who he is: Sam.

He freezes when he sees us. So does the soldier accompanying him. Skylar's helmet hides her blond hair and the lower half of her face from view, but her short stature and the fierceness in her eyes give her away.

The traitor. She used to be a pilot for the Alliance, but she was working for Commander Charlie all along.

"Lieutenant," Dean says, giving Sam a quick salute. "We have the rebels. I'm taking their wounded to the sick bay, with your permission."

Sam takes another slow step. There's a limp in his gait and a dark stain on the side of his pant leg that must be blood. Clearly I did some damage when I shot him back at Alliance headquarters. But he's still breathing, so it wasn't enough.

His gaze sweeps over the group of us, cold and calculating, coming to rest on me. "You have permission to take the commander's daughter to the sick bay. Lock the rest of them in the brig."

He's been looking for an excuse to hurt me again—he told me so earlier tonight, before we entered the Alliance compound with his troops. I'd been turned into the perfect obedient soldier under the control of the Developers' serum, but he still saw me as a threat. He wanted me out of his way. Since he didn't manage to kill me during the fight, locking me up is his next best option.

"We want to bargain for a truce," Beechy says swiftly. "We'll help you face the Mardenite raiders if you let us remain free until we reach the Core, and if you treat our wounded. I'm sure you could use three more pilots and a ship mechanic—"

"I have no interest in bargaining with traitors," Sam says, cutting off Beechy. He looks at the soldiers behind us. "Take them away."

A soldier grabs my arm from behind—my wounded one. The pain spreads hot and fast, but I'm too weak to pull away from him. Another soldier grabs Darren and another takes Fiona by the wrists, who looks like she might punch Sam in the face.

"Listen to me," Beechy says, his voice rising in frustration. "Did you see how many warships are heading for the mountains? We shouldn't be arguing about this. We should be figuring out what we're going to do if they attack, and how we're going to get off the Surface."

Skylar clears her throat behind Sam. "With all due respect, sir, I could use Beechy's help piloting the hovercraft. And Fiona might be able to get the comms working again between our ships."

I stare at her, unable to believe she's actually arguing for our side. But Sam looks so enraged, I'm not sure he's going to listen to reason.

"Sam," I manage to croak. "Please."

He turns his eyes on me again, glaring. "Get them inside the ship."

The soldier pushes me forward, up the boarding ramp.

I'm dimly aware of Dean saying something to Sam, something that makes Sam look even more furious. But I don't hear what he says. The pain in my arm consumes me, and everything turns hazy again.

*Keep going,* I urge myself. But I can't.

Another wave of dizziness rushes over me, and this time my strength gives out completely. Darkness spreads across my vision.

A body breaks my fall, and it's the last thing I remember.

I swim back into consciousness, with no idea where I am. I can feel I'm lying on a padded table with a blanket over me. A haze of blue light glows above me, and there's a strong antiseptic smell in the air.

I must be aboard the hovercraft, in the infirmary. There are voices coming from beyond the foot of the table I'm lying on.

"I don't like this," a person who sounds like Beechy says.

"Neither do I," a deeper voice replies. Lieutenant Dean. "But it's too late for that now."

Their voices are hushed so I pretend I'm still asleep and listen.

"We just need to keep her as safe as we can until we get to the Core," Dean says. "She's our best hope for survival."

Who are they talking about? Sandy?

"Will you help me?" Dean asks.

"Fine," Beechy says. "I'll do what I can."

"Good. I'll send someone for you as soon as we call the strategy meeting," Dean says. There's the sound of his boots clunking out of the room, and the hiss of a hatch door shutting behind him.

I open my eyes again and look around the room. The infirmary is small, with counters and cabinets lining the walls. There's a door to my left, probably leading to a storage closet. Beechy stands with his back to me near the foot of my bed, by the hatch door leading out of the infirmary. He's still wearing his safety suit, but he's taken the helmet off and he's running his fingers through his dark hair. When he turns around, I see hardness flickering across his expression. Annoyance at what he and Dean were discussing, or something else?

"What's going on?" I ask. My voice is weak from exhaustion.

Beechy startles, but quickly regains his composure. "Hey," he says, walking around to the side of my bed. His forehead creases with concern. "How are you feeling?"

I hesitantly move my right arm, which someone bandaged in my sleep. There's still a dull ache where the laser seared my skin, but the pain is a lot less than it was earlier. And I don't feel light-headed anymore.

"Better," I say, exhaling in relief. "How long was I out?"

"Not long," Beechy says. "Twenty minutes. We're still in the valley."

My stomach clenches. Twenty minutes isn't long, but it could've been enough time for the Mardenites to put the first wave of their attack into motion. They could've discovered the city on the other side of the Surface by now—all the thousands of people trapped there could already be wiped out. Or they will be soon. Commander Charlie wasn't on the Surface when hundreds and hundreds of raiders poured out of the battle stations; he doesn't realize sacrificing everyone in the city won't cripple even half of Marden's fleet.

The longer we take to get to the Core and convince him to put a different defensive strategy into motion, the more innocent people will die.

"What happened to the raiders that were heading this way?" I ask.

"We don't know." Beechy sighs. "We haven't had a visual of their location since just before we reached the hovercraft, because of the storm. They didn't get close enough for our radar to pick them up, so we have no idea which way they went."

Since they didn't target the valley, they must not know we're here yet. We should leave while we still can.

I sit up too quickly, and the dizziness rushes back.

Beechy grabs my shoulders to steady me. "Careful. You were hit pretty bad back at the compound. You need to take it easy."

"I'm fine," I say, though it's a lie. I'm exhausted and I want to sleep until the pain in my arm goes away. But there isn't time. "We can't stay here. We need to get to the Core."

"I agree," Beechy says. "Sam's about to call a strategy meeting so we can discuss our options and work out a plan."

"What needs to be worked out?"

The plan seems simple to me: we depart immediately and take the shortest route to the Pipeline—the entrance to the lower sectors—keeping the hovercraft and the X-wings in a defensive flight formation. There's not much more we can do to prepare, since we hardly know the enemy we're dealing with. We'll be going in blind no matter what we do.

Beechy rubs his temple. "Well, some of the soldiers—including Sam—are afraid to leave until we've managed to make contact with flight control in the Core and let them know our situation. They'd be able to direct us on a clear flight path to the Pipeline. And there's some hope they could also send us back up from a Core squadron. The radio signal is still facing serious interference from the electrical systems aboard the Mardenite fleet, but Fiona's working on trying to patch it. We could set up a temporary camp here until she's finished. The problem is, it could take hours."

In a few hours, it'll be daylight, which will make it much easier for the raiders to spot us, even with the trees providing cover. Setting up camp here is not a permanent solution.

"Even if we're able to make contact with someone in the Core, it would take too long for help to get here," I say. "It's not just about us, Beechy. It's about the other people on the Surface. Every minute we stay here, more people die."

"I know." Beechy's cheeks pinch together. He was there at the meeting where Commander Charlie explained how he planned to put all those child workers in the city and detonate the bombs inside them to save the rest of Kiel. Beechy saw how big the fleet is; he knows the plan isn't going to save us. "We need to leave tonight. Dean and Skylar are on my side. We just need to get Sam and the other pilots to agree."

"You're working with Skylar?" I can't keep the accusation out of my voice. Even though she argued with Sam on our behalf, and she was the person who warned us Marden's army had arrived in the first place, there's no way that makes up for all the other times she betrayed us. I can't forgive her for pretending she was part of the Alliance, acting like she was my friend when she was spying for Commander Charlie the whole time. He didn't inject her with any serum, but she still gave him every Alliance name and other bit of information he wanted. I can't forgive her for helping him break into our headquarters and capture everyone inside.

"Yes," Beechy says, quite calmly. "I know what she did, and I know we can't trust her. But right now she can help us get out of here. So, yes, I'm going to work with her. I suggest you do the same."

How can I possibly get along with Skylar? I don't trust her at all.

Although, as much as I hate to admit it, there are ways she could still be useful. She's a liar and a traitor, but she's also one of the best pilots I've ever met. And Sam is far more likely to listen to her than to us. Beechy's right; we need her on our side, in some capacity, however much I can't stand the thought of playing nice with her.

"Can't promise I'll be able to, but I'll try," I say. I push off the blanket and notice my weapon holster is empty. Sam must've taken my gun. I guess I should be thankful that's all he did instead of throwing me and the other rebels in the brig, like he wanted. "How come Sam didn't lock us up?"

"Dean convinced him this is the smartest strategy. He's agreed to set aside our differences and work together to escape the Mardenites, for now." Beechy's gaze drifts past me.

I still want to know what he and Dean were talking about before I woke up. But he seems distracted, troubled by something.

My stomach pinches as I remember. "Where's Sandy?"

"With Uma. She and the ship doctor are performing emergency surgery in the other room."

I follow his gaze to the door on my left, the one I thought led to a storage closet.

"They took a scan of Sandy's internal injuries and . . ." Beechy exhales, trying to keep calm. But his voice comes out hoarse. "We didn't get her here fast enough."

I reach out and squeeze his hand. "She's a fighter. She'll make it. Once we're back in the Core, a surgeon will be able to fix her."

Beechy says nothing, but he doesn't let go of my hand. His golden brown eyes are anxious, glued to the door.

I can't help remembering the last time I saw his eyes this close, when he was still subdued by the serum. They were blank, wiped of life. The Beechy who'd been my friend since I'd been transferred from the Surface work camp to the Core, who'd comforted me when I was terrified I'd fail Extraction training, had been replaced with someone more bot than human. I wish I could do more to comfort him, now that he's the one feeling hopeless.

"The baby's a girl," Beechy says softly, breaking the silence.

"Is she?" I'd hardly thought of his baby as a person until now. A tiny human with scrawny limbs and a faint beating heart, growing inside Sandy, getting bigger by the day. I wonder what she'll look like, whether she'll have more of Beechy or Sandy's features. If we can find a way to defeat the Mardenites and overthrow the Developers, their daughter could be born into a world made peaceful and whole and new. Or she might not even make it through the night.

"Sandy has a name in mind for her," Beechy says. He blinks fast. His eyes glisten with tears. "She told me right before we left for Crust. Said she would tell me the name when we saw each other again."

"When she wakes up, you can ask her."

There's another interlude of silence. The crease of worry in Beechy's forehead tells me the question he's thinking, but afraid to ask aloud: *What if she doesn't?*

I don't know what to tell him. When I think of losing Logan, of never again seeing his lazy smile or hugging him close or waking up to his arms around me, I'm not sure how I'd be able to go on. I'm not sure I'd be strong enough to live in a world without him. But if there was still a hope of saving the other people I cared about, I'd have to find way.

Beechy drops my hand. His eyes glisten with water. "If she dies, it'll be all my fault. I'll never forgive myself."

I set my hand on his shoulder. "What happened to her wasn't your fault—"

"Yes, it was," he says in a hard voice. "I told Charlie the location of the compound. I gave up the Alliance. It's because of me that Sam's troops broke in. If they weren't there, she never would've been hurt."

"The troops would've reached the compound with or without your help," I say. "Skylar would've given up the location if you hadn't."

"I'm still responsible."

"Beechy, you were under the serum, remember? Don't blame yourself for what you did while Charlie was controlling you."

He lets out a short, husky laugh. "Oh, what, and you don't blame yourself for everything you did?"

I stop short of answering him. A lead weight drops into the pit of my stomach. I do blame myself, for all of it. For every word I said to Charlie while I was under the serum, for everyone I hurt against my will.

Beechy doesn't know the worst of it. He was already onboard this hovercraft, in the cockpit readying us to depart the Core and invade Alliance headquarters. But I was outside the ship, in the flight port with Charlie. He ordered Dean to bring him a gun. Then he handed the gun to me and told me to shoot Logan. I tried to ignore him, but it was impossible; the serum was calling the shots.

My fingers squeezed the trigger and Logan fell to the floor, blood pouring from his leg. I screamed and screamed inside my head, but the serum wouldn't let me make a sound. Logan couldn't hear how sorry I was, how much I needed him to forgive me. I still don't know what Charlie did with him after I left.

I swallow the tightness in my throat. *Logan's okay. You're going to see him again.*

Beechy's expression is riddled with guilt. He must know he struck a nerve. "Clem, I'm sorry—"

"It's fine," I say automatically.

"No, it's not." He sets both his hands on my shoulders. "You were right. You shouldn't blame yourself. Nothing you did was your fault, either."

I take a shaky breath. "I know."

His words stir anger inside me—not at him, but at the people who do deserve the blame: Commander Charlie and the other four leaders of Kiel. The Developers. They're the ones who controlled us with injections and ordered us to hurt the people we cared about. They're the reason for every loss we've ever faced, and every person we've had to say good-bye to.

Their faces fall into my head, one by one: Laila, Ella, Oliver, Buck, James. People I knew in the Surface work camp, Karum prison, the Core, and the Alliance. People I cared about. All dead because of the Developers.

# 3

Sam calls the strategy meeting into session an hour before midnight. He only permits eight people into the main cabin upstairs: Lieutenant Dean and the two soldiers in the squadron with corporal rank; Beechy, Skylar, and the other two head pilots; and Fiona, since she's working on fixing the radio transmitter in the cockpit.

The rest of us are stuck waiting downstairs in the cargo bay. It's emptier than the last time I was in here, since most of the boxes of ammunition were used to blow up Alliance headquarters. But there are several supply crates stacked against the walls, stocked with rations and other rudimentary supplies we'd need to survive aboard the hovercraft for an extended period of time.

The soldiers have laid out bedrolls on the floor. A couple people are trying to catch a few winks of sleep, but most are huddled in groups talking in low voices, or standing by the open air-lock doors looking out at the snow swirling in the darkness. Four patrolmen are stationed on watch outside, ready to alert us in case of a raider sighting. But the storm's getting worse by the minute, and I doubt they'll be able to see any enemy ships until it's too late.

I can't sit still, so I pace back and forth near where Darren rests on one of the bedrolls with his injured leg propped up on a pillow. Someone bandaged it while I was unconscious, and he doesn't seem to be in pain anymore. He's wide awake, looking around at the other people in the room, his eyes narrowing with distrust. A couple soldiers keep glancing in our direction, including the one patrolling the room—the soldier who met us when we first arrived at the hovercraft. I bet Sam told him to keep an eye on the two of us.

"I don't like this," Darren says in a low voice, almost a growl. "I wish they'd hurry up with the meeting."

"So do I." They've been talking for almost thirty minutes. I should've argued my way in so I could hurry along the decision making, but it wasn't worth potentially compromising the truce we made with Sam.

Every minute we're stuck in the valley, I can't help fearing what we're going to find once we're able to see beyond these mountains. A barren wasteland with bombs raining from a sky swarmed with Mardenite raiders? A Surface completely destroyed?

The years I lived on the Surface were terrible. I was so hungry some days I wished for death. I witnessed kids tortured and worked until they bled in the fields. I saw them dragged away to kill chambers when they turned twenty and it was time for them to be replaced. I dreamed of being Extracted. It was the only thing that kept me sane.

But this place is still my home more than the Core. The thousands of child workers trapped in the city where I grew up are my family more than anyone else. Just because the Developers believe all those young men and women are nothing more than bodies to be used and cast by the wayside doesn't mean they deserve to die.

If they deserve to die, so do the rest of us. There's no reason we're more special than any of them, no matter what the Developers might say.

Pacing is starting to make me restless. I stop walking and drop onto the bedroll beside Darren's, pulling the blanket over me to block out the chilly air coming in through the open air-lock doors.

"You know something?" Darren says. "I don't understand how this happened."

"What do you mean?"

"The Mardenite army appearing out of nowhere. An entire fleet of ships shouldn't have arrived without any warning. The Developers, at least, should've known they were coming."

I'm confused by what he means, because we did know the army was coming. Then I remember: Darren, Sandy, and the other rebels who stayed behind in the Alliance compound have been completely in the dark. Beechy and I only found out Marden's fleet was on its way after we were captured and taken to the Core, and we didn't have a way to get a message to our friends. There's a lot we haven't had a chance to tell them.

I hesitate, not sure where to begin. "There wasn't zero warning. Astronomers in the Core picked up the fleet's position over a week ago. Commander Charlie had them continue tracking its movements, so we knew it was supposed to arrive within the next few days."

The fleet was supposed to enter Kiel's gravity pull two days from now. Either the scientists miscalculated its trajectory, or the battle stations turned on secondary engines and picked up a lot of speed in the last few hours. Any warning the Core might've tried to transmit to Sam's squadron wouldn't have reached us after we made it to the Surface, since the radio transmitters have been facing interference.

Darren raises an eyebrow. "So Charlie thought it would be a good idea to send troops to the Surface and demolish our headquarters, knowing his soldiers could end up stranded here?"

"Like I said, we were supposed to have more time. Charlie wanted his daughter safely underground before the fleet arrived." As I say the words, I realize there is the possibility Charlie lied. He could've known the fleet would arrive tonight and sent us to the Surface with the intention of stranding us here.

Except I can't think of any reason he would've wanted Sam and the rest of his squadron dead. And if he did, why would he have wasted ships and ammunition to blow up Alliance headquarters? No, Charlie must've been as thrown off guard by the army's arrival as the rest of us.

Darren frowns. "I see. . . . What about the rest of the Alliance?"

I sift through my memories, thinking back to what Charlie said in the meeting room in Recreation Division, the night before we left for the Surface. "His instructions were to capture all of you alive, unless you put up too much of a fight. He didn't say what he plans to do with you once you're in the Core."

"The commander told you all of this?" Darren asks, skepticism in his voice.

"I was at the strategy meeting for the mission," I say stiffly.

"Huh. Well, that seems convenient."

I narrow my eyes. "What's that supposed to mean?"

"You're telling me he captured you while you were working

undercover for the Alliance, took you back to the Core, and gave you a spot in his strategy meeting? It sounds more like you went over to his side willingly in exchange for him sparing your life."

He's accusing me of being a traitor. I'm so angry, I can barely speak. "You want to know what happened? His soldiers captured me in Crust after I'd blown up the control room in their security hub. They locked me in a cell and starved me for more days than I could keep track of. Then they blindfolded me, dragged me into a hovercraft, and took me to the Core, where Charlie threatened me and forced me to inject myself with a new strand of his serum that was powerful enough to control me. I couldn't disobey any of his commands, not a single one. He forced me to shoot Logan, and I had to do it. He forced me to help Sam invade our headquarters and capture all of you, and I couldn't say no. I was fighting the serum the whole time, as hard as I could, and I managed to break free of it before I could hurt anyone else. I fought for the Alliance again even though Charlie threatened to kill Logan if I did. So don't you dare accuse me of working with him."

Darren holds up his hands. "I'm sorry—I didn't mean to accuse you of anything, I swear." He looks a little afraid of me. "I don't think you're a traitor. I'd just . . . heard some things about you, and I wasn't sure."

"What do you mean?" I ask, now confused as well as angry. Darren and I weren't good friends at the Alliance compound. All I knew about him was he was one of the fighter pilots who volunteered for the recon mission to the Surface city. The most interaction we'd had before today was when I accidentally shot down his ship after he returned, mistaking it for a Core transport. My stomach pinches at the memory. It wasn't my proudest moment. Another Alliance rebel, Cady, died because of my incompetence—because I was letting my fears have too much power over my actions.

But I've grown stronger since then. I don't let my fears control me anymore. I shouldn't let anger control me either, so I take a deep breath and exhale.

Darren seems to sense I'm calming down, so he answers me. "I know you're the one who helped Beechy fly Charlie's bomb contraption to the moon and destroy the acid generator. And I know before that, you escaped from Karum prison, where you were sent because he couldn't control you with his serum. You've done plenty of things that should've angered the Developers, yet they keep pardoning you. It just seems strange."

"It's not like I'm the only rebel they've pardoned," I say. "They pardoned Beechy too."

"Yes, but Beechy's different. He's Commander Charlie's son-in-law, even if he is a rebel," Darren says slowly. "You, you're just another Extraction. So I've been wondering . . . what makes you more special than the rest of us?"

I bite my lip. I know exactly why Darren is confused, because I've been wondering the same thing. After I was captured and taken to Commander Charlie in the Core, he told me the reason he's kept me alive more than once is because I have a higher intellectual capacity than any Extraction he's ever met, and because he's fascinated by my reaction to his control serums. He called my genes "remarkable" and said he's been observing me since I was a little girl.

But there must be more to it than what he was telling me. I'm not the only person who's been able to fight his serums, nor am I the only Extraction with high intelligence. There's a bigger reason he keeps forgiving me for my disobedience and trying to control me, despite how many times he's failed. As soon as we make it back to the Core, I'm going to find out what it is.

Out of the corner of my eye, I see the door leading to the main cabin open at the top of the staircase. The strategy meeting is finally over. I get to my feet as Sam steps out onto the landing.

"Attention, everyone," he says, tense authority in his posture. The other soldiers immediately quiet down. "Twenty minutes ago, we sent an emergency transmission to the Core to let them know our position and request assistance. We have yet to receive a response. It's possible they heard our transmission and the signal's interference is preventing their response from reaching us, or our transmission may not have reached them at all. But as long as we stay on the Surface, we remain in danger. So, we've decided to prepare for immediate departure. The corporals and head pilots will pass out your mission assignments."

Four soldiers move through the door behind Sam and head down the staircase. Beechy and Skylar aren't with them; they must've been assigned as the hovercraft pilots.

"We're hopeful the flight path to the Pipeline will be clear," Sam says. "But we need to prepare for the possibility we'll run into enemy raiders. It's imperative you all stay alert and follow any commands you're given. If you have any questions, direct them to your assigned mission leader." He casts a solemn look around the room. "Good luck."

Turning on his heel, Sam heads back into the main cabin. Dean steps out onto the landing a moment later.

The corporals and head pilots begin shouting everyone's mission assignments. There's a flurry of movement around the cargo bay. Soldiers roll up the beds and stuff them back into the supply crates. Others hurry into the weapons locker to arm themselves with better guns before heading down the boarding ramp to go to their assigned X-wing.

"Can you help me up?" Darren asks, wincing as he tries to stand up on his own.

I take his arms and help him to his feet.

"Thanks," he says.

Lieutenant Dean's coming down the staircase. When he reaches the bottom, he walks over to the two of us. "You were both assigned to the hovercraft crew. Head upstairs and buckle in. Switch on your ear-comm."

I twist the dial at the base of my helmet. Static comes through the speaker, but there's a lot less than there was earlier tonight. Whatever Fiona did to strengthen the radio signal definitely helped lower the interference, thank goodness. The hovercraft pilot needs to be able to communicate with the X-wings once we're up in the air.

Darren starts for the staircase, limping on his wounded leg. I move after him so I can help him climb the stairs, but Dean touches my shoulder to stop me. "Wait."

I turn around. "What?"

He glances over his shoulder, then beckons me to follow him behind a supply crate, out of view of the other soldiers. I hesitate, but go with him. Once we're there, Dean pulls out one of the small pulse guns he carries in his holster belt and pushes it into my hands. "Keep this with you. Don't let anyone take it."

I tuck it into my holster belt. I doubt Sam wants me carrying a weapon, but I don't care. I feel much safer with a gun on my person. "Thanks."

Dean takes a step closer to me and drops his voice. "If anything goes wrong on our way to the Core, promise me you'll do everything you can to stay unharmed." He touches my shoulder, and I frown. His eyes are intense, almost fearful. "If we're shot down, you need to get yourself as far away from the ship as you can and take cover. Don't worry about anyone else. Just save yourself. Understand?"

I frown. He wants me to abandon the other rebels—my friends—if we end up under attack. I couldn't possibly do that.

"Do you understand?" Dean repeats.

I can see he's not going to take no for an answer. "Yes, I do," I say. "I will."

"Good," he says, releasing his grip on my shoulder. He pauses, as if he might say something more.

"Lieutenant Dean!" A soldier calls his name.

Without another word, Dean moves past me. I almost stop him. I want to ask him why he cares so much about protecting me, and if it has anything to do with why Commander Charlie pardoned me when he captured me in Crust.

There isn't time to press for answers to all my questions, not when we're scrambling to get ourselves to safety. But soon I will demand them.

# 4

Shortly before midnight, we leave the valley.

I'm strapped into a passenger seat in the main cabin of the hovercraft, at the two-person round table behind the cockpit. Fiona sits across from me, nervously chewing on her lip, ready to jump up if we run into any mechanical problems in flight. Darren is at one of the other tables. Sandy is still in surgery, and there's been no word from Uma or the doctor yet as to how she's doing.

I grip my armrests tightly, bracing myself against the jolting of the ship from the stormy turbulence outside. Thick snow swirls in the darkness beyond the cockpit window, making it impossible to see more than a few yards ahead of us. The defroster is on high so the window won't freeze over. We're relying on flight instruments to follow a clear flight path to the Pipeline, and to pick up the signal of any approaching raiders. I hate not knowing where the swarm went after we lost it in the storm. It could be on the other side of the Surface by now or a hundred miles ahead of us, flying in our direction.

Beechy's keeping us close to the ground, in case we need to make a quick landing. I'm glad he and Skylar are the ones up in the copilot seats; they're the only pilots I'd trust to get us through a storm like this.

"Bird one, ease off thrusters." Skylar's voice comes through my ear-comm, speaking to one of the X-wing pilots. "You're going too fast."

"This is bird one," the pilot answers through the static. "Copy that. Slowing down."

Sam paces behind Skylar and Beechy with his arms folded, the slight limp still visible in his leg. Beneath his stony gaze, I can sense his nervousness.

I spoke to him a couple minutes before take-off. He intercepted me on my way to my seat, acting as if he were ordering me to carry out a task for him. But the words he said under his breath were far less kind.

"Don't make the mistake of thinking you're safe, just because I pardoned you and your friends until we reach the Core," he said. "You might've convinced Lieutenant Dean to argue on your behalf, but I'm still the commander of this ship. I could throw you out the air-lock if I wanted. So, I need you to understand something." He took a step closer to me, his eyes cold as ever. "If you or any of the rebels make any move to defy my commands, I will strand all of you on the Surface. I doubt you'd last more than a few days before you'd freeze to death. And I will personally make sure you have no way of calling for help or returning to the Core."

The smile he gave me was a vicious one. Before I could say anything in response, he turned away to answer Skylar, calling him up to the cockpit.

It was likely a ploy to scare me; I doubt he has the guts to really throw all my friends and me off the ship, especially with the Mardenite army so close. He wouldn't give up bodies that could help defend the rest of his squadron. Still, I glare at his back and grip the barrel of the gun tucked out of sight under my holster belt. I wish I'd shot him in a better spot than his leg back at headquarters. If only I'd crippled him enough that he was no longer fit for command of the ship.

My fingers brush something hard inside the zippered pouch in my holster belt. Three thin, tubelike objects—the three syringes full of Charlie's serum. The ones he gave to me with instructions to readminister the serum to myself every twenty-four hours, before it wore off. I'd forgotten about them. I should get rid of them before someone, namely Sam, finds out I have them and tries to use them to subdue me or any of my friends.

But as I stare at Sam pacing up in the cockpit, an idea begins taking shape. If I could get him alone, if I had the opportunity, I could inject him with all three of the syringes. One dosage is powerful enough to trap a person—even one with a mind strong enough to resist control—inside his body for twenty-four hours. And I doubt Sam has the strongest mind of the lot. Three dosages at one time could be enough to kill him, or at least knock him unconscious for several days. And if I could do it quickly, when no one else was around, it would be a lot less messy than shooting him, and a lot harder for someone to find out I was responsible.

I'd just have to make sure he didn't wake up.

The sliding door opens at the other end of the cabin, and I quickly drop my hand away from the zippered pouch. Dean walks into the room. He was downstairs closing the air-lock doors when we took off. He moves swiftly down the aisle between the passenger seats, his eyes meeting mine for a fraction of a second longer than seems normal.

Shifting his gaze away from me, Dean joins Sam in the cockpit. "How are we looking?"

"We're on course to reach the Pipeline in twenty minutes," Beechy says off comm, tilting the nose of the hovercraft up to avoid the mountain pass slowly becoming visible ahead of us in the snowstorm. "Should be a relatively smooth ride."

"No sign of raiders yet," Skylar says. "All the birds are still with us."

I can't see the X-wings out the cockpit window, but I know they're flying in tight formation with the hovercraft.

There's no point in staring out the window the whole time. It won't get us to the Pipeline any faster.

To distract myself, I look around the cabin. About half the passenger seats are filled, since only seven of Sam's soldiers remained on the hovercraft, while the rest split up among the X-wings. All the soldiers look as tense as I feel. I'd expect them to be more used to dealing with scenarios like this, since they've been training for war all their lives. Then again, an army of aliens hasn't invaded Kiel in any of their lifetimes.

"Any return transmissions from the Core yet?" Sam asks.

"Still none," Skylar says.

Sam grinds his teeth together. "Try re-sending the emergency transmission."

"Copy that."

Across the table, Fiona shakes her head in disbelief. "The fleet must be generating a huge electromagnetic field for it to be causing this much interference. We're lucky other flight equipment hasn't started malfunctioning."

"Do you think the Mardenites are targeting our radio signal?" I ask.

"If they are, they're doing a poor job of it, since I got our ear-comms working again. All I had to do was secure the grounding of the wires connected to the transmitter box." Fiona's eyes drift past me, staring off into space. "No, if the Mardenites are targeting anything, it's some other electrical equipment. And our transmitters are just being affected as well."

"Or maybe our transmission actually went through," I say. "And the Core is just not responding."

"Yeah. That's crossed my mind too."

"Fifteen minutes to the Pipeline," Beechy says up in the cockpit. "Flight path still looks clear ahead."

I look back out the window, at the snow swirling through the darkness. If we can make it just a bit farther, we'll escape the storm as well as the raiders. The war won't be over, but once we're belowground we'll be out of immediate danger.

"Clementine," Fiona says.

I turn back to her. "Yeah?"

She hesitates. "Can you tell me something?"

"Anything."

"How many other Alliance rebels have been captured?"

My stomach twists. I wish she'd asked an easier question. "I don't know for sure. When I was captured, Charlie had taken three others prisoner: Beechy, Skylar, and Logan. But Charlie forced Beechy to hand over a list of people working for the Alliance. That was last night. Charlie said he was going to put out the call for their capture to all of his soldiers in the lower sectors."

"Was my sister on the list?" Fiona's voice is small, nervous.

She means Paley, her twin. They were inseparable whenever I saw them at the Alliance compound, spending their days fixing engine parts and refueling ships in the flight port. But the two of them were forced apart when the Alliance infiltrated the lower sectors to launch our uprising against Commander Charlie and the other Developers. Paley went with the crew led by Beechy; Fiona stayed behind to keep headquarters running. She and the others who stayed behind were supposed to join us at a certain point and help us invade the Core, but nothing went according to plan.

I twist my mouth, trying to recall the list of names. It wasn't complete, not by a long shot. It gave me hope Beechy was fighting his injection too. "I don't think she was."

Fiona exhales in relief. "Thank stars. Ever since she left, I've been terrified something horrible had happened to her."

"Last I heard, she was working undercover in Crust," I say. "She'd helped blow up the quarantine facility."

Fiona smiles proudly. "Guess we'll have a lot of catching up to do when we see each other again."

I smile back, but I can't help wondering: *Will* they see each other again? Even if we make it back to the Core, Crust will be far away.

There's a loud beeping up in the cockpit. A sharp intake of air from Skylar.

"Enemy sighting," she says. "Raiders are approaching from the southeast."

Both Fiona and I snap our attention to the window. I search frantically for the shapes of warships on the horizon. The snow is starting to clear a little outside, but I can still see hardly anything in the darkness. The lights beaming from our ship fall on the faint figures of trees below us on the mountainside. Of course I wouldn't see any raiders; we're heading north, so they must be approaching us from behind.

Sam takes two strides forward, leaning over Skylar to see the radar screen. "Can you tell how many?"

"Seven."

"How far away?" Dean asks.

"Three miles."

"Turn us northwest," Sam says. "Let's see if they follow."

Skylar quickly relays the order to the X-wing pilots through the ship-comm, while Beechy rolls the hovercraft to the right, tilting the nose upward to take us higher in the sky.

I dig my nails into the cushion of my seat and stare at the snowstorm. I count the seconds as they tick by in silence.

*Twenty-seven.*

*Twenty-eight.*

*Twenty-nine.*

"They're flocking this way," Skylar says, a tremor in her voice. "They've locked onto our signal."

They know we're here. They're following us.

We're about to be under attack.

# 5

W e need to lose them," Sam says.
           Even if they don't catch us, if we can't get rid of them
before we reach the Pipeline, they'll follow us underground. We'll
lead them straight to the lower sectors. The underground cities
didn't exist the last time we faced the Mardenites in combat, so
those sectors are our biggest advantage right now, our strongest
defense. We need to hold that advantage as long as possible; we
need to keep the raiders from discovering the tunnel entrance.

Up in the cockpit, a look passes between Beechy and Skylar,
a silent, uneasy conversation.

"Should we?" Skylar asks.

"Might as well give it a shot," Beechy says, unbuckling.

The two of them quickly switch seats, and Skylar takes over the
main flight controls. She inhales a deep breath and focuses, switch-
ing on her ear-comm speaker again. "Pilots, do you copy?"

The static is getting worse. We're losing the radio signal again;
there's too much interference with the raiders closing in. But the

pilots' voices still come through, one after another, saying they copy.

"We're gonna pull a Mad Jack and lose these bastards," Skylar says. "Birds one and two, on my left. Three, four, five, stay on my right. On my mark." She grabs hold of the control clutch.

I double-check my seat belt is secure around my waist and shoulders. I have no idea what a "Mad Jack" is, but it sounds like the flight could get rough. My gun is digging into my stomach, so I tuck it into the actual holster.

"Now!" Skylar says.

I barely have time to grab my armrests again before the hover-craft swerves to the left. The force of gravity presses me back against my seat. Out the window, a mountain peak comes into view through the snow and the fog. Skylar rolls our ship farther to the left, taking us around the other side of the peak. For an instant I see one of the X-wings with a red light flashing on its right wing, but then it falls behind us again.

As we speed past the peak, Skylar abruptly turns the hovercraft in the other direction. My right arm bangs against my seat, and a sharp pain shoots through the muscle beneath the bandage. I clench my teeth, trying to ignore it.

Bright moonlight peeks through the falling snow. I can glimpse the full moon beyond a mountain ahead of us, rising higher in the sky. Before it, the acid shield shimmers in the darkness. But I don't see any of the Mardenite battle stations; they must've passed out of sight in their orbit.

Skylar tilts the nose of our hovercraft toward the ground, and we speed for a low pass between the mountains ahead of us. I think we're circling back in the direction we came from. I wish I could see more of the flight panels up in the cockpit, particularly the radar screen. Then I'd have a better idea where the raider swarm is in relation to our ships, and whether or not we're losing them.

This maneuver needs to work. Right now they only have seven ships to take on our five, but I wouldn't be surprised if they have more nearby. There were at least twenty in the swarm we saw heading for these mountains earlier tonight. And we have no way to call for backup, no one close by to save us.

I'm not ready to die tonight. I wouldn't have a chance to tell Logan how sorry I am for hurting him while I was under the serum's control. I'd never be able to hug him again, or kiss him again, or tell him I love him.

Maybe I should feel lucky we found our way back to each other for a short time. Months ago, after I was picked for Extraction, I never expected to see him again. I feared he'd be replaced long before I could find a way back to the Surface. But we beat the odds, and we had a week in the safe confines of the Alliance compound to wake up beside each other every morning and know the comfort of a life that had only ever been a dream. Still, it wasn't enough. We deserve more days; we deserve more weeks; we deserve more years than we've had.

The hovercraft evens out again and I catch my breath. Though I can't forgive Skylar for betraying the Alliance, I can't deny she can fly the hell out of a ship.

"How are we looking?" she asks, out of breath.

"They're still on our tail," Beechy says heavily. "And more are coming. They must've signaled the rest of the swarm."

Skylar curses loudly.

I squeeze my eyes shut. *It's going to be okay.* We'll fight them if we have to. We'll find a way to take them down.

"Lieutenant Sam, what are your orders?" Beechy asks.

Sam has stopped pacing in the cockpit. He stands completely immobile, paralyzed with fear. I've never seen his face so pale.

"Sir?" Skylar says.

"They're going to catch us," Sam murmurs. "We're all going to die."

Dean makes a low grunt of annoyance and pushes past Sam to get closer to the control screens, swiftly taking over command. "How far is it to the Pipeline?"

"Thirty miles," Skylar says.

"So all we need to do is outrun them a few more minutes. Can you make us go any faster?"

"I'm giving her all I've got," Skylar says through clenched teeth. "I can't do anything more from the cockpit."

"Fiona," Beechy says. He swivels his head in our direction.

Fiona jerks her head up. "Yes?"

"I need you to go down to the engine room and boost our power to full velocity." His jaw is hard, his voice breathless with worry.

"I'm on it." Fiona gets to her feet. "Clementine, come with me."

I glance back at Beechy, who nods. "Go."

I unbuckle and hurry after her, glad I can finally do something to help. Hoping we haven't already run out of time.

We access the engine room through a door in the cargo bay, near the infirmary. Down a short set of steps, we move through another door and the loud hiss of the ventilation system fills my ears.

I've been in an engine room before, on the spaceship Beechy and I flew to the moon the day we destroyed the generator that used to bleed acid into Kiel's atmosphere. But this room is much bigger. A rail separates us from the fuel tanks and a huge cylindrical shape that must be the engine, surrounded by a mess of metal tubing and parts I can't identify. The wall to our right is covered in pressure gauges, buttons, and panels, while the left-hand side of the room has two passenger seats and a cabinet full of mechanical tools.

Fiona hurries over to the cabinet and rummages inside for the tools we need. A tremor runs through the floor, and I grab on to the engine rail. Hopefully that was just turbulence, not a blast hitting the hovercraft.

"How can I help?" I ask.

"We need to cut the hydraulics," she says. "Open the red panel on the wall, beneath the fuel-pressure gauge."

Finding the pressure gauge and the red panel is easy enough. But when I lift the panel cover, I'm faced with a tangle of wires— blacks and reds and yellows crisscrossing each other. Nothing I can make sense of, since I know hardly anything about engineering.

"What now?"

Fiona appears beside me and shoves a pair of wire cutters into my hand. "Cut the thickest black wire where it connects to a red one."

She leaves me, slipping under the rail and disappearing around the far side of the engine. I bite my lip, leaning into the tangle of wires to find what she's referring to. There, a black wire that's definitely thicker than the rest, and it merges with a red one before it runs into the wall.

Before I can second-guess myself, I snip the end of the wire with the cutters. Nothing seems to happen. Only the hum of the vents grows louder.

"Good," Fiona says, reappearing at my side. "Now we just need to—"

Another tremor runs through the ship, and a loud beeping sound comes from the wall next to me. One of the bigger screens flashes the bright red words:

HULL DAMAGE

Almost immediately, the walls shudder from another hit. Every inch of my body stiffens with terror. The raiders have caught up to us.

There's a crackle in my ear-comm. The static is getting worse again—something aboard the raiders must be causing more interference. Beechy's voice cuts in and out, sounding frantic: "Clem— we're taking fire—get out of there."

"We're almost finished," Fiona says, her voice shaky. "We need two more minutes."

If Beechy heard us, his answer doesn't come through; there's too much static. I switch off the ear-comm so I won't go crazy.

"What's left to do?" I ask.

Fiona tosses me a wrench. "Unscrew the panel on the engine cover and press the red button underneath."

I spin around, find the panel on the engine, and work the wrench on the screws as quickly as I can. *Come on, come on.* We have to finish this, or we're dead.

The hovercraft shakes again as I lift open the panel and press the red button. "Done."

"Okay," Fiona says, frantically tapping something into one of the wall screens. "One last thing."

Before she can give me any more instructions, there's a horrible grinding sound like a huge chunk of metal is splitting in two.

I barely have time to inhale before the wall behind the engine blasts apart.

The force of the explosion sends me crashing back into the opposite wall. Smoke and bits of tubing and metal parts fly in the same direction. Shards catch in the fabric of my safety suit, and something hard slams into my helmet.

I don't black out, not all the way. But it takes several moments for everything to come back into focus.

My ears are ringing, and I can feel blood trickling out of my left one. A trail of smoke rises from the engine cover. Hail swirls into the room through the small hole in the wall behind the engine, where the hovercraft was hit. Beyond the icy rain, trees on the side of a mountain below us rush past in a blur. We're losing altitude fast and picking up speed when we should be decelerating. Skylar must've lost control of the ship. We were hit too hard.

The hovercraft is going to crash.

A few feet away from me, Fiona staggers to her feet, wind whipping at her safety suit. She's steadying herself on the rail with one hand, while using her other to turn a lever on the wall. There's another set of words flashing on the beeping screen above her head:

### ENGINE DAMAGE

As if we couldn't already tell.

"We need to strap ourselves in," I say.

"Hold on," Fiona says.

I don't know what she's doing, but I don't have time to argue with her. I need to get to one of the passenger seats on the other side of the room.

I push myself off the floor, wincing from the tendrils of pain shooting through my body. I lose my balance and stumble into the engine rail. The floor is shaking, and the wind blowing through the hole in the wall threatens to drag me outside.

Somehow, I make it across the room. I heave myself onto one of the passenger seats and click the safety strap into place. Through the hole in the wall, I can see a forest-covered hillside growing bigger ahead of the ship. And we aren't veering out of its way.

"Fiona!" I cry.

She turns and looks at me, across the room. "I was trying to slow us down. I couldn't. I'm sorry."

The hillside is straight ahead of us. Fiona doesn't have time to strap in.

I open my mouth to scream at her to hold on to something. But it's too late.

The hillside rises toward us through the blur of rain and darkness. There's a vicious bump as we slam into the ground, and my head jerks back against my seat. I'd be flying if not for my seat belt.

There's a shrieking sound of metal, of more machinery being ripped apart. My scream is lost amid the noise. It feels like we're still moving, skidding across the hilltop. I don't know how long it goes on—could be seconds or hours. I'm bracing myself in my seat as hard as I can and begging it all to be over.

At last, the quaking stops and the engine room goes dark.

6

I cling to the one thing I know: the mad thumping of my heart, a sign I'm still alive even if the ship is broken.

When I try to move, a bolt of pain shoots from my neck down my spine. It's almost too much to bear.

*You have to get up.* I have to get off the hovercraft. The Mardenites who shot us down are still out there, and they could bomb us again. I have to make sure Fiona and the other rebels are alive and help them off the ship.

I take deep, steadying breaths and fumble to unbuckle my seat belt. The pain is worse when I stand up. But as long as I keep moving, keep focusing on what I have to do—save my friends—I can ignore it.

The air is thick with dust and smoke. Coughing, I step carefully, feeling my way through the darkness to make sure I won't trip over anything on the floor. There's a faint glow of light on the other side of the engine, a soft crackle of flames. Some of the electrical lines must've caught fire.

As I move closer to the light, I make out the shape of Fiona's body slumped on the floor, amid the debris of the wrecked engine parts. She's lying on her back, unmoving. When I call her name, she doesn't respond.

I drop to my knees beside her. There's a crack in her helmet and a dark stain of blood seeping from her forehead. A broken piece of machinery must've hit her head hard. *Please, don't be dead.*

I feel for a pulse in her wrist. It's faint, but still there.

The loud crackle of flames draws my attention back to the fire. It's spreading along the broken electrical lines, moving steadily in the direction of the fuel tanks. I need to get both of us out of here before there's another explosion.

There's a chunk of rubble trapping the lower half of Fiona's legs. I try to push it off her, but it doesn't move an inch; it's a lot heavier than I realized. I push and shove, gritting my teeth against the pain spreading through my body. But the machinery won't budge.

The engine room's growing hotter and thicker with smoke, and the flames are climbing higher, inching ever closer to the fuel tanks.

Fear sets adrenaline pumping through my body. I grab one of Fiona's arms and heave it over my right shoulder. Then I slide my other arm under her torso and try to heave her out from beneath the debris. But it's no use; her legs are completely stuck. I'm not strong enough to pull her out on my own.

I twist the dial at the base of my helmet, turning on my ear-comm. "Help! I'm in the engine room and I need help!"

There's nothing but static in answer. There's too much interference. I doubt anyone can hear me on the other end, and even if they could they wouldn't get here fast enough. The flames are mere centimeters from the fuel tanks. Any second now, the whole room is going to explode.

Dean's warning from earlier echoes through my head: *Don't worry about anyone else. Just save yourself.*

There's nothing more I can do for Fiona. I have to get out of here.

With one final, broken look at her, I turn and push through the exit door. I take the stairs two steps at a time, coughing from the smoke and choking back sobs because I can't believe what I just did. I feel numb all over. But I can't go back.

Five more steps.

Three more.

One more.

I reach the top of the stairs just in time—there's a booming sound as the fuel tanks explode behind me. The floor lurches beneath my feet, and I trip forward, landing on my hands and knees. Dust and hard bits of rubble strike me from behind, from the door blasted open at the bottom of the staircase. Thankfully the engine room seems to have contained most of the damage.

I pause there on my knees, giving in to the weakness for a moment. Letting the reality of what just happened sink in.

Fiona is dead. I left her behind.

The sorrow consumes me, tearing me apart inside. Once again, I wasn't strong enough. No matter what I do, I keep losing people who don't deserve to be lost.

But there's no time to dwell on my guilt over her death, or anyone's. There's an army of aliens outside and I still have to escape. There's only time to keep moving.

*On your feet, Clementine.*

I push off the ground and pull myself through the door at the top of the staircase. The cargo bay is filled with the sounds of voices and boots pounding and people breathing heavily. The ship lights are out, but there's some moonlight coming in through the open air-lock doors. People are making their way across the room, some of them leaning or limping on each other as if they're hurt. Someone's helping tend to those who were injured, while another person is passing out water canteens. The sky must be clear of raiders for the moment.

"Everyone, stay alert," Dean says, somewhere on the other side of the bay. "Be ready to move when you're given the order."

I head toward the group, wiping away the blood still trickling from my left ear. It's throbbing like crazy and I can't hear much of anything out of it, which is lovely. But not my biggest concern at the moment. I need to make sure Beechy and the rest of my friends are all right. There are too many bodies and not enough light for me to make out faces.

"Clementine!" Beechy calls my name from somewhere behind me. I spin around and see him rushing out of the infirmary doors. He must've gone to check on Sandy first, as he should have.

When he reaches me, he grips my shoulders. "Are you okay?"

"I'm alive."

"Where's Fiona?"

There's a suspended moment of silence, and then I force out the sentence: "She's dead." The words feel like rubber in my mouth. "The fuel tanks exploded and I couldn't get her out."

Pain bleeds through Beechy's eyes.

"I had to leave her," I say, my voice cracking. "I didn't have a choice."

He exhales a shaky breath and pulls me into his arms. "I'm sure you did everything you could. I'm just glad you're okay."

I squeeze my eyes shut, clinging to him and his warmth. Pretending he can make all the bad go away.

But he can't. This war is far from over, and things are sure to get worse before the end. Somehow, we have to find a way to keep surviving.

I pull away from him just as a soldier runs into the hovercraft from outside. "Lieutenant, sir, the raiders are in sight," he says in a rush.

There are gasps and panicked movements around the room.

I swallow hard. I knew the Mardenites would come looking for survivors, but part of me hoped they'd take longer to target us again. That we'd have more time to work out a way to escape them.

"How many?" Sam asks over by the air-lock doors. His dark figure is silhouetted by faint moonlight.

"At least ten ships."

Ten raiders swarming us on the hillside, and they've already broken our hovercraft, our first line of defense. We could hole up here in the cargo bay and shut the air-lock doors, but the Mardenites would blast the ship apart and find a way inside.

"Skylar, you're sure you can't get us in the air again?" Dean asks.

"We've had major damage to the hull and the engine," Skylar says. "I don't think I can fix her."

"What about the X-wings?"

"We've lost all contact with them. There's a good chance they were also shot down."

We have no working ships, no means of escaping the Mardenites. We have two choices: try to escape on foot, or fight them. And even if we do manage to escape or fight them off, how are we going to fly off the Surface?

"What are your orders, Lieutenant Sam?" Dean asks. There's something spiteful in his tone. I'm sure he wishes he were the one in charge. I'm starting to wish that too—anyone would be better than Sam.

"We're going to try to bring them down," Sam says. "Everyone, move the missile guns outside and form defensive lines." He looks around at all the soldiers frozen in terror. *"Now."*

There's a flurry of movement as everyone races to carry out his orders.

"But, sir," Skylar says, "half our crew was aboard the X-wings. We're completely outnumbered—"

"Our missiles are strong enough to bring down far bigger ships," Sam says. "Now, get into formation outside. That's an order, soldier."

Skylar clenches her fists, but she doesn't argue anymore. She hurries to help the other soldiers haul the missile guns out of the weapons locker.

This can't be the smartest plan. The Mardenite raiders will have all the advantage from the sky. Even if we're able to shoot some of them down, surely their firepower will be stronger.

"Listen," Beechy says, grabbing my arm and pulling me away from the soldiers. "I want you to go with Dean."

"Excuse me?"

"Go outside and pretend you're following Sam's orders, forming rank with everyone else. But as soon as you're able, break away from them and take cover in the forest. Get as far from the hovercraft as you can until the battle's over. Dean will help you get away."

I glance over at Dean, who's ushering the soldiers out the airlock doors with their missile guns. "You really think he's on our side?" I ask.

"I do," Beechy says without hesitation.

My mind wanders back to the conversation I overheard him and Dean having in the infirmary earlier. Maybe they weren't talking about Sandy. Maybe they were talking about me.

Whatever they think they're doing, I'm grateful they're trying to protect me. But that doesn't mean I'm going to abandon any more of my friends. Especially not Beechy. "You're coming with me," I say.

"I'll be right behind you, after I get Sandy out of the infirmary. She's still in surgery, but Uma and the ship doctor are closing her up right now so we can move her."

"I'll stay here so I can help you."

"No." Beechy's jaw is firmly set. "You need to get outside now and take cover before we're under fire, if you can. Get to the trees and wait for me there."

I shake my head. "I can't." I won't leave him.

"You have to," he says. "Then, if something goes wrong, at least you'll be out of danger. Dean can help you get to the Pipeline. It's only a few miles away, and there's a transmission station there that should have an emergency transport. You can use it to get back to the Core, so you can rescue Logan."

There's a lurch of guilt in my stomach. Logan is depending on me to make it back to him. He would tell me I'm crazy for not immediately doing what Beechy wants and getting myself out of danger. I need to survive this, for him.

"But what about you, Beechy? I can't lose you."

"You won't." Beechy takes my hand and squeezes it. "I promise I'll be right behind you."

A tremor runs through the hovercraft, another explosive hitting the hull. There are shouts from outside, where most of the soldiers have gone. The Mardenites are firing at us again. If I'm going to make it to the forest before it's too late, I have to leave now, with or without Beechy.

I gulp down the worry in my throat. "Hurry. Please."

Beechy's hard expression cracks a little, enough for me to know he's even more scared he won't make it than I am. "I will. I'll see you soon."

He drops my hand. I turn and race for the air-lock doors.

# 7

There's another fierce shudder through the ship as I stumble down the boarding ramp. The night is a blur of rain and fire streaming from the heavens. The shapes of Mardenite raiders weave through the clouds above the hillside, moonlight glinting off their dark, rugged bodies.

They're so much closer than when I saw them before. They're not small, harmless buzzards anymore—the raiders are bigger than our X-wings and look far more formidable. Real alien warships come to destroy Kiel. Lasers shoot from the tips of their curved, V-shaped wings.

There's fire all over the hillside in front of me, too much for the rain to put out. A burst of blue flames erupts in the grass at the foot of the boarding ramp. I barely scramble away from it in time. Sam's soldiers are running all over the place, ducking under pieces of debris to avoid the lasers. Only a few ranks are still standing with their missile guns. I don't know how long they're going to be able to stay in one place.

"Now!" Sam yells, somewhere in the chaos.

Missiles fly from the huge guns. Most of them miss their targets—the soldiers underestimated how fast the ships were moving—but one missile hits the wing of a raider, causing it to swerve violently to the left. It falls beyond the hillside, its wing smoking from the explosion.

One raider shot down, but there are at least ten others left. Sam and his troops are far too few to stand a chance against so many ships. They should be running to take cover.

I draw the pulse gun Dean gave me earlier and click off the safety. I shouldn't care what happens to Sam and his men. All I need to worry about is getting to the forest.

The trees are about twenty yards away, just visible beyond the slope of the wide hillside. Huge pieces of hovercraft debris and an open stretch of sky under which I'll have no cover from raider fire stand in my way. But there's nothing else for it—I have to reach the trees.

*Go. Now.*

I scurry off the boarding ramp. Flames in the grass lick at my boots, and I have to swerve to the left to avoid another laser from the sky. There's smoke everywhere. Beechy told me to find Dean, but I have no idea where he is. All the soldiers look the same in their armor.

Sam's soldiers launch another missile and take down a raider. If they had more visibility and better protection from the raider fire—if they'd had time to dig trenches—they might actually have a chance of bringing down most of the swarm. But I don't see how they're going to survive for long the way things are. Soon there won't be any part of the ground not covered in flames.

Already, some of the soldiers are giving up, trying to escape to the trees for cover. A man not far ahead of me stumbles into the path of a Mardenite laser, and he doesn't have time to scramble out of the way. He lets out a horrible shriek and falls to his knees as the fire sears through his armor.

Bile rises in my throat. I tear my eyes away and race around him.

I'm almost to the forest, but many of the trees on the edge of it are alight with flame. I search frantically for the safest path in—there, on my right-hand side. There's a massive piece of ship junk in my way, a chunk of the hovercraft hull that tore off during the crash. I duck my head from another laser and scurry around the debris.

That's when I see Dean running toward me through the smoke. He has an arm over his head to block his helmet from the rain, and his other hand clutches his pulse rifle. He yells at me, "Clementine, get to the trees!"

"I'm trying!"

He reaches me and grabs my sleeve, wrenching me out of the way of another laser. The two of us keep running toward the clear spot between the trees.

Twenty more feet.

Fifteen.

Ten.

Out of the corner of my eye, I see a flash of light. The lights on the wings of a raider soaring overhead. I look up just in time to see an object drop from a hatch in the warship's underside—something that looks like a grenade. Aiming right for the trees ahead of us.

Every part of me seizes in terror. I try to scramble away from the grenade, but there are too many pieces of debris in my way, and I can't get anywhere quickly enough.

Dean pushes me to his right, so hard I fall to the ground. I feel his weight press on top of me as he crouches over me, shielding me from the explosion.

There's a thump as the grenade hits the ground. I brace myself for a *BOOM!*

But the explosion doesn't come.

There's a hissing sound. I lift my head and see the object that fell a few feet away from us. It's a round object made of some sort of metal, almost like a cam-bot but bigger. Whitish vapor streams from openings in the metal ball, seeping in every direction.

The gas engulfs my body and I feel a burning sensation all over, like someone's stabbing me in a thousand points with needles.

The vapor is poison.

# 8

Dean climbs off me, sputtering and coughing. "Go!"

I'm on my feet before he can help me up. Soldiers are shrieking and yelling behind us. More poison bombs drop from the raiders, all over the hillside. Soon the whole place will be drenched in burning vapor.

I run as fast as I can into the forest, stumbling in pain, trying to escape. I'm blinking back tears, and I can hardly see. I trip over a rock and fall to my knees, then pick myself back up, gasping for air. The whitish gas is seeping through the trees ahead of me. The raiders must've dropped bombs everywhere.

My safety suit was designed to protect me from a particular kind of toxin—the moon's acid. Whatever this poison is, its particles are able to seep through the fabric. I bet it's some new chemical the aliens devised, a weapon meant to destroy us.

I pump my legs even faster. The trees are growing closer together, and the slope of the hill is steepening. I don't know how much farther I can make it. I'm losing energy with every step. How much more vapor can there be?

I don't see the fallen branch in my path, not until my ankle catches on it and I fall, tumbling over sticks and rocks down the side of the hill. After only a few feet, I ram into a tree trunk and stop, groaning.

The vapor still surrounds me, but I'm too exhausted to move. So I lie there. Rain patters on my helmet and on the forest floor all around me.

I slowly become aware that my skin isn't burning anymore, though vapor still clings to my clothes. I frown. When did the burning stop? While I was running, maybe. I feel sweaty under my clothes, a little feverish, but I'm wide awake.

The forest seems quieter than before. There's still the soft sound of the rain and the wind rustling the branches, but I don't hear anyone screaming anymore, not even far away. I don't hear anyone running behind me, either.

Wincing, I push myself off the ground. My legs are unsteady; I grab on to the tree to hold myself upright.

"Dean!" I call, not too loudly, but loud enough that he should be able to hear me if he's close by.

When he doesn't answer, worry settles in the pit of my stomach. He should've been right behind me. The poison must've slowed him down. I have to go back and find him.

I take a few tentative steps forward, moving into the vapor that's slowly clearing up, bracing myself for pain. But there's still no burn. The poison seems to have suddenly stopped working. I have no idea why, but I'll take it.

Gritting my teeth, I start back up the hill in the direction I came. I don't know how far away I am from the hovercraft. The silence doesn't comfort me. It makes me think the battle must be over. What will I find if I go back to the crash site?

I can't help picturing the worst: Everyone else is dead. The Mardenites poisoned all the soldiers and set their bodies on fire.

I shake the thought from my head. There's still a chance Beechy made it off the hovercraft, and others could've escaped into the trees. First I'll find Dean and then I'll look for survivors.

I pick up my pace, trying to stick to the same path I took to get here. It's difficult, since I could hardly see where I was going. At least I know I'll eventually reach the top of the hill.

"Dean!" I call again.

The low hum of a sky engine reaches my ears. I press back against a tree trunk as a raider passes by overhead. It's moving a lot slower than I'd expect, hovering over the treetops and beaming a light down into the forest. Looking for something—probably bodies of the people the poison knocked out.

I hold my breath as the light skims past me, waiting for the Mardenites to spot me. But the light doesn't reach me in my hiding spot, and soon the hum of the engine grows fainter.

I keep scrambling up the hillside. "Dean!"

A couple yards ahead, I nearly trip over his body. He's lying in some underbrush. His eyes are closed and his skin shines with sweat. When I check for a pulse in his wrist, it's barely there at all.

I drop to my knees beside him and shake him. "Dean, wake up."

He doesn't respond, no matter how many times I shake him and say his name. More of the vapor must've entered his system than mine, or the poison affected him more than it affected me.

I look around helplessly. If the raiders are searching the forest,

I can't stay here in case they come back. Dean should stay safe in the underbrush while I go see if there are others alive. But I can't risk getting closer to the hovercraft until I know for sure the raiders aren't still there. I need a better vantage point.

On my feet again, I quickly pick out the tallest tree in the vicinity. I pull myself up onto the lowest branch. The bark is coated with moss that's wet from the rain and slippery to stand on. I make sure I have a firm grip on the branch above me before I climb higher.

I'd forgotten how wonderful it feels to climb up in high places. I used to escape to the tops of buildings all the time when I was growing up in the work camp on the other side of the Surface. It wasn't a true escape, not really, but it was something that was mine. Officials couldn't bother me as easily if I was up high. The only danger was falling, and I wouldn't let that happen.

It doesn't take long to reach a branch that gives me a view of the hilltop. Pushing the leaves aside, I can see smoke rising from the hovercraft wreckage. It's maybe fifty yards away.

Two of the raiders have landed in the crash site. Three more circle overhead like monstrous krails.

An alien stalks into view through the smoke. It's walking on two legs, but it's much taller and leaner than any human I've ever seen. It carries a weapon, a huge black gun similar to our missile launchers. There's a strange, translucent quality to the alien's skin—or maybe what I'm seeing is armor.

I hadn't given much thought to what the Mardenites would look like, but I never would've imagined a creature like this. So alien, yet there's something strangely familiar about it—not just the fact it's walking on two legs. There's something else. Something I can't place.

The alien turns away and disappears into the smoke before I can make out more of its features. Anyway, it's too far away.

One of the raiders lifts off the ground. The second follows, and the third. The raiders still up in the air lead the others to the north, and I watch the swarm grow smaller and smaller until it's lost in the moonlit clouds.

I hurry down from the tree. Maybe I should feel relieved the Mardenites are gone, but I don't, and I won't until I find more survivors. There's a tight wad of fear in my chest, a worry that I might be the only person left.

I refuse to believe it until I've scoured the crash site and checked every part of the forest.

I go back to Dean in his hiding spot and find him stirring, swimming back into consciousness. "What happened?" he asks.

"The poison gas knocked you out. How do you feel?"

"Horrible," he says, groaning. He tries to sit up and I help him. He's sweating so much, I can feel it through his glove. But he has enough strength to ask, "Are you okay?"

"I'm fine," I say. "A lot better than you."

"Good. I had a feeling you would be."

I'm not quite sure what he means. But I brush the comment aside. "The raiders took off. I'm going back to the crash site to look for survivors."

"I'm coming with you," Dean says, struggling to his feet. He looks like he might pass out again. All he's going to do is slow me down.

"You should stay here and rest. I'll come back for you."

"No, I have orders and I'm following them," Dean says, grabbing his pulse rifle from the grass. He cocks it so it's ready to fire. "Lead the way."

I can see there's no arguing with him, so I don't bother trying. I turn in the direction of the hilltop and Dean follows, wincing with every step.

9

The smoky battlefield is silent when we reach it. There're no signs of raiders among the clouds drifting across the starry sky. The Mardenites won the attack and fled the scene.

Rain drizzles on the grass, hissing as it lands on a few spots where flames still lick the debris. My boots squelch in the mud as I hurry through the smoke, scouring the hill for any sign of survivors. But the only people I find are three dead soldiers. Corpses with flame-eaten clothes.

There were more than three soldiers in the battle. Where did the rest go?

There's a clanging sound behind me, and I spin around. But it's just Dean, pushing a piece of rubble off the body of another fallen soldier. The man I saw struck by a laser earlier. Dean feels for a pulse in his wrist, but the look in his eyes tells me there's nothing.

"I'm going to search the hovercraft," I say.

"Be careful," Dean says, straightening and continuing to survey the battlefield.

I turn and hurry up the boarding ramp into the cargo bay. "Beechy! Darren! Uma!"

My voice echoes in the dead hull of the ship.

There's no one in the cabin upstairs, or in the weapons locker, or in any of the smaller rooms attached to the cargo bay. The engine room would've been too full of smoke and ashes for anyone to use it as a hiding place. I'm afraid to look in there for fear of running into Fiona's body.

I check inside the infirmary and find the empty surgical table where Sandy was undergoing her operation. The IV bag on the stand next to the table is half full of blood the doctor must've been giving her to replenish what she lost.

Beechy must've carried Sandy off the ship. The question is what happened to them afterward.

Back outside, Dean meets me near the foot of the boarding ramp. "Did you find anyone?" he asks, breathless. His body is still trembling.

I shake my head. "We should check the forest."

"Maybe we should rest first," Dean says. "If anyone's out there, they'll still be there in a few minutes."

"No. We have to find Beechy." I push past him. If Dean won't help me search the forest, I'll go myself.

"Clementine, you're hurt." There's authority in Dean's voice now, beneath his weariness. And real concern. "You need to change your bandages."

I look down at my arm, where I was shot last night. Sure enough, the bandages are in dirty shreds from my fall in the forest. The wound has opened up again and there's blood on my safety suit.

I grind my teeth together. "Fine. Five minutes of rest and we'll go."

"I'll get a medi-kit," Dean says, starting up the boarding ramp.

The question I've been wanting to ask him spills out: "Why do you care if I'm hurt? Why are you helping me?"

Dean pauses halfway up the ramp. His voice is stiff when he answers: "I've told you why. Commander Charlie ordered me to make sure you're safely returned to the Core."

"Right." I don't hide my sarcasm. "He thinks I possess 'extraordinary genes,' so he wants to keep me safe, even though I've done nothing but disobey him and ruin his plans. You expect me to believe that?"

"I don't know why he wants to keep you safe." The muscles in his back are rigid, visible through his armor. "I don't question the commander's orders. I just follow them."

"You're lying."

"If that's what you want to believe, I don't care," Dean says, continuing up the ramp. "I'll be back with the medi-kit." He disappears inside the hovercraft.

I kick a piece of rubble in the grass, letting out a yell of frustration. I'm sick of all the lies. They have to stop. From now on, I'm going to demand the truth until someone gives it to me.

Out of the corner of my eye, I catch movement on the edge of the forest. I spin around, focusing on the trees. Four figures limp onto the battlefield—four more survivors from the battle with the Mardenites. Dean and I aren't the only people left alive.

I run forward, ready to shout Beechy's name—he has to be with them. But I stop in my tracks as soon as one of the figures lifts his gun and I realize he's not an Alliance rebel. He's Sam, limping along but alive as ever.

"Halt right there," he says.

I put my hands up, so he'll know I'm not one of the Mardenites. "Don't shoot. It's me—it's Clementine."

Sam's arm falters a little, but he doesn't lower his gun. He's close enough now that I can make out his face and the people he's with: Skylar, Darren, and a corporal whose name I don't know.

Beechy isn't with them.

"How did you get here?" Sam asks, his voice unsteady with anger. His eyes seem bloodshot in the moonlight.

A step behind him, Darren's eyes flicker between the two of us nervously. His face is shiny with fever sweat, his body shaking. The rest of them are in a similar state. Skylar has a hand pressed against her side, covering up a dark stain that looks like blood. She makes no move to calm Sam down. Her gaze drifts past me, looking around the battle site.

"I'm not alone," I say, trying not to sound as agitated as I feel. Sam shouldn't be pointing his gun at me after everything, but he's clearly not in a normal state of mind. "I came with Lieutenant Dean. He and I escaped into the forest."

"Where is he now?" Sam demands.

"I'm right here," Dean says behind me, his boots clunking down the boarding ramp. "Lieutenant, put your weapon down. We've lost enough people today."

After a long moment, Sam slowly lowers his gun. I drop my hands. The look he gives me is full of pure hatred. I'm sure he can't stand the fact I survived yet another battle.

"It's good to see you," Skylar says between coughs, as Dean

steps into view beside me. "We weren't sure if anyone else got away before the raiders landed."

I swallow hard against the bulge of fear in my throat. I have a question, but I'm worried I already know the answer. "Where is everyone else?"

"They're gone," Darren says through a ragged breath.

"They were taken by the Mardenites," Skylar says.

Their words slice through my chest like a knife. Taken. Captured.

"You're wrong," I say.

They have to be.

"How do you know?" Dean asks.

"We saw the aliens drag people aboard their ships." Skylar's voice doesn't waver, and she meets his eyes directly. I don't think she's lying.

I feel cold all over, drained of every last bit of hope. In my head, I see the Mardenite stalking across the hillside through the smoke. Had the creature just hauled Beechy's body aboard a ship? And Sandy? And Uma?

"How many were taken?"

"At least seven people," Skylar says. "Everyone on the battle-field who was still alive. Most of them were trying to escape into the forest, but the poison gas knocked them out. We were lucky we'd already started running, or we would've been captured too."

"We need to get off the Surface," Sam says, his voice still cold. "We're in danger of being captured as long as we're up here."

"We don't have a ship," the curly-haired corporal says. He's clutching his arm to his chest like it was wounded. "The hover-craft's useless and the X-wings are gone."

"The Pipeline isn't far—we can reach it on foot in a couple

hours," Skylar says. "There's a transmission station there. They'll have an emergency transport we can use to get to the Core. Unless someone has a better plan." She looks around at the rest of us.

No one says anything in response, not even Sam. This was the plan Beechy had meant for me to follow before he was captured. I owe it to him to go through with it.

"It'll be light in a few hours," Dean says, turning in the direction of the hovercraft. "We'd better get moving if we want to reach the Pipeline before dawn."

As we start toward our ship to grab the supplies we'll need, I search the sky again for signs of the raiders that took Beechy and the other prisoners. But they're long gone, likely on their way to the battle stations floating beyond the acid shield. They're not coming back.

The guilt rips me apart inside. I did what Beechy wanted; I left him and I escaped. But if I'd stayed, maybe I could've saved him. Maybe he would've avoided capture too.

I focus on the one thing Skylar said that gives me hope: The Mardenites only captured those who were alive.

Beechy is still alive. For how long, I don't know. I don't know what the Mardenites will do to him and the other prisoners. But as long as there's a chance he and Sandy and Uma are alive, there's a chance I can find a way to rescue them once we return to the Core.

# 10

We take as many supplies from the hovercraft as we can: meal rations, water canteens, sleeping rolls, and extra ammunition stuffed into backpacks.

Darren helps me dress the bullet wound on my shoulder, and I treat his leg. The damaged tissue below his knee is starting to fester. I wipe it as best I can with the antiseptic packets in the medikit, but he needs stronger antibiotics or the infection's going to get worse. One more reason we need to get off the Surface as soon as possible.

With our sacks slung over our shoulders, we take one last look around the battlefield. Dean and the corporal, Cormac, moved the bodies of the dead soldiers into the hovercraft and shut the air-lock doors behind them. Normally we would've set their bodies on fire, but we didn't want to attract any more raiders to the hilltop while we're still in the area. Now all that's left of the battlefield is the silent hovercraft, the smoke trailing from the piles of rubble, and the lingering smell of the poison gas.

My stomach pinches at the sight of it. If the raiders found our group and attacked us out here in the middle of nowhere, I can only imagine how they've ravaged the city halfway across the Surface. The settlement where I grew up.

"We must be too late," I say.

"For what?" Darren asks.

"To save the Surface city."

"Hopefully the commander's plan worked," Skylar says, adjusting the straps of her sack on her shoulders. "If he triggered the Strykers, the Mardenites were destroyed along with the people."

I snort. "You saw how big the fleet is. Those bombs couldn't have crippled even half the raiders. Thanks to your precious commander, thousands of people are dead for nothing."

Dean hesitates. "We don't know that for sure."

"We will soon enough."

Skylar's cheeks pinch together, but all she says is, "Let's move out."

Dean leads the way into the forest, away from the silent battlefield. He keeps a compass in his hand to make sure we're moving in the right direction. He and Skylar plotted out the quickest path to the Pipeline using a map we found in the cockpit. At a fast pace, we can reach the transmission station in three hours, just before sunrise.

I'm worried it's going to take us a lot longer. We're all exhausted from fighting and from lack of sleep. Especially once we have to hike uphill in the snow, it's going to get difficult to keep going.

Darren's breath hitches with every step as he walks beside me. We're a few feet away from the others, walking on the other side of some of the trees. The wind is freezing cold, and my teeth won't stop chattering.

"You can lean on me if you need to," I say.

"My leg isn't the main problem," he says, though he touches my shoulder to steady himself. "It's that vruxing poison gas. My skin is still burning."

I bite my lip. "I'm sorry."

"Guess I should just be glad I'm alive, instead of a corpse in the engine room or a prisoner of those aliens." Darren's jaw tightens and he shakes his head in disbelief. "I can't believe we lost everyone else."

"We'll see them again," I say firmly. "We're going to find a way out of this. We have to."

Darren doesn't say anything in reply, just exhales a heavy sigh.

I glance over at Sam, crunching through the leaves on the other side of the trees. He catches me looking at him and meets my gaze head-on. There's a threat in his eyes, and his fingers play with the gun in his holster.

Pressing my lips together, I turn my head away. We're stuck with him and Skylar and Dean because there's no one else left, but we need to remember they're not our allies. Even Dean is only helping so he can hand me over to Charlie again.

The air grows even colder as we begin the trek up the mountains. The storm has finally passed on, but there are fresh patches of snow glistening between the trees. The higher elevation makes it harder to breathe, and my legs are becoming heavier and heavier to lift. I don't see how I'm going to make it much farther.

The Pipeline is just on the other side of these mountains, and so is the transmission station. Another hour and we'll be there. If we take much longer, we'll lose the cover of darkness.

Still, when Darren finally asks if we can rest for a little while and the others agree, I'm glad. All I need to do is close my eyes for a few minutes and I should be able to keep the pace.

"We'll stop for half an hour," Dean says, setting his pack at the base of a tree. He's shivering and his face is soaked in sweat.

Sam has a hand pressed to his helmet like his head is hurting. Cormac unrolls his bedroll, wincing with every movement.

Skylar takes a seat on a boulder and continues fiddling with the hand-comm she brought from the hovercraft. She seems less sick than the others, though her eyes are also slightly bloodshot. She's been trying to make contact with someone in the Core, now that there's less interference from the raiders.

"This is Cadet Skylar," she says for the fiftieth time, her voice scratchy from weariness. "I'm with Lieutenants Sam and Dean and we are stranded in Surface Sector H-9, close to the Pipeline transmission station. We are in need of a rescue team. Does anyone copy?"

"Just give up," Sam says, rummaging through his pack for his water canteen. "If they'd heard our transmission, someone would've answered by now."

"We might not be able to hear their answer through the interference," Skylar says.

"That doesn't mean you need to keep saying the same thing over and over. It's not going to make them get here any faster."

Skylar catches my gaze and rolls her eyes at Sam's comment. I start to smile back, then stop. Rolling eyes at each other and smiling is something friends do, and she and I aren't friends. Not anymore.

I turn away from her. Out of the corner of my eye, her expression hardens and she turns away too.

I take out my sleeping roll and set it on a semi-dry area of the ground, as far away from Sam as possible. I'm anxious to get a few winks of sleep, but first I need to relieve myself. And I'm not going to do it in front of everyone.

"I'll be right back," I tell Darren, and slip away from the group, moving through the trees.

Soon the camp is out of sight, but I don't stop walking yet. It's nice to finally get away from everyone. It's still dark out, but there's enough moonlight that I can see where I'm going.

I find a bush and unzip the outer layer of my safety suit. There's a special apparatus in the suit that lets me go without being exposed to the air. It's kind of a pain, but it's better than risking moonshine.

It hits me that all the time we've been out here in the mountains, I haven't seen any animals. Not a krail or mountain bird in sight. When Commander Charlie took the acid shield down and the acid seeped into the atmosphere, it must've killed thousands of animals. But then, he never intended for the Surface to continue existing at all. If he'd had his way, his bomb would've blasted the outer sectors apart so his Core battleship could fly far away to Marden, to take back the planet that was our home long ago.

But Beechy, Oliver, and I used his bomb to destroy the acid generator on the moon instead, so Charlie couldn't go through with his plan. Not that it would've worked, anyway. The Mardenite army was already on its way.

I've finished relieving myself and just re-zipped the outer layer of my suit when there's the crunch of boots in the snow behind me.

I spin around as Sam steps out from between the trees.

# 11

He's only a dark shape in the shadows, but I know it's him because of the way he's breathing. He watches me like he's waiting for something.

Now I regret going so far from the camp. "What do you want?" I ask, clenching my hands into fists at my sides.

"I want to know how you did it." Sam's voice has airiness to it, a quality that makes me think he must still be in a lot of pain from the effects of the poison gas. He takes a slow step forward.

I've been in this scenario before, alone with Sam, and it didn't end well—he attacked me and nearly took advantage of me. Maybe if I act like I'm not afraid of him, he won't try anything. I'd run, but I'm sure he'd chase after me.

"How I did what?" I ask.

"How you avoided capture. I saw the poison bomb drop two feet away from you. You should've been knocked out like the rest of us. The aliens should've found your body in the trees."

"The poison did knock me out," I lie. "But I was already far away. You escaped too, didn't you?"

"Barely. The poison was so painful I felt like I was dying. Almost wished I was. But you? You don't even have a scratch." He takes another step toward me, his eyes full of viciousness. "You keep escaping death, even when you shouldn't. But it's going to end as soon as we return to the Core."

"Commander Charlie won't hurt me," I say forcefully. "He wants me alive. He needs me." I'm grasping at threads of hope here, at things I'm not sure I believe.

Sam lets out a short, cold laugh. "I think you overestimate your worth to him."

"So do you." I'm sick of Sam believing he's better than me. "Charlie sent you to the Surface knowing Marden's army could arrive any day now, knowing you could end up in danger. He didn't even trust you with all the information about their return. Think about it, Sam. He's lied to you as many times as he's lied to me, if not more. You're not special to him. You're nothing but a pawn, and if you keep fighting for him, you're going to die for him too."

In a flash, Sam moves to strike me. I jump back, blocking his punch with my forearm. But Sam comes back faster. His fist slams into my ribs, knocking the breath out of me.

Before I can recover, he's pummeling me again, smacking my chest and shoulder with his fists so hard I lose my balance. I hit the ground on my side, gasping from the pain.

There's no time to rest. He comes at me and I kick at his leg, knocking him a step backward.

As I scramble to my feet, he punches me square in the chest. There's a cracking sound and a hot flash of pain in my chest that makes me scream. He snapped one of my ribs.

Sam knocks me onto the ground a second time, and this time I'm too weak to get back up. My chest feels like it's on fire, and the pain worsens every time I draw in breath.

Sam gets on top of me, pressing his weight into my body. I struggle beneath him but I'm pinned to the ground. I can barely move my arms.

"Help me!" I yell as loud as I can.

Didn't anyone notice Sam come after me? Why hasn't anyone come looking?

Sam wraps his fingers around my neck. He squeezes hard, making it impossible for me to speak or get any air in.

My gun. I need to get it out.

"You think you know who I am," Sam says. "But you're wrong. You have no idea what I would do for Commander Charlie."

I draw the gun from my holster, but I lose my grip on it and Sam kicks it out of my reach.

I flail beneath his weight, trying desperately to get air into my lungs. He's squeezing my neck too hard. He's going to choke me to death.

No one's coming to help me. I have to escape on my own. *How?*

Suddenly I remember—the syringes in my holster pouch.

Everything's becoming hazy, but somehow I manage to open the pouch. I wrap my hand around one of the syringes and pull it out. Sam is wearing armor that protects him almost everywhere, but there are a few weak spots, including the place where I shot his leg earlier tonight. The way he's crouched on top of me, his ankle is within reach.

Gathering all my energy, I stab the needle through the bandage on his leg and press the plunger. Sam lets out a gasp and releases my neck a little, enough for me to get some air in.

I kick at his groin as hard as I can. His weight gives out and I shove him off me, scrambling to my feet. He's hardly fighting me anymore; he's groaning from the kick to his groin, and he seems dazed and confused. The serum is working fast.

I pull the second syringe out of the holster pouch and stab the needle into Sam's leg. Within moments, his body falls limp on the ground. His eyes glaze over in his head. I bet his pulse is weakening.

Anger still courses through my veins. I draw the last syringe from my pouch. I take a step toward Sam.

A third dosage might kill him. A simple stab and press of the plunger, and I'd have one less enemy to worry about. If Sam were in my shoes, he'd give it to me without a second's thought.

But as I stare at him, helpless on the ground, I realize I can't go through with it. Sam can't hurt me anymore. And if I killed him when he was completely incapable of defending himself, what would that make me?

It would make me exactly like the Developers, the people I've been fighting.

Sam isn't my real enemy—he's just a pawn. A stupid boy who's been manipulated and warped into following orders, bred to be a ruthless killer like his commander.

Commander Charlie is the one I need to kill. And I will kill him, once the threat of Marden's army has been removed. I'll make him pay for everything he's done.

There's rustling in the trees behind me. I spin around and a light shines in my eyes, from Dean's armor. He and Skylar step into view, both of them out of breath.

"Did you call for help?" Dean asks.

"I did," I say, suddenly nervous.

His light lands on Sam's crumpled body on the ground behind me, and he freezes. Skylar's eyes slide from Sam to me, still standing with the syringes in my trembling hand. I just subdued an officer. People have been put to death in gas chambers for much less than this.

"H-he attacked me," I explain. There's water in my eyes, and I blink it out. "He tried to choke me to death."

Skylar stares at the syringes in my hand. "Did you subdue him?"

"I had to," I say. "He was going to kill me."

Dean curses loudly.

"I'm sorry—"

"Don't be. The idiot had it coming." Dean moves toward me, his boots crunching in the snow. "How much did he hurt you? Are you okay?"

"My neck hurts," I say, wincing. "And I think I fractured a couple ribs." Every time I draw in breath, the pain is excruciating.

He touches the bandage on my arm. When he pulls his hand away, there's blood on his fingers. My wound must've opened up again.

Behind Dean, Skylar kicks at Sam's limp leg with her boot. He doesn't respond, not in the slightest. His eyes are still open, but they're glazed over. He seems like he's drifting in some other world inside his head.

"How much serum did you give him?" she asks.

I bite my lip. "Two dosages."

Skylar snorts. "That explains it."

She's laughing now, but what's going to happen once we're back in the Core? I don't think the Developers will be so amused when they hear what I did to Sam.

"I'm going to get in trouble for this, aren't I?" I ask.

"No, you're not," Dean says. "Because no one's going to find out you gave him the serum. We'll say it was me. Sam attacked you, Skylar and I heard you call for help, and I took care of him."

I frown. "You'd do that for me?"

"Yes," Dean says, his voice unwavering.

"What if Sam wakes up and tells the real story?" I ask. Maybe he won't have any memory of what happened while he was doped up, but I doubt he'll forget I'm the one who stabbed him with the syringes. And I doubt he'll forgive me.

"It will be his word against ours," Dean says. "As long as Skylar agrees to back us up."

We both glance in her direction. Skylar's eyes meet mine, and for a moment I can see her debating whether or not she wants to help me. Weighing whether it's worth it to lie for me, or whether it would help her prove her loyalty to Commander Charlie if she told him I subdued Sam.

"Sure, I'll back you up," she says, folding her arms. "Stars know the lieutenant needed someone to shut him up." She smirks a little.

Dean glances at me again, looking for my reaction. I don't have anything to say. I don't trust Skylar, but what choice do I have? If it becomes clear reporting me for what I did could work in her favor, I'm sure she'll betray me again. But there's no point worrying about that until it happens.

"Okay, we'd better get him back to camp," Dean says, stomping over to Sam's body. "Skylar, help me get him up."

While the two of them heave Sam off the ground, I grab my pulse gun from where it landed and tuck it back into my holster. I toss the empty syringes and the one still full of serum into the bushes, where they can't hurt anyone else.

Sam makes a strange moaning sound as we start back to camp, and his eyes roll back farther into his head. I can't help smiling a little seeing him like this. Now the monster who's used his hands against me too many times is a weak, helpless human who can't even walk on his own, let alone wield a weapon. I still have plenty of dangers, but Sam is no longer one of them. At least until he recovers.

Back at the camp, Dean and Skylar tuck Sam's body into his sleeping bag. Darren and Cormac are both still awake; they'd also heard me call for help. I let Dean explain what happened, and avoid Darren's gaze when he hears I was nearly strangled to death by Sam. I don't need anyone's pity.

We only have a few minutes left until we have to leave if we're going to reach the Pipeline before sunrise. Hopefully I can still catch a few winks of sleep, enough to feel a bit more rested. I slip inside the warmth of my sleeping bag and finally close my eyes.

Exhaustion quickly drags me under. I dream I'm chained to a stake in the ground in the middle of the desert, far from civilization. The world is on fire all around me. Flames rain down from the sky, and the cacti and the tumbleweeds are alight. The air is so thick with smoke, I can barely breathe.

Amid the cacti and tumbleweeds, I make out human bodies. People with familiar faces. Nellie and Hector and Evie, the friends I made in the Crust camp. Their eyes are wide open, their mouths screaming. Their bodies are paralyzed. I call to them, but they only scream in reply.

I pull against my chains, trying to get to my friends before the fire does, but I can't save them. The flames scorch their clothes and lick their skin until their faces aren't recognizable anymore. They are charred corpses.

The flames drift closer and closer to me, licking my boots. I wrench and wrench to break free of the stake, but my chains only grow tighter. They cut into my wrists and make them bleed.

I wake just before the fire reaches me. Darren is shouting. It takes me several moments to understand what he's saying.

"Raiders! There are raiders in sight!"

The blood drains from my face, and every part of my body turns rock-solid with fear.

We didn't escape the Mardenites.

# 12

I scramble out of my sleeping bag and get to my feet. A slice of pain shoots through my injured ribs and I regret standing up so fast. My hand fumbles for my pulse gun.

Skylar, Cormac, and Dean are already up, their eyes on the sky through the trees overhead. The sky is growing lighter as the day moves closer to dawn. There are three dark forms flying above the mountain pass. Three raiders.

"What do we do?" Darren asks. His eyes are wide with fear.

"Stay out of sight," Dean says, moving away from the opening in the branches. "The trees should hide us unless they get a lot closer."

Skylar crouches beside a tree trunk with her gun in her hand. "As soon as they're gone, we hightail it for the transmission station so we can get the hell off the Surface."

I move beneath the branches of another tree and drop onto my knees, not taking my eyes off the raiders. They're circling lower and lower like they're searching for something.

STEPHANIE DIAZ / 88

How did they find us again? They can't have known we survived, or they would've captured us back on the hillside. Surely these ships don't know we're here. It's just a coincidence they're flying overhead.

"We shouldn't have stopped in the first place," Cormac says through gritted teeth.

"We needed to rest," Skylar snaps back. "If we hadn't and the Mardenites ran into us before we reached the station, we'd have been in no state to fight them."

I don't think we're in any state to fight them now. There are six of us, and Sam is completely useless. Which is why I'm hoping with all my might we remain unseen.

"I'll start packing up everything so we can leave," Dean says, slinging his rifle over his shoulder and moving around the camp to stuff the sleeping bags into our sacks.

"Do we need the bedrolls?" Cormac asks. "We should just leave them here and go."

"No," Skylar says swiftly. "We should keep them with us in case something goes wrong at the station and we end up stuck on the Surface longer than we intended."

"We're getting off the Surface tonight. We'll die if we stay out here much longer."

While Cormac and Skylar continue to argue, I keep my eyes glued on the sky. The closer the Mardenite ships get, the more details I'm able to make out. They don't have curved, V-shaped wings or rugged bodies like the last raiders we ran into. Two of the ships are round like flight pods; the third is a small hovercraft.

"Wait!" I say, interrupting Skylar mid-sentence. "Look at the ships. Those aren't raiders."

The others immediately stop talking and look at where I'm

pointing. One of the flight pods is so low I can make out a symbol on its hull, the bronze shape of the moon.

"She's right," Darren says. "They're Core ships."

Maybe it's a rescue mission. Maybe they finally heard our transmission.

"We need to make contact with them," Dean says.

Skylar quickly pulls out the hand-comm and twists the signal dial to the correct channel. "This is Cadet Skylar. I am with Lieutenants Dean and Sam, and we are stranded in Surface Sector H-9, close to the Pipeline transmission station. Does anyone copy?"

There's a long stretch of nothing but static. My heart pounds as I wait for an answer, if anyone's going to answer at all.

*Please, please, please.*

A voice crackles through the comm speaker: "Cadet Skylar, this is Lieutenant Patrick. What are your coordinates?"

Skylar lets out a whoop! of excitement. Relief, so much relief floods my bones.

She relays our exact coordinates to Lieutenant Patrick, and the Core ships lower into the clearing. The lieutenant disembarks with several soldiers and the ship medic. He takes one look at the disheveled state of our group and asks, "What happened?"

"We were attacked by Mardenites," Dean says. "Didn't you hear our transmission from earlier tonight?"

"We received a transmission, but there was a lot of interference," Lieutenant Patrick says. "I don't know exactly how much got through—I wasn't the one who intercepted it. All I was told was you were in trouble and we needed to help you get back to the Core."

Commander Charlie did send a rescue mission. Help just didn't get here fast enough.

"What happened to the rest of your crew?"

"They were captured," Skylar says.

"We'll tell you everything once we're on board," Dean says. "We need to get to the Pipeline before any Mardenite ships come roaming the area again."

"Right," Patrick says, glancing fearfully at the sky. "Let's hurry. Get the wounded onto stretchers."

Sam is hauled onto a stretcher by the soldiers. So is Darren, because of his leg infection. My ribs still ache, but I can walk well enough, so I go up the boarding ramp into the hovercraft on my own.

Inside, someone wraps a blanket around me and thrusts a canteen into my hands. The sweet, frothy drink warms my belly. Hopefully my teeth will stop chattering soon.

We buckle in for takeoff. I watch through one of the cabin windows as the pilot takes us over the mountain pass. The sun comes into view, casting sweeping rays of red across the snow-topped mountains ahead of us. I grip my armrests, bracing for any sign of raiders. But there are no ships on the horizon. No enemy contacts appear on our radar screen.

We descend into the valley below us, where the Pipeline entrance lies well hidden between the forested hills. The trees grow bigger and bigger, and finally I see the dark hole of the tunnel entrance. I don't let out my breath until we're well into the tunnel. The Mardenites don't know this tunnel or the lower sectors exists, so we're out of their reach. For now.

But the raiders are still out there with my friends aboard their ships. They're still attacking the Surface. Soon we'll know exactly how much damage they've done.

Soon I'll have to face Commander Charlie. I'm going to have

to explain why I disobeyed his orders and broke free of his serum's control. I'll have to convince him not to go through with his threat to kill Logan.

But for now, I push aside those worries and focus on the fact I've escaped one of my enemies alive.

Lieutenant Patrick sends a transmission ahead to the Core, to let them know he has injured passengers on the way. In the meantime, the ship medic does what she can to treat our wounds.

First she checks my vital signs. Blood pressure is a bit high, but not a real cause for concern. Temperature is normal. Unlike the other survivors, I don't have a high fever or symptoms of nausea. My biggest medical problems are obvious: my ruptured eardrum, broken ribs, and the bullet wound that reopened thanks to Sam's attack. The medic stuffs a small bit of gauze into my ear to help it stay dry and heal on its own, though at this point I'm afraid I'll never recover my hearing completely—not without surgery or an implant. My ribs will also have to heal on their own, but the medic gives me a pain pill to take so it won't hurt as much when I breathe and cough. After all the times medicine has been used to control me, I'm wary of taking any pills. But my chest pain is becoming too much to bear, and I can't afford to let it slow me down. It's only a mild pill, anyway. The medic says I'll probably need stronger medicine, but I'll have to wait until we're back in the Core.

While she cleans and re-bandages my gun wound, I wonder about why the poison gas didn't affect me. It can't be because I ran faster than the others to escape it, or because I didn't inhale as much as them. I was right next to the bomb when it fell. Somehow, I was able to resist the poison the same way I've resisted the control serums better than everyone else. And I don't think it's a coincidence.

After the medic is finished with me, I'm given a fresh pair of clothes to change into. I won't need my safety suit in the Core, as the moon's acid can't reach us there.

I go into a supply closet, so I won't have to change in front of everyone. But the closet isn't empty, as I'd hoped it would be. Skylar's changing in here too. She pauses when I walk in.

"Hey," she says, clearly uncomfortable to be in such close quarters with me.

I don't say anything in response. Just because she's agreed, for the time being, not to get me in trouble for the Sam situation doesn't mean anything has changed between us.

I turn my back on her.

Changing proves to be a difficult task. I remove my helmet easily enough, but I have a harder time getting out of the suit. The pain medicine hasn't sunk in yet, and even reaching my hand behind my back to unzip the suit sends slashes of pain through my chest.

"Here, let me help you," Skylar says, behind me.

I hesitate. But clearly this is going to take forever if I try to do it on my own. "Fine."

She finishes unzipping the suit for me and helps me ease it off my arms. After I've stepped out of it, she helps me remove the outfit underneath and pull on a new shirt and set of trousers. The process is painful enough with her help. I can't imagine how much worse it would've been without her.

When it's finally over I say, "Thanks."

"Don't mention it," Skylar says.

There's a long, awkward stretch of silence. She shifts from one foot to the other, looking like she wants to speak.

She starts to open her mouth, but I blurt out: "Why aren't you going to turn me in for what I did to Sam? You know Commander Charlie was waiting for me to do something like this on the mission. And I'm sure he'd praise you for your loyalty if you ratted me out. That's how you get your fix these days, right? By betraying people you once pretended to be friends with."

"Sam attacked you first," Skylar says, ignoring the second part of what I said. Her cheeks are turning pink. "I'm not that cruel of a person."

I snort. "Oh, really?"

"Yes. And I don't think you should be punished for making a decision you had to make in order to protect yourself." Her eyes meet mine, hard and challenging. "We do what we have to do."

She's trying to say the things we've done are the same. She betrayed the Alliance in order to save herself from harm, so she doesn't deserve blame.

But what she did was unforgivable. Skylar handed other people—*innocent* people—over to Commander Charlie in order to earn her freedom. People who should never have died are dead because of her.

"Thank you for helping me," I say in a flat tone, picking up my helmet from the floor. "But don't think this means I've forgiven you for being a traitor."

"You're welcome," Skylar snaps. "And that's fine. I wasn't asking for your forgiveness."

She leaves the room before I can, slamming the door shut behind her.

⚔

I don't remember falling asleep in my passenger seat, but I wake to someone shaking my shoulder. "What?" I mumble.

"We're here," a soldier says. "Time to go."

Blinking, I lift my head and take in the scene around me. The hovercraft isn't moving anymore. I must've slept the rest of the hour-long journey through the Pipeline.

Beyond the open doors at the back of the pod, I see transports of various shapes and sizes, and mechanics in orange uniforms pushing tool carts between the ships. We've landed in a flight hangar in the Core.

Most of the other passengers have already disembarked. The gurneys with Darren and Sam are gone.

I quickly unbuckle and get to my feet. My neck is stiff from the position I was sitting in, and the pain medicine is no longer doing anything for my ribs. I keep a hand on my chest as I follow the soldier out of the pod.

There's a group of people waiting for us at the bottom of the ramp. I immediately search for Commander Charlie in the group, but he is missing. There are only soldiers and a few nurses, one of whom is wheeling Darren's gurney toward the hangar exit.

Cadet Waller, the woman who oversaw my Extraction test and serves as one of Charlie's aids, is standing near Sam's gurney, next to Lieutenant Dean and Skylar. Waller's dressed in her usual scarlet uniform, wearing her hair in a slick, high ponytail, clutching the tablet she always carries with her. She steps closer to Sam on his gurney. He's babbling incoherent speech in his overdosed haze.

"Take the lieutenant to the health ward," Cadet Waller says. She glances at me with no pity in her gaze. Then she looks over to Skylar and Dean. "Commander Charlie is waiting to speak with the three of you in the debrief room."

My heartbeat picks up. I thought we'd all be taken to the health ward first. I thought I'd have more time to figure out what I'm going to say to Charlie.

"Clementine was hurt," Dean says. "She has fractured ribs and a bullet wound. She needs rest." He sounds wearied, exhausted; yet he isn't even mentioning the fact he's still feverish from poison.

Cadet Waller takes in my injuries—the blood-streaked bandage on my arm, the muddy spots on my safety suit covering up the bruises Sam gave me. All she says is, "She seems well enough to walk, so she's coming."

There's annoyance in her expression, and distrust. She didn't agree with Commander Charlie's decision to send me on this mission.

I might've tried to kill Sam and help the Alliance rebels escape, but I failed. It's not my fault we were attacked by Mardenites. I hope the Developers will believe that.

Dean's eyes flicker to me, a question in them. I bet he'd continue arguing on my behalf if I needed him to, but this isn't worth a fight. I can handle the pain a little while longer. As nervous as I am, it's probably smart to get this meeting over with.

"I can wait," I say, even as I wince from another flash of pain in my ribs. "I'll be fine."

"Good. Follow me," Cadet Waller says, leading the way out of the flight port.

※

The hallways look exactly as they did the first time I arrived in the Core: crisp and clean. That day I was nervous for a different reason, because I didn't know what to expect in this new life I'd won. Now I know the truth: I'm no safer in the Core than I was all those years I lived in the work camp on the Surface. I escaped the hard labor and the starvation, but I didn't escape the ruthless dictator and the lies.

But this time, I'm facing Commander Charlie with more strength and more knowledge. He's tried to control me with two serums now and failed. Giving me another injection won't work; I'll just break free of it again. He's lost the biggest power he had over me. And with the arrival of Marden's army, his mind is preoccupied with a bigger threat, so there's no time for him to create another serum. He's going to have to accept the fact I can no longer be controlled.

If Charlie truly ordered Lieutenant Dean to protect me and bring me back here safely, my life must be worth something to him—something more than what he told me before. I'm going to find out what he needs from me, and I'm going to use it to get what I want: a truce. Freedom for Logan and myself, at least until the Mardenite army has been defeated. That will buy us time to figure out a more permanent means of securing our freedom.

I hold my helmet under my arm as Cadet Waller leads Dean, Skylar, and me down a narrow corridor in Restricted Division, the area of the Core where only the Developers, their personnel, and citizens granted special access are allowed to go. I've walked down some of these corridors before, but the first time I was about to be sent to Karum prison and the second time I was a mindless soldier. Now, I pay closer attention to the path we're taking, trying to memorize it so I can navigate these hallways on my own. We pass doors marked ENGINE ACCESS, CREW QUARTERS, and HALL OF COMMANDERS. Rooms that would allow the Core to function as a space station if the outer sectors of the planet were blasted away.

Ahead of me, Dean is talking to Cadet Waller about the Mardenite invasion. He asks whether she knows anything about the extent of damage to the Surface thus far.

"I don't have the latest updates," she says. "Everything's been chaotic. I've been working with citizen control, so I haven't been able to hear any damage reports. But I'm sure the commander will inform you."

Cadet Waller stops in front of a door marked CONTROL ROOM A. She presses her hand to an access panel on the door, and it opens. We step into a massive room filled with voices and the loud beep of monitors. Giant screens cover the walls and form partitions throughout the room. Each screen has a different label: CORE, CRUST, MANTLE, LOWER, or SURFACE. Images on the screen directly in front of me, labeled CORE, show me Recreation Division, the area of the Core with war simulations, antigravity machines, and other games Core citizens can play in their pastime. This must be the room where the Developers keep an eye on all the happenings in Kiel's five sectors, through the video footage from their security cameras and cam-bot patrols.

As Cadet Waller leads us farther into the room, my eyes jump to one of the partition screens playing a live feed from the Surface. There are more techs crowded around this screen than any other. They're sifting through images at lightning speed, but sometimes they pause long enough for me to catch a flash of something familiar: the education building in the Surface city, or a street in the work camp. Enough for me to see that the skyscrapers in the city are still standing. If the Developers had detonated the Stryker bombs inside the child workers, the buildings would've been completely demolished. Which means the Strykers haven't been detonated yet.

The child workers are still alive. I exhale in relief. Something must've made the Developers decide to abandon that strategy.

My relief splinters when another image pops up: the black shapes of four Mardenite raiders circling over the skyscrapers. The techs start talking faster into their ear-comms. Bits of what they're saying reach my ears over the hubbub of noise in the room.

"We have another sighting—four raider planes—"

"Circling over blocks ten, eleven, and twelve."

"No sign of poison bombs, but we'll let you know."

"This way, quickly now," Cadet Waller says, ushering us past the screens.

I almost stop and wait to see what the raiders will do on the screens. But it's not like I can do anything to stop an attack from this control room, anyway. I can only hope the techs are communicating with a military squadron on the Surface.

Cadet Waller leads us to a door on the far side of the room. She pauses in front of the door and presses a speaker button on the wall. "Commander Charlie, sir, this is Cadet Waller. I have the survivors of the Alliance mission, as you requested."

A moment passes before an answer comes through the speaker. "Bring them in," Charlie says.

Just hearing his cold, hoarse voice sends a shiver down my spine. The words he said to me before I left for the Surface mission replay in my mind, burning in my memory: *The more you fight the serum, the more you will lose.*

But it was nothing more than an empty threat, meant to scare me into thinking he still has power over me. I won't let him control me anymore, or hurt Logan or anyone else I care about ever again.

Cadet Waller opens the door and leads us into the debrief room, her high, black ponytail swinging behind her. I follow Dean and Skylar inside, hardening my jaw. Trying to control my breathing so the pain in my ribs won't distract me from what I have to do.

It's not just Commander Charlie waiting for us.

# 13

Charlie sits on the other side of a large, circular table, between three men and one woman. All of them wear matching navy blue uniforms with small golden moons pinned to their chests. These are the five scientists and military leaders who rule Kiel.

The unease worsens in my stomach. Cadet Waller should've warned us they'd be here. This means I have to make all of them, not just Commander Charlie, agree to the truce I want to make.

The only other time I've seen all five Developers together was the day I completed my Extraction training, when I became an official citizen of the Core. I shook hands with each of them, and they offered me congratulations. Behind their warm, smiling exteriors, I'm sure they were celebrating that they'd soon have one more person to use as a pawn for their own purposes.

Right now, it seems we've interrupted them. They're in the middle of communicating with someone via a live video hologram on the table in front of them.

"If you want this to work, I'm going to need it as soon as possible," the person on the video feed says. I can't see his face from this side of the table, but he sounds like Colonel Parker, the soldier Charlie sent to the Surface yesterday morning to oversee the transport of all the child workers from the internment camps into the resident buildings. The colonel must still be in one of the outer sectors or else he'd be talking to his commanders in person.

"You'll get it," Commander Charlie says. "Be patient."

He glances up at the others and me. The wrinkles around his eyes are exaggerated by tension. Whatever he's talking to Colonel Parker about, it's causing him stress.

"We'll talk again soon," says the woman sitting on Charlie's left-hand side. She shuts off the video hologram as we approach the table.

The back of my neck prickles as the eyes of the Developers focus on Lieutenant Dean, Skylar, and me. There's a stark contrast between us and them—them in their navy blue suits and slick white gloves, us in our disheveled uniforms with the smell of war clinging to our clothes. They sit with their shoulders back and their hands clasped on the table in front of them, emitting authority and power. Commander Charlie isn't the only one who looks stressed; the others have sweat on their foreheads and tightness around their mouths.

I don't know what they've done so far to combat the Mardenite invasion, but I don't think they have a handle on the situation yet. They aren't confident they're going to win. That knowledge makes me breathe a little easier. Hopefully it will make them more willing to accept my help.

"Commanders," Dean says, saluting them.

"Thank you for coming," Commander Charlie says, clearing his throat. "We're glad you made a safe return. I apologize for not dispatching a rescue team sooner, but it took us some time to clear up the transmissions you'd sent. I hope you understand."

"Of course," Dean says, sounding calm. "Thank you for sending a rescue team, nonetheless. Without their help, we might still be stuck on the Surface."

"I'm glad you were able to survive until our people found you." Commander Charlie's gaze pauses on my face, studying my features. He's looking for a sign I'm still under the control of his serum. I don't have a smile painted on my face like I did the last time I saw him. "Clementine, did you follow the orders you were given?"

I stare resolutely back at him. But my palms are sweaty. "No, I didn't."

He shakes his head, disappointed. "Even after we discussed what would happen if you disobeyed. I expected more of you, I must admit." He makes a *tsk* sound.

*He can't control you anymore. Don't let him scare you.*

"I lost the extra syringes of your serum during the Mardenite attack," I say in a steady voice. "And the serum wore off. It wasn't my intention to disobey you."

"I can confirm she's telling the truth," Dean says without hesitation.

"If you wanted me to follow your orders," I say, "you should've made a serum that didn't have to be readministered."

Charlie's jaw twitches. I have a feeling he's angrier than he's letting on. "We'll discuss this more later," he says. He looks at Lieutenant Dean. "I understand the rest of your crew was captured during a Mardenite attack."

"That is correct," Dean says. "And at least four soldiers were killed."

"Where is the mission commander, Lieutenant Sam?" the woman sitting next to Charlie asks. Her hair is a bob of graying brown, and her lips are painted bright red. Her skin has a tautness that makes me think she must've had operations to reduce her wrinkles.

"He's incapacitated from a field injury and he's been taken to the health ward," Dean says. "I took over his command after he was injured."

The woman smiles at Dean, an exaggerated smile that stretches her painted lips. "You must be Lieutenant Dean."

"Yes, sir."

"And you must be Skylar, and of course you're Clementine," she says, looking at each of us in turn. There's a curious spark in her eyes when they land on me. "I've heard a lot about both of you, but I don't believe we've had the pleasure of meeting in person, except for at your citizenship ceremonies. Commander Charlie usually speaks for us in public so the rest of us can focus on keeping the sectors running smoothly."

Funny, I was under the impression Charlie made most of the decisions on his own, and the other Developers simply existed for show.

"You may address me as Commander Regina," the woman says. "I'm the head of culture and public relations. This is Commander Talbin, our head of history." She gestures to the man on her left, the eldest Developer, a balding man with a nervous twitch in his fingers. "Commander William oversees health care." She motions to the man on the other side of Charlie, a man with a thick black beard. "And this is Commander Marshall, our head of science and technology." The dark-skinned, gray-haired Developer on the far left side of the group nods his head.

Commander Marshall must be the father of Fred, the man I met in Karum prison, who first told me about the existence of the planet Marden. He had unknowingly helped Charlie construct the bomb that nearly destroyed all of Kiel's outer sectors. Fred was training to replace his father as a Developer before he rebelled against Charlie. But in prison, Fred began working for Charlie again in order to escape execution. He handed over information about me to the Karum doctors in order to help them break me. Fred hasn't stopped working for the Developers since.

"Please, take a seat." Commander Regina gestures to the empty half of the table. "We know you all need rest and medical attention, so we'll try to make this as brief as possible. But we need you to give us a full account of what happened on your mission."

"It's crucial you tell us as many details about the Mardenite attack, specifically, as possible," Commander Marshall says.

Dean takes a seat at the table and I follow suit, sitting between him and Skylar. I set my helmet on the table.

I can't help staring at Commander Charlie, wondering why he's letting these other Developers take over the interrogation when he's the one who supposedly called us here. Maybe it's my imagination, but he looks a bit uncomfortable.

"Can we bring you anything?" Regina asks. "Some breakfast, perhaps?"

"Breakfast would be wonderful," Dean says.

Regina signals to Cadet Waller, who relays an order to someone through her ear-comm. In the meantime, Dean takes a deep breath and launches into the story of our mission to invade Alliance headquarters. "We departed for the Surface yesterday at Core 1300 hours. We landed a mile away from the facility the Alliance rebels were using as their headquarters, just before night fell.

We loaded the X-wings with explosives and infiltrated the compound's tunnels, following instructions from Beechy and Skylar to break through the security barriers. The rebels didn't seem to have been alerted we were coming, but by the time we reached the center of the compound they'd boarded their transports for a counterattack."

I'm holding my breath, waiting for Dean to come to the part that could incriminate me, the part where I shot Sam. But he skims over many of the details of the fight. He doesn't mention Sam or Sandy getting shot, or that the explosives were detonated sooner than they were supposed to be.

"We overpowered the rebels and they surrendered," he says. "So we set the timers on the explosives and departed the Alliance compound. This is when things stopped going smoothly. Our comms started malfunctioning before we were out of the Alliance tunnels. We couldn't make any contact between our X-wings. That's when we caught sight of the Mardenite fleet invading the Surface."

Skylar abruptly cuts in: "You had people tracking the fleet's movements. We shouldn't have run into this sort of trouble without any warning." She speaks in a calm voice, but I can sense her annoyance underneath.

"You're right, and we apologize," Charlie says stiffly. "It was a mess of miscommunication. Our trackers informed us the fleet was on course to make an early arrival about an hour after you left for the Surface."

"They'd quadrupled their speed in a very short amount of time," Marshall says. "They must've had an extra fuel supply on board they were saving for the final stretch in order to catch us off guard."

"Warning transmissions were immediately sent to all military personnel in the outer sectors, including your crew," Regina says.

"Unfortunately we weren't aware they hadn't reached you until it was too late. Please continue with what happened next."

The door opens and someone comes in with three trays of breakfast food for the three of us. Hot shir cakes with sweet syrup and yazo juice. I pick up my fork and take small bites of the cake as Dean continues the story. I need energy after everything I've been through in the past twelve hours, but I don't want to overwhelm my body by eating too fast.

Dean tells the Developers how the raiders attacked us as we tried to escape the valley.

When he gets to the poison gas, Charlie's brows furrow in concentration. "Please describe the effects of the gas."

"A burning sensation all over the skin," Dean says. "Fever. Dehydration. Temporary loss of consciousness."

"The medic from your rescue team informed us most of you were still feverish," Marshall says. "What about any of the other symptoms?"

"The burning is still a bit of a problem," Skylar says with a grimace. "Though it's not unbearable anymore."

"We'll get you checked into the health ward for treatment as soon as possible," Regina says before turning to me, the only one who hasn't spoken yet. "Clementine, can you describe your symptoms for us?"

I rub the handle of my fork with my thumb, considering whether or not to tell the truth. I know it means something that the poison gas didn't affect me like the others, and I have a feeling the Developers might have some idea why. There's a strong possibility I'm about to arm them with knowledge they could use against me. But maybe if I tell the truth I can finally get some answers.

"The only symptom I had was the burning sensation on my skin," I say. "But it went away after a couple minutes."

A look passes between Regina and Charlie.

Out of the corner of my eye, Skylar gapes at me. She must've thought I'd had other symptoms and I was just keeping quiet about them.

Dean doesn't look surprised. In fact, he seems like he's purposefully avoiding my gaze. The short conversation we had in the forest, right after he'd stirred from unconsciousness, comes back to me: He asked how I was feeling, and when I said I was in a lot less pain than him, he said he had a feeling I might be. He somehow knew I'd be resistant to the poison.

I wonder what else Dean and the Developers have been keeping secret from me.

"Now, what happened after the poison bombs fell?" Regina asks, tapping her fingers curiously on the table.

"The Mardenites landed their ships and captured most of our squadron," Dean says.

"Did you see this happen? Or did you wake up and, finding them gone, assume they'd been taken?"

"I saw it happen," Skylar says. "When I recovered consciousness, I went back closer to the crash site and hid in the trees. I saw the aliens drag people inside their raiders."

"How many were captured?"

"At least seven soldiers, along with Commander Charlie's daughter and her husband, Beechy."

I've never seen Commander Charlie's cheeks turn so pale. "Sandy was taken?" he asks. "You're sure of this?"

"Yes, sir. I'm sorry."

"They were still alive," I say. "We can rescue them. We can bring them home."

"We don't know that for sure," Regina says gently. "They've been gone for several hours now. There's a good chance they've already been slaughtered by the aliens. The Mardenites are vicious creatures."

"No, you're wrong," I say. She has to be wrong—Beechy has to still be alive. "They wouldn't have captured them if they only meant to kill them in the next couple of hours. They would've kept bombing us from the sky until we were all destroyed."

"Regardless," Regina says, brushing my comments aside, "attempting to rescue the prisoners isn't something we can accomplish right away. At the moment we have bigger problems."

I look to Charlie, hoping he'll argue on my side for once. He might be a monster, but he has tried to protect his daughter in the past. Yet all he does is press his lips together in silence.

"What's the current situation on the Surface?" Dean asks.

"Not good," Charlie says tersely. "Due to the fleet arriving ahead of schedule, the transfer of the child workers to the Surface city was still under way when the invasion began. There were transports stuck in the Pipeline on their way to the Surface. Detonating the Stryker bombs would've caused too much damage to the lower sectors. Not to mention Colonel Parker's squadron—a good chunk of our army—was still in the city. We couldn't get him and his men out in time."

"So what happened?" I ask.

Charlie's jaw is so tense, I'm afraid to know the answer. "The Mardenites began their first wave of attack. Colonel Parker's troops were able to take out some raiders from the ground, but not enough. The Mardenites dropped poison bombs all over the city, we're guessing the same ones they used to attack your party. The child workers inside the buildings were affected, as well as the squadron of soldiers. Many of Colonel Parker's men are deathly ill. They were forced to retreat to underground bunkers outside the city limits."

"And the raiders?" Skylar asks.

"We've spotted a few ships scouting here and there, but most are well outside the city limits. It's likely they're gathering for a second, larger attack. We anticipate it coming within the next twenty-four hours."

"So there's still time," I say. "You need to get everyone out of the city. Empty it before the next attack."

"We're not abandoning the Surface without a fight," Regina says. "It would only be a matter of time before the Mardenites discovered the entrance to the lower sectors and invaded the Core."

I gnash my teeth together in agitation. "But if you leave the child workers in the city, they're all going to die."

"They will die when we trigger the Strykers, but it's a necessary sacrifice. They'll help us destroy the fleet." The fake, sweet smile Regina gives me makes me want to cut her eyes out with my fingernails.

My stomach jolts. They're still planning on going through with Operation Stryker.

"When will you trigger the Strykers?" I ask.

"Once Colonel Parker's squadron is safely out of range, as soon as the next attack begins."

"Triggering the Strykers won't demolish even half of Marden's fleet," I say, spitting the words in my anger. "There will still be enough raiders to overrun the Surface. Your plan isn't going to save you, but it's going to cost you thousands and thousands of lives. And what will you do next, when the raiders continue their attack? You won't be able to keep the lower sectors a secret forever. They'll find their way to the Core and they will slaughter you."

Regina looks amused by my frustration, but Marshall asks me in a serious voice, "What would you propose we do instead? Do you have a better plan?"

My mind races to collect my thoughts. I need a plan that would protect the child workers in the city, even if the Developers refuse to get them out. "If the city falls, it's like you said—it's only a matter of time before they'll discover the entrance to the lower sectors. So you should draw attention away from the city. Send more ships and soldiers to the Surface, immediately. Target the raiders wherever you can."

Regina frowns, but the rest of them—even Charlie—look thoughtful. I have them paying attention to me, so I need to keep going.

"While you're keeping the raiders occupied," I say, "send another fleet of ships to attack their battle stations. Without those, they won't be able to refuel their raiders or pack more ammunition, and they won't have a means of escaping. We take out the stations and we'll have a much better chance of winning the war. You can rescue our people they captured while you're there. You can bring Commander Charlie's daughter home."

Charlie hesitates. "Of course, I intend to do everything I can to bring her home."

"But what you're suggesting would require an incredible amount of ships and firepower," Marshall cuts in. "And we have no familiarity with the layout of the battle stations, or their weaknesses. Trying to put a plan like this into motion in the next twenty-four hours . . ."

"So send probes to the stations and collect as much data as you can," I say. "I know you have the weapons and forces for this; you're just afraid to use them because of the casualties. And you should be afraid. You haven't seen their raiders in person, but they're at least as powerful as our battleships, if not more, and they have thousands. The Mardenites are going to wipe out our entire race if we don't stop them."

There's silence around the table. Charlie, Regina, and Marshall look at each other, having some silent conversation. I wish I knew what they were thinking, but their expressions give nothing away.

Finally, they look back at me. Charlie's mouth is tight. Regina is the person who answers. "Thank you for your advice, Clementine. I'm hopeful we can make your plan work."

I frown. Is she joking? I didn't expect them to agree so easily.

"However, there are some things we need to discuss with you first," Commander Charlie says in a slick tone. His eyes have grown cold again.

Of course, there's a catch.

"Lieutenant Dean, Skylar, you're dismissed," Charlie says, motioning to the door behind us. "Cadet Waller will escort you to the health ward."

Skylar lets out a sigh of relief as she stands up without a glance in my direction. But Dean looks at me before pushing his chair back. There's a warning in his eyes: *Cooperate with them.*

The two of them head out of the room with Cadet Waller. She pauses in the doorway, calling someone in to remove the breakfast trays from the table. I let the man take mine too though I didn't finish my food. I'm not hungry anymore.

I fiddle with my hands in my lap, nervous again. But I need to stay calm. Whatever Commander Charlie and the others want with me, I can handle them. All I need to do is show them I'm not afraid.

The door slides shut behind Cadet Waller, and I'm alone with the Developers.

# 14

Silence drips over the room. All five of the Developers watch me across the table, as if they're waiting for me to initiate the conversation. Or trying to break my confidence. It won't work.

"What do you want with me?" I ask, not hiding my annoyance.

Commander Charlie presses his fingertips together. "Tell me, Clementine, what really happened to the dosages of serum you took with you to the Surface?"

I knew he didn't believe my story. "I told you—I lost them. But they wouldn't have worked anyway. The serum wore off much faster after the second dosage."

"It's interesting how easily you're able to overcome the serum," Commander Marshall says. He has warm eyes, the kind that should belong to nice men, not ruthless dictators. "You seem to build up more resistance every time we alter the formula."

"I'm not the only person who can resist it," I say. All the people I met in Karum prison, who'd been branded "Unstables," couldn't be controlled either, and neither could most of the rebels in the Alliance. That's why they stopped believing the lies of the Developers and started fighting to overthrow them.

"No, you're not," Marshall says. "But you're . . . shall I say . . . the most interesting of the people we've come across. No one can fight our serum quite like you, nor are many people as strong-willed and intuitive."

"So I've heard." I cross my arms. "But that's not the whole story, is it? You need me for something. You don't have time to develop a stronger serum to force me into helping you. If you want me to cooperate with you, you'll tell me the truth. All of it. No more secrets."

Commander Regina leans forward in her seat and replies, "Here's the truth, Clementine. In order for us to have any chance of defeating the Mardenites, there is something we require from you."

My heart's pounding in my chest. I keep quiet, waiting for an explanation.

Regina and Charlie look to Commander Talbin, the twitchy, balding man who serves as head historian of Kiel. He clears his throat. "I believe you already know this isn't the first war we've had with the Mardenites. There've been skirmishes between us throughout all our recorded history. In the most recent centuries, there've been two major wars, both within a twenty-year period, brought on by famine here on Kiel. We attempted to return peacefully to Marden and reestablish our civilization there, but it turned into a bloody fight. The Mardenites wouldn't accept a peaceful return."

His story doesn't match up with everything I've heard before. He's warping what happened to make it sound like the Mardenites were the instigators. But I'm pretty sure humans started both of the wars. "Colonel Fred told me we tried to enslave the Mardenites and they fought back," I say.

"Yes, well, there were instigators on both sides," Talbin says, his eyes nervously shifting to Commander Charlie. "Prejudices and hard feelings that hadn't been forgotten. Regardless, war began and it didn't end quickly. We refer to a short period of time between the two wars as 'The Calm,' but it was really fraught with preparations for the war that would follow it, when we sent even more battleships to Marden, an army we were sure would wipe them out. We'd enslaved many of their people in the first war, so their numbers were far fewer than ours by this time.

"But our second attempt to overtake their civilization also failed, as you know. The Mardenites unleashed new weapons unlike anything we'd seen before: chemical gases and poisons capable of crippling us in remarkable ways, even manipulating our thoughts and the decisions we made. The only reason any of our troops were able to return to Kiel was because some of them weren't affected by all of the chemicals the way the rest were. They made the decision to pull us out of battle before we could be completely demolished. Of course, the Mardenites followed us back and you know what happened next: They built the acid generator on our moon, meaning to wipe out more of us without injuring any more of their kind."

This is interesting and all, but most of it isn't new information. "What does this have to do with me?" I ask.

"Everything," Commander Charlie says.

"When we were all belowground, out of harm's way of the acid," Talbin continues, "the leaders at the time turned their attention to investigating the effects of the Mardenite chemical weapons on the wounded, and testing those who had been largely unaffected by the poisons. There was something in their genes that made them more resistant to the side effects."

The back of my neck tingles as I put the pieces together.

"We knew the Mardenites would be back for revenge, whether in a hundred years or a thousand, and we knew their chemical weapons would be even stronger," Talbin says. "We had to be ready. We began working toward creating a superior race of humans, one that would be more resistant to their weapons. We chose to speed up evolution."

Talbin glances at Marshall, who says, "We call it the Mod Project, short for Genetic Modification."

The definition of that phrase floats out of my memory, from a textbook I read in school years ago.

Genetic Modification: (Noun). *The alteration or manipulation of an organism's genetic makeup using biotechnology.*

I remember learning that Core scientists genetically engineer many of the plants we grow on Kiel, in order to make them as rich with nutrients as possible. Scientists also genetically engineered the silver aster flower, which they used to create the basic form of the control serum. The serum I'm allergic to.

But the Developers aren't talking about genetically modifying plants right now. They're talking about humans.

"For a little over two centuries," Marshall says, "we've been carefully controlling the genetics passed down from person to person, selecting the genes that would help us defeat the Mardenites in a future war. You know the primary ones as 'Promise'—strength, intelligence, and obedience. When it comes to obedience, we've actually been selecting for two different types of people: the first, people with weak wills who can easily be manipulated; the second, people who can't be controlled. The serum we use to control citizens is a derivative of the strongest poison the Mardenites used against us in the last war. The goal has been for a portion of our population to build up resistance against the serum. You, Clementine, are our strongest prospect yet. We've been watching and testing you since the day you were born, to assess how well your modifications worked."

The Developers haven't just been controlling who lives and who dies—they've been breeding us. Building soldiers in their labs.

"That's why you picked me for Extraction," I say.

Charlie laughs softly. "You weren't picked for Extraction. You were *created*."

A faint memory tugs at my thoughts. Flashes of light on needles; nurses leaning over me in bright rooms that smelled like bleach and antiseptic. When I was young, a new child in the sanitarium on the Surface. Finally, I know where the memories came from: the Mod Project.

Charlie taps three fingers on the table, turning on a holographic screen, and pulls up a file with my name at the top. My citizen file.

NAME: CLEMENTINE
CITIZEN NUMBER: S68477
GENERATION: 11
SUBJECT: 7
PRIORITY: HIGH

There's a mess of data and observation notes underneath: test scores from school and lab results from health examinations. I scroll down the file and find pictures they've captured of me with their cam-bots over the years. Hundreds and hundreds of pictures. Me sitting in classrooms in the education building, my head bent over lab work. Me walking hand in hand with Logan down the street to my shack. The two of us curled up in the cot inside my shack.

A sick taste fills my mouth, and it doesn't go away no matter how many times I swallow. I knew people had been watching me all my life, but I had no idea it went so deep.

"Every generation, we select individuals in the work camps who show the strongest potential for Promise based on the genetic makeup of their parents," Commander Charlie says. "Before birth, we engineer their genes to strengthen a particular set of traits, and once they're born, we make sure they receive the proper training to enhance those traits."

"Wait," I say, suddenly remembering something that doesn't make sense with all of this. "My mother, Mae. Beechy knew her when he was younger. He told me she kept her pregnancy a secret and I wasn't taken to the sanitarium until after I was born. So when did you modify my genes?"

"Yours was an interesting case," Regina says, pulling up a new file on the hologram.

My mother's file. Her picture renders me speechless. It's the first time I've seen her face. She had hair like mine—stringy, red-orange curls—and she was even skinnier than me. She looks so small in these pictures, it's hard to believe she was able to give birth. The fierceness in her eyes makes me smile. I bet she caused plenty of trouble for the Developers.

"Mae showed great resistance to control, but she was too sickly for us to pick her for Extraction," Regina says. "She wasn't supposed to be paired with anyone to conceive an offspring. But she became pregnant by one of the officials in her camp. A lieutenant who was later sent to an early quarantine for his refusal to carry out orders. Because Mae didn't want anyone to know she was pregnant, you were born in the camp almost two months early. But that was lucky for us. We can continue to modify genes until babies reach full term. Yours already showed remarkable potential, thanks to your parents."

"So," I say carefully, trying to make sure I understand all of this, "the reason why I can't be controlled by your serums is because you made me this way. You engineered the genetics of my parents and then my own, making me strong and intelligent but also resistant to your control serums, so one day you could use me or my offspring to defeat the Mardenites in war."

"Indeed," Regina says. "There are others with similar modifications, of course, but you're the one who's shown the most resistance to our serums. And with the arrival of Marden's army, there's no more time to test all the others. Which is why you've become our most important subject."

"And you want to send me and the others like me into battle?"

"That was our original intention," Commander Charlie says. "We hoped to be able to continue the Mod Project for five more generations, in order to build a larger force of people who would share your resistance. If all had gone according to plan, we would've separated the Core from the rest of the planet and prepared to launch an attack on Marden with our battle station a hundred years from now. But that didn't happen." Charlie's eyes bore into me across the table.

I'm the reason that didn't happen. I screwed up their plans.

"When you and the Alliance rebels destroyed the weapon the Mardenites had placed on our moon," Charlie continues, "it seems you triggered some sort of signal that alerted them and made them fear we would be infiltrating Marden. So they sent a fleet of battleships to our planet instead of waiting for us."

There's a pinch in my gut. If all these theories are true, this war is partially my fault. I thought I was saving everyone in the outer sectors by getting rid of Charlie's bomb, but I was wrong. I only prolonged their suffering.

"Now we've had to come up with a new plan," Charlie says. "There aren't enough trained soldiers with your type of resistance to the Mardenites' chemical weapons. But we believe we can change that."

"Based on our previous studies," Regina says, "we believe we can synthesize antibodies that will protect our soldiers from the Mardenite poison gas, using samples of your blood. A new serum that will give non-modified soldiers immunity. Of course, poison gas isn't the only weapon in our enemy's arsenal, but it is a powerful one. A resistance serum won't make us invincible to their attacks, but it will enable us to send warriors and battleships to the Surface with a much stronger defense than we currently have. Those who've already been infected by the poison, Colonel Parker's sick soldiers and the others who returned from your mission, will take days to recover without the proper antibodies. And we don't have days; we need all our soldiers fit for battle as soon as possible. Which is why we need your help."

"You need my blood," I repeat.

"Yes," Regina says, smiling sweetly. "And your bone marrow. You'll have to have a few small procedures and tests so we can extract what we need. But it won't cause you any major discomfort, nothing a little pain medicine can't fix. We've done many of these procedures on you before, most recently when you were under observation in Karum prison, but it's likely your body has built up more resistance since our last tests. We need to be sure we have the strongest samples to work with."

My stomach clenches at the mention of Karum prison. They did perform procedures on me there, operations and tortures that made me sick. They even took my eggs without my permission. Now I know why—so they could genetically engineer my offspring to make them even stronger mods, if they'd had more time to build their army.

"But you won't treat me like you did in Karum," I say carefully.

"When you were in Karum, you'd broken our laws," Commander Charlie says in a voice as smooth as silk. "You were being punished for your crimes, as everyone who rebels must be, no matter how important they are to the Mod Project. But if you help us now, we'll pardon you for past misdeeds, including any false moves you made while you were on the Surface. This is your only chance to ally with us, Clementine. I can assure you none of the procedures will be painful."

I hesitate, searching Charlie's face for a sign he's lying to me again. But his face is unreadable.

"If we have your cooperation, we can begin your tests immediately," Commander Regina says. "There isn't time to waste."

I run my teeth over my bottom lip. "What will happen if I don't agree to help you?"

Charlie's jaw twitches, and Regina's lips purse ever so slightly. They weren't expecting any more argument from me, it seems. But Regina answers in an even voice, "There are other Mod subjects we can go to, but it will take longer. And your genes would provide the best opportunity for helping us develop a strong resistance serum for our troops. We can't afford to send them to the Surface without the strongest serum possible, seeing how many soldiers in Colonel Parker's squadron have already been crippled. In other words, we need you to agree to help us if you want us to follow through with the war plan you proposed. Otherwise, we'll return to our previous plan. We'll put Operation Stryker in motion and sacrifice all the child workers in the Surface city."

The only way the Developers will abandon Operation Stryker is if I agree to give them what they want.

My heart is beating at a faster pace than normal, but I feel calmed by this new information. Finally, I understand: The Developers have kept me alive because I'm their best hope for defeating the Mardenites. That day I ruined their plans and used their bomb to destroy the acid generator on the moon, Charlie was so angry with me, he would've killed me. But now the army is coming and there isn't time to find anyone else. The Developers need me.

I can do this. I can ally with the Developers, just for a little while. Just until they've helped me take out the bigger enemy—Marden's army. Then I will turn against them and make sure none of them are able to control Kiel's government ever again.

I take a deep breath. The Developers need my help, then they need to earn it.

"I want to help you," I say. "But you must understand, it's hard for me to trust everything you're telling me when you've lied to me about a hundred times before. And even if I help you, it won't ensure the survival of everyone I care about. Whether or not my blood is enough to make everyone resistant to the poison gas, you said yourself the Mardenites have lots of other weapons. They still greatly outnumber our war fleet. There's no certainty this serum will help us defeat them. So if you want my cooperation, I need you to promise me a few things in return for my help."

"We can consider your requests," Regina says, an edge of impatience to her voice. "What is it you want from us?"

*Who do I care about saving?*

"First," I say, "I want you to grant pardon to all the Alliance prisoners for their past misdeeds and release them from their cells. I'm guessing many of them are your stronger Mods. They were once your best soldiers, pilots, and analysts. You'll need their help to defeat Marden's army, as we need yours. Make a temporary truce with them until the war is over."

I pause to let the Developers talk among themselves. I don't expect them to agree to this, but maybe they'll give me something. And starting with this request will make the rest seem smaller.

Finally, Commander Charlie turns back to me. "Those who cooperate with us in any assistance we require for the war effort will be granted pardon once the war is over. But we will decide when to release them from custody."

"It's a matter of Core security," Commander Marshall says. "I'm sure you understand."

"Fine," I say, trying to sound less agreeable than I really am. That's much better than I expected them to give me. "Second, Logan. If you won't release him from custody, you have to let me see him anytime I want. I want to talk to him before I go through with the tests, to make sure he's alive and healthy. You can't harm him anymore, in any way. Nor will you transport him anywhere without notifying me, under any conditions."

"So long as you cooperate, you can visit the boy and he won't be harmed," Regina says, waving her hand as if that request is nothing substantial.

There's amusement in Charlie's eyes. It makes me angry. He should not be amused by any of this; he needs to understand I will not cooperate if any of these requests are broken.

"Third," I say, raising my voice, "you'll agree to rescue Beechy, Sandy, and the others who were captured by the Mardenites at the earliest opportunity."

"Once it's possible to rescue them without endangering the safety of our citizens, of course we will," Charlie says. "Do you really think I would abandon my daughter to the aliens?"

"Anything else?" Regina asks.

My mind's racing. This might be my only opportunity to get what I want. What have I forgotten? I need to ensure I'll have some future influence over what happens in the war. And I want to learn as much about the enemy invading Kiel as possible—not from the half-baked lies of the Developers, but from the old war records. The primary and secondary sources.

"I want a seat in all your strategy meetings. I want to know what's happening in the war, every step of the way. I want access to your records concerning the last war. And I want clearance to speak with the Mardenite you have in captivity here in the Core. Alone."

"Your terms are acceptable," Charlie says with a smile. He pushes his chair back and stands up, and the rest of the Developers follow suit. "We have an agreement."

I get to my feet as they move around to my side of the table. Regina is at the front of the group and offers her hand. I shake it. Her skin is warm through her glove.

"We'll have a guard take you for a quick visit to your friend in his cell," she says, dropping her hand. "And we'll inform the doctor in charge of the Mod Project you've agreed to help us, so we can begin your tests right away and get started on developing a resistance serum. You Mods are the best hope we have of winning the war."

When she smiles at me again, showing her perfect white teeth, I smile back. But staring into her cold gray eyes, an itch of worry crawls across my spine. I hope I've made the right decision.

Regina turns and heads for the door, her high heels tapping on the linoleum. The other Developers approach me one by one and shake my hand.

When Commander Charlie reaches me, he gives me a demure smile. "I'm pleased to finally have you working on our side, Clementine," he says.

"I'm pleased to work with you too," I say.

He grips my hand so tightly, it feels like he might crush my fingers. I bite hard on the inside of my cheek, trying not to let him know I'm in pain.

Finally, he lets go. But instead of walking away from me, he holds out his arm for me to take. Another challenge; he knows how much I hate being near him, let alone touching him. I smile and slip my arm through his. My heart's beating fast.

As we walk out of the room, I notice there's an odd, pungent aroma wafting off his clothes, some sort of perfume that reminds me of the bleach smell in the quarantine facility in Crust, where the worthless—people without the strongest modifications—are taken to die. I wonder if he put it on just for me once he heard I was returning from the Surface mission.

I know what he's trying to tell me with this demonstration: No matter what I think, he is still in control of me. He and the other

Developers might have agreed to my conditions for helping them, but when it comes down to it, once I've cooperated with their tests and operations, they won't need me anymore. I will be disposable, easily cast aside.

So I need to prolong the tests as long as possible.

# 15

A guard escorts me to Cell Block A, where they've locked up Logan. I have only twenty minutes to see him. Then I have to go to the health ward to begin the Mod tests.

I look inside the other cells as we walk past them, wondering if I'll find other Alliance prisoners here. I still don't know how many were captured in Crust and the other sectors after the Developers received the list of names from Beechy and Skylar. Probably something I should've asked about, although the Developers might've tried to pry more names out of me.

But if they've captured others, they aren't in Cell Block A. All the cells are empty except the very last one, Logan's cell. I clench my sweaty hands at my sides and the guard unlocks the door with his thumbprint.

The last time I visited Logan in this cell, yesterday morning, I was still trapped by the control serum. I tried to make him see the real me was there underneath, fighting to be heard, but he didn't understand. All he saw was the girl with a smile plastered on her face who was about to go to the Surface and help Sam destroy the Alliance compound. The soldier who'd willingly taken Charlie's serum and agreed to fight for him.

But it was all for Logan. I never would've taken the serum if he hadn't been captured in Crust, injected with a bomb that could've killed him. Every choice I made was to protect him. Yet I couldn't even protect him from myself.

Logan's voice drifts through the door, sounding husky. Tired and wounded. "What do you want?"

"You have a visitor," the guard says.

"If it's the commander, you can tell him to go to—" Logan stops talking as soon as I step into view. He must've been hobbling across the cell on his crutches, but now he's frozen.

I can't get any words out of my mouth; I'm so relieved to see him. His hair is messy from lying on it and there are specks of stubble covering his jaw. My Logan, the boy who has defended me since we were young, who was strong enough to let me go knowing I might not come back to him.

Logan's eyes are wide, full of cautious hope. "Clementine?"

"You have twenty minutes," the guard says. The door slides shut behind me.

Five steps and I reach and fling my arms around Logan. He greets me with as much enthusiasm, dropping his crutches and pulling me tightly against his chest. There's a flash of pain through my ribs, but I ignore it. I won't let anything ruin this moment.

"You're not dead." Logan kisses my hair, my forehead, my cheeks. Everywhere he can reach. "They told me the Mardenites attacked and they hadn't been able to make contact with anyone on your mission. I didn't think you'd make it back."

My eyes are watering, but I don't care. I was so scared I wouldn't see him again, or I'd come back and Charlie would follow through with his threat to execute him.

"I'll always come back," I say. "I'm not saying good-bye yet."

Logan touches my cheek, his stormy gray eyes searching my expression for something. "Is it really you?"

He means: Is it the real you? Or am I still trapped inside myself, screaming to get out?

I take his hand from my cheek and slide our fingers together. "I'm here. I'm real. No one's controlling me." I stand on my tiptoes and plant a kiss on his lips to prove it.

Logan kisses me back harder, wrapping his arms around me again. I pull him closer. I want all of him, the heat of his body against mine, his legs tangled up with my own. But we're in a cell with a security camera, not alone. And the slight hitch in Logan's breath reminds me he's hurt.

I pull away and pick up his crutches from the floor. As I hand them to him, I look closer at the cast on his leg, tight slips of gauze around his left thigh. I shot him a few inches above his knee.

"Are you okay?" I ask as he adjusts the crutches under his arms. "What happened after I left?"

A shadow touches Logan's face for the slightest moment at the memory of what happened in the flight port. Then it vanishes, replaced by warmth as he smiles at me. Forgiving me in a single gesture. "I'm okay. I was in the health ward until a couple hours ago. They sewed up the skin. Said it'll take a few weeks to heal."

He turns away from me and hobbles over to the bed. I can see the strain in his neck as he sits down; even that slight movement causes him pain. Logan already had a limp in his left leg that made it harder for him to fight like the rest of us, and now I've given him another injury to slow him down.

"I'm so sorry, Logan," I say softly. "I swear I didn't mean to hurt you. I tried to stop my hands, but I couldn't . . . I wasn't strong enough to fight the serum."

"I know," Logan says, reaching for my hand. He pulls me over to the bed. "I don't blame you one bit. I just wish I could've stopped you from taking the serum in the first place."

"You couldn't have stopped me." I sit down next to him. "Charlie was going to kill you if I didn't."

Logan opens his mouth to say something, then stops, frowning. "Wait. You're not subdued anymore. Why is he letting you visit me?"

I hesitate. Part of me doesn't want to tell him about the conversation I had with the Developers, because I know it will make him worry. But I need to be honest with him. I kept him in the dark about what I was going through before, and it only put walls between us.

I meet Logan's eyes and tell him straight: "I've made a deal with the Developers. I'm going to help them fight the Mardenites, in exchange for my freedom and a few other conditions."

"What do you mean?" Logan asks, uneasy.

"They need my blood," I say. "My antibodies and DNA. Whatever it is in my genetic code that allows me to break free of their mind-control serum could protect the army from the Mardenites. The aliens have chemical weapons—poison bombs. They hit my squadron with them while I was on the Surface. It crippled most of our soldiers and led to their capture. Beechy and Sandy and Uma were taken."

There's a sharp intake of breath from Logan.

I continue: "The poison hardly affected me at all. The Developers think my blood can be used to synthesize antibodies for the toxin, which they can administer to everyone else to make them resistant. The Mardenites hit the Surface city with the poison too and it affected all the soldiers stationed there. If we send any more troops to the Surface without a defense against the poison, they're going to end up captured or killed before they even have a chance of fighting."

Silence lingers as Logan takes in all this information. "The Developers told you all this," he says slowly.

"Yes," I say. "And I saw it for myself. I saw how the poison affected the others while I was on the Surface. Lieutenant Dean and Darren and Skylar are still sick from it."

"But the Developers said they need your blood to protect everyone, so you're giving it to them. Just like that, without any proof that's really what they'll use it for."

I nod. There's a rock in my throat.

"After all the times they've lied to you?" Logan's voice is losing its steadiness. "All the times they've tortured you and threatened you and made you do things against your will?"

I shake my head. "It's not that simple, Logan. This isn't about what they've done. It's about the people I can save if my blood works the way it should. And after what I went through on the Surface . . . I don't think the Developers are lying about it."

"What if you're wrong?" The tremor in Logan's voice isn't out of anger; it's out of fear.

The truth is, I'm terrified I am wrong. I'm terrified I've put myself in a position where I'm giving the Developers everything they want, and they'll use it to control me again. "It doesn't matter. I need to keep you and the rest of our friends safe. Working with the Developers is the best way I can do that right now."

A moment of silence passes. I can sense Logan still struggling to come to terms with the situation. "What are they giving you in return?"

"They've agreed to pardon me for my past crimes, and they've promised not to subdue me again, or hurt you anymore. They're also going to pardon any Alliance rebels that agree to help them. They're going to help me rescue Beechy, Sandy, and everyone else who was taken at the earliest opportunity. And once they've created a resistance serum for their soldiers, they're going to put an attack plan into motion that doesn't involve sacrificing the child workers in the Surface city. We might have a real chance of saving them."

Logan looks me straight in the eye. "You know Charlie might not keep his word."

I remember how Charlie looked amused at my requests, how he gripped my hand too hard when he shook it after we made the deal. "I know," I say in a small voice. "And I don't know if helping him will be enough to win the war and get Beechy and the other prisoners home safe. This serum is only the first step. But it's something only I can do, and it could give us a much better chance of surviving the war. That's the best I can hope for right now."

"I understand." Logan takes a long, shaky breath and gives me a tight smile. "If you think it's the right move, you should do it," he says, but he still looks troubled. "I'm just worried about you, Clem. I don't want you to get hurt trying to save me or anyone else."

I hear the cell door slide open behind me. The guard's come back. My twenty minutes are up.

Before I stand up, I reach for Logan's hand and squeeze it. "You don't have to worry about me. The Developers can't subdue me anymore; I've broken free of all their serums. They need me to cooperate with them in order for this to work. So I have the power this time, at least for right now. I'll make sure I keep it."

Logan squeezes my hand back. "I hope you're right," he says.

In the health ward, I'm led to a pre-operation room. It's bare, with only an examination table and a blue light in the ceiling. I blink and for a moment I feel like I'm back in Karum prison, about to be put under by the cruel doctors. I remember their cold hands and sharp needles, and panic twists my stomach. But I quickly control it.

This will be different. Commander Charlie promised.

A nurse helps me out of my clothes and peels the old bandages, crusted with dried blood, from my shoulder. She replaces them with a fresh pair, and also replaces the gauze inside my left ear. Afterward, she sends me into the steam-clean shower in the attached bathroom for a full-body sanitation. The steam is a special kind that won't mess up the gauze.

I linger in the shower longer than I need to, letting the warm steam wash away the lingering feeling of cold from all those hours we spent in the freezing weather of the mountains. My weariness is catching up with me again, making my eyelids heavy. I've been shot, gassed with poison, and attacked by Sam all in the last twelve hours, and I've only had an hour or so of sleep. Hopefully I can rest after I'm through with the Mod tests.

The nurse calls into the bathroom to make sure I'm okay. I take that as my cue to finish up. Stepping out of the steam-clean, I move to stand in front of the bathroom mirror while I dry off with a towel. My short, stringy curls are their normal reddish-orange color again, now that all the bleach I used as a disguise for the Alliance has washed out of my hair. I'm glad to look more like myself again. But I'll be happier once my hair grows longer, the way it used to be.

The bruises Sam gave me on my neck and shoulders are a horrible shade of black-and-blue. He really meant to kill me when he attacked me—and he almost did. It'll be a miracle if he doesn't try again when he wakes up. But that's something I'm not going to worry about until the time comes.

Until then, I need to make sure the bruises stay hidden under my clothes, so they won't raise questions from people like Commander Charlie. Right now he believes I lost the syringes of control serum during the Mardenite attack. If he finds out I lied, I don't know what he'll do.

I return to the pre-op room and the nurse helps me change into a hospital gown, a thin slip of fabric that barely feels like clothing. As she finishes tying up the back, there's a knock on the door.

"Come in."

Another nurse walks into the room, a young woman with long, shiny blond hair and creamy skin. She's Ariadne, my old friend from Extraction training who was transferred to the Core from the Surface work camp, same as me. Her bright, shining smile doesn't match the eerie blankness of her eyes. Ever since she received her first monthly injection of control serum, Ariadne has been more bot than human being.

"It's good to see you again, Clementine," she says brightly.

We saw each other yesterday morning, before I left for the Surface. She was the nurse who oversaw my second injection of the serum. Commander Charlie planted her in that room to remind me he has people under his control I care about, people he could toss aside without a care if I make one wrong move. No doubt that's why she was assigned to be my nurse again today.

"I can take over, June," Ariadne says to the nurse.

June nods and heads for the door. "I'll be back as soon as we're ready."

Ariadne walks over to one of the counters and opens a drawer.

"Did Commander Charlie send you?" I ask.

"No, Dr. Jeb did," she says, removing various medical instruments from the drawer. She sets them on a tray. "He's the doctor who will be overseeing your tests. I'll be assisting him, as part of my medical training."

She looks so pleased with herself, I force my mouth to smile back. "I'm glad you'll be there."

Ariadne snaps on gloves. "If you'll take a seat on the bed, I'll do your preliminary checkup."

I sit down on the examination table, and Ariadne walks over with a stethoscope. I notice the circles under her eyes are darker than yesterday. There's more slowness in her movements. Maybe she also didn't get much sleep.

"How are you feeling?" she asks, before I can ask her the same question.

"Been better," I say, wincing as she presses the stethoscope to my chest. I still need another dosage of pain medicine. I adjust my position on the table so my ribs won't hurt as much.

One of my gown sleeves slips down a little from the movement. I quickly push the sleeve back up, but not before Ariadne notices the bruises on my neck.

She freezes, her eyes widening. She pushes down my sleeve and takes in all the markings Sam gave me. "Who did this to you?"

I hesitate. But why can't I tell her what happened, as long as I leave out the part about the serum? She needs to know he's dangerous. Sam tried to seduce her after she received her first monthly injection, and she didn't stop him.

"It was Sam," I say, fixing my sleeve again. "He attacked me on the Surface, after we'd escaped the Mardenites."

"Mardenites?" Ariadne repeats, her brows furrowing at the word. "What do you mean? I didn't know you had to escape anything on the Surface."

It takes a second for me to process her confusion. I frown. She doesn't know about the alien invasion. What other story would the Developers have told her about the reason behind these Mod tests?

"Don't you know the planet is under attack?" I ask.

Ariadne stares at me for a long moment. Then she lets out a peal of laughter. "I don't know what you're talking about, Clementine." She presses the stethoscope to my chest again. "If you can take a deep breath for me, please."

"But, Ariadne—"

"Inhale and exhale. Don't speak."

I grind my teeth together in frustration, but do as she says. I can't believe she's completely clueless. Does *anyone* in the Core know there's an invasion going on? If Ariadne was fed some lie, I bet all the other citizens were too. Maybe Commander Charlie and the others don't want to cause a panic, but it's not their right to keep something so big a secret. Everyone is in danger, and they deserve to know.

When Ariadne finishes listening to my heart, I speak before she can do anything else: "Ariadne, listen to me. The whole planet is under invasion. There are creatures attacking the Surface."

She pauses. Worry flashes through her eyes. "Creatures?"

"Aliens. They have ships and guns and bombs, and they've captured our people. Beechy and Sandy were taken prisoner on one of their battle stations. The aliens are going to take control of the Surface, and then they'll come for the rest of us underground. Even the Core won't be safe anymore."

Ariadne shakes her head, taking a step backward. "No, you're wrong. The Developers will keep us safe. They'll protect us if anyone threatens our home."

"Look at me," I say, pointing to the bruises on my neck and the bandage on my arm. "I was attacked, and they didn't protect me."

"You must've done something wrong, then. You must've disobeyed them. They always protect people, as long as they remain loyal citizens." She's spitting words out of her mouth because she's subdued, but there's no way she actually believes them. The real Ariadne has to be somewhere underneath, still able to hear what I'm saying even if she can't tell me she agrees.

"Ariadne, please." I stand up from the table. "You have to listen to me—"

There's another knock on the door. Ariadne turns away from me as June comes back in, this time with a third nurse. They're pushing a gurney between them.

"Dr. Jeb is ready for you, Clementine," June says, smiling sweetly.

It's time for my tests to begin.

"Climb onto the gurney and we'll take you to the operation room," Ariadne says. She starts toward the counter to put the stethoscope away.

I grab her arm to stop her. "Wait."

"What?" she snaps.

I don't care if she's annoyed. I have to try to reach her while

I still can. "I just want you to know . . . if you're still in there, I see you. I know you're trapped. I'm going to help you break free."

Ariadne roughly pulls her arm away. "I don't know what you mean. Now, you need to come with us quietly and cooperatively," she says in a forceful voice. "Or I'll call for a guard. Do you understand?"

I press my lips together. "Yes."

"Good."

Even if she can hear me, she's buried too deep. She'd need a strong dosage of an energy injection to snap her free of the serum's control, the kind I used to free our friend, Oliver, before he died. But I doubt an energy injection would be easy to get my hands on.

And even if I freed Ariadne, the Developers would just subdue her with another injection.

When she turns away again, I let her go.

# 16

The operation room has a blue bulb in the ceiling, a metal operating table, and a medi-bot—a rectangular bot nearly the size of a person—that's holding a tray of metal instruments in its arms. Through a wall of glass on the far side of the room, I can see Commander Charlie talking to the doctor who must be overseeing my tests.

Now the nervousness kicks in about what I've gotten myself into. What if these operations aren't simple, like they told me they'd be? Surely uncomplicated procedures wouldn't require a surgical room like this.

But whatever happens next, I can't go back on my word. Refusing to go through with the Mod tests means the Developers will kill all the child workers in the Surface city. I can't let that happen.

As Ariadne helps me climb onto the operating table, the doctor comes into the room. He's a skinny man in a white lab coat, with glasses over his blue eyes and a splatter of freckles on his cheeks. He seems familiar, but I can't place where I've seen him before.

He holds out his hand for me to shake. "I'm Dr. Jeb," he says. "You must be Clementine. We've met before, though you may not remember me."

When he smiles, I realize where I know him from: He's the doctor who took my brain scans the day I left for the Core. "You performed part of my Extraction test, didn't you?"

"You are correct. In fact, I also performed some of your Mod tests when you were a little girl. But you would've been too young to remember."

I have almost no memory of the years of my life before I was sent into the work camp. Only flashes of bright lights and needles and nurses.

"Let's begin, shall we?" Dr. Jeb says, snapping on a fresh set of gloves. "Today's procedures shouldn't take long. I'm sure you're eager to get them over with. If you could lie back on the table for me."

I do as he says, settling my head onto the thin pillow. Commander Charlie is still looming on the other side of the glass. I wish he'd leave. But I'm sure he wants to make certain I cooperate and the tests go smoothly.

"What exactly are you going to do?" I ask.

"I'm going to take a pint of your blood and also extract samples of your bone marrow and muscle tissues. After that, I'm going to hook you up to a machine and take some new brain scans."

I exhale. It sounds easy enough.

"However," Dr. Jeb says, and my stomach sinks, "we need samples of some deeper muscle tissues. I can do it laparoscopically, but it's quite a painful procedure. So, you have the option of going under general anesthesia. I'd knock you out for about an hour. It's what I would recommend."

"I'm not going under," I say immediately. Every other time I've done that, the surgeon has done something to me without my permission.

"All right, it's your choice," Dr. Jeb says. "I can give you a local anesthetic, then. If at any time the discomfort becomes too much, you can always change your mind."

I won't change my mind. No matter how painful it is, I'm staying awake so I can watch the procedure.

Ariadne moves around the table to administer the anesthesia. A small prick of a needle to my hip, and my whole abdominal area becomes numb. The good news is it also makes my ribs finally stop hurting.

"We'll begin with the bone-marrow sample," Dr. Jeb says.

He has me lay on my side on the table. My hospital gown covers most of my naked body, but he uncovers part of the back to do the procedure. I try not to think about Commander Charlie watching through the glass, and what he might be able to see.

The needle for this procedure is much bigger than the one for the anesthetic, and it's attached to a huge syringe. I bite hard on the inside of my cheek as Dr. Jeb pushes the needle into my hipbone. Pressure spreads all through my hip and lower back, but it's not unbearable. The meds are doing their job, so far.

When he's finished, he tells me to roll back over. I glimpse murky blood in the syringe before he sets it on the medi-bot's tray.

"Now for the deeper tissues."

The needle goes into my belly button this time. The pain

spreads like pinpricks of fire. I clench my teeth harder and harder, breathing deeply through my nose. The material Dr. Jeb sucks into the syringe is a grayish material, mingled with more blood. The sight of it makes me nauseous.

"One down," he says, pulling the needle out. "Five more to go."

"That wasn't so bad, was it?" Commander Charlie asks from beside my hospital bed.

I sit up in the bed, wincing. They've transferred me to a recovery room, now that my operations and brain scans are finished. Dr. Jeb gave me stronger pain medicine after the anesthetic wore off, but there's still a little discomfort when I move. "Is that it? Or will you need me for another procedure?"

"We should have everything we need," Dr. Jeb says on the other side of the bed. He's checking my blood pressure, while Ariadne arranges the pillow behind my back. Commander Charlie hands me a cup of water, which I sip gratefully.

"How soon will you know if you can create a resistance serum?" I ask.

"Within a few hours," Charlie says. "We'll test it on the other survivors who returned from the Surface with you."

"If your antibodies work," Dr. Jeb says, removing the blood pressure scanner from my wrist, "their symptoms should decrease significantly as soon as we administer the serum."

It has to work. Otherwise, Commander Charlie will put his old Stryker plan into motion. Thousands of people will die.

"Dr. Jeb is going to keep you under observation here for the next few hours, so you'll be close by if we need you," Charlie says. "But you're welcome to get some rest. I know you didn't get much sleep last night."

As if in answer, a yawn stretches my face in two.

Dr. Jeb chuckles. "We'll leave you to it, then."

He and Commander Charlie make for the door at a quick stride, talking to each other in low voices. Before Ariadne follows them, she shows me a button I can press if I need anything.

I'm so exhausted I should be able to fall asleep without any trouble. But as soon as I close my eyes, my mind drifts to thoughts of Beechy aboard one of the Mardenite battle stations. I picture the aliens stringing him up to a ceiling by burning hot iron chains, or slicing him open on a table in a dark room, or torturing him with tiny croacher-like insects that crawl under his skin.

How many hours has it been since he was taken? He could be dead by now. He could've given up all kinds of information that will lead the Mardenites to the Core to capture the rest of us.

Beechy is stronger than that. He's still alive. He has to be.

Once we have a serum to make everyone resistant to the poison, we can send more troops to the Surface. We can infiltrate the battle stations and get him and the rest of the prisoners out. We'll find a way.

Beechy could've left me to rot in Karum prison when I was imprisoned there weeks ago, but he came and saved me. So I'm not giving up on him.

There's a figure looming over my bed. A dark shape wearing a navy blue suit and white gloves.

Commander Charlie leans over me and brushes a stray curl out of my face. His mouth curves into a cruel smile. Slowly, he removes an object from his pocket—an injection syringe. He presses the needle against my forehead and shoves it through the skin.

I wake screaming. There's a pounding of footsteps in the hallway outside.

Ariadne rushes into the room. "What's wrong?"

I'm scrambling to untangle from the bedsheets. "Commander Charlie—he was in here."

She glances around the empty room, looking confused. "No, he wasn't." She touches my shoulder. "You need to calm down. You're okay. You were dreaming."

I touch the spot on my forehead where he'd plunged the needle in. There's nothing there, no blood or anything. I swallow hard. It was just a dream. Charlie has more important things to do than subdue me in my sleep.

Still, I hesitate. "You're sure no one came in here?"

Ariadne shakes her head. "No one can come in without passing the nurse's station, and I've been there the whole time."

I close my eyes briefly, exhaling to help slow my racing heartbeat. It was just a dream, like all the other nightmares I've had about Charlie. I shouldn't be afraid of him anymore; his serums can't control me. But fear will control me, if I let it. So I have to let it go.

"What time is it?" I ask, rubbing the grogginess out of my eyes.

"You just missed dinner, but I can bring you something to eat."

Dinnertime? I can't remember what time it was when I finished the Mod tests. "How long was I asleep?"

"About four hours."

I sit bolt upright in bed. "Where's Dr. Jeb? Did he finish the serum?"

"He's testing it right now," Ariadne says. "I can take you to him as soon as you have something to eat."

Her voice is firm, commanding. She's not going to let me leave any sooner.

"Fine," I say.

She leaves and comes back with a dinner tray for me. There's a thin slice of smoked coura and cheese, along with a serving of hodgori, baked custard.

"Take your time," Ariadne says as I start to eat too quickly. "We don't want you scarfing it down only to throw it all back up."

I force myself to slow down, though I don't have time for this. Someone should've come for me as soon as the resistance serum was ready for testing. I want to be there when they find out whether or not it works, to make sure the Developers won't go back on their promise.

After I finish eating, Ariadne takes me down several corridors to a room that seems to be a small laboratory. There are counters lining two of the walls, and machines emitting beeps and sputtering sounds, such a high frequency I can't hear the sounds when my left ear is facing the machines. A bluish liquid pumps through a giant tube on the counter to my left.

The left half of the wall on the far side of the room is made of glass, like the wall in the operation room earlier. The right half is covered in data screens. Commander Charlie and Commander Regina stand with Dr. Jeb in front of the monitors.

On the other side of the glass portion of wall, Lieutenant Dean and Skylar are sitting in exam chairs in a smaller room, hooked up to machines. Nurses hover over them. Both of them still have foreheads shiny with sweat from the fever, and they look even more tired than earlier. Dean seems to be staring right at me as I walk forward. But when I wave, he doesn't seem to notice. I'm pretty sure the glass is darker on the other side.

"Dr. Jeb," Ariadne says. "I've brought Clementine."

Charlie glances in my direction, and my throat closes up momentarily. He looks exactly the way he did in my nightmare, minus the cruel smile. He's even holding something in his hand. But as I step closer, I see it's not a syringe—it's a vial of liquid. It must be the resistance serum.

"It's good to see you again," Charlie says, sounding strangely chipper. Things must be going according to his plan. "I hope you had a nice, long rest."

"I did. Thank you." I move closer to the screens so I can see what they're looking at. Heart rate, oxygen levels, and other vital signs, it looks like. But some of the screens have data I can't interpret. One has three rotating images of a double helix shape: DNA. I wonder if one of them is mine. "How's the serum coming?" I ask.

"We've just administered your antibodies to Lieutenant Dean and Skylar," Regina says. "We should know if it will work in the next few minutes."

"I've already tested the serum we synthesized in a simulator," Dr. Jeb says, making a note on a tablet he's holding. "The antibodies attacked the molecules of the poison gas, as we hoped they would. It's looking like we have a working serum. But keep your fingers crossed."

I glance at Dean and Skylar on the other side of the glass. There's no outward sign that they're getting better. *Please get better.*

"You're dismissed, Ariadne," Commander Charlie says. "Thank you for bringing Clementine here."

Ariadne plasters that mindless smile of hers on her face. "Of course, sir," she says, and backs out of the room.

Seeing her respond to him like that reminds me of the fact she still knows nothing about the war against Marden's army. Or rather, she doesn't believe what I told her. She must think we're producing another control serum or something.

Dr. Jeb moves his tablet to his side. "I'd like to check with our subjects and see how they're feeling."

He and Commander Charlie head for the door to the other room. I start to follow them, but Commander Regina touches my shoulder to stop me. "You'd better stay here," she says. "There isn't enough room for all of us in there."

I shake her hand off my shoulder. "Fine."

The door closes behind the other two. I watch them approach Lieutenant Dean and Skylar on the other side of the glass, but of course I can't hear their conversation. I'm all too aware of Regina breathing over my shoulder.

"I'm surprised you cooperated with us so well," she says. "After all the times you've fought Commander Charlie before, I was worried you'd resist the procedures."

"Well, we had an agreement," I say. And it's not like the Developers gave me much of a choice. I turn to face Regina. "I have a question."

"Yes?" she says.

"Why haven't you told the Core citizens what's going on? They should know Kiel is under invasion."

She purses her lips slightly. "For now, it's better this way. They can continue feeling safe and comfortable while we take care of things. Of course, if the situation progresses and the Core becomes endangered, we'll inform the citizens as we see necessary."

That's the way they always do things—keep up their lies as long as possible, until they have no choice but to tell the truth. It's not a policy for citizen protection; it's a policy for control.

"You should tell them now, instead of waiting until they're about to die," I say, my nostrils flaring in anger. "They deserve to know what's happening. Maybe you don't realize it, but the more lies you tell them, the more they'll despise you once the truth comes out. One day your system's going to splinter, and your serums will stop working. Then everyone will know. And they won't stand for it anymore. You can't keep them all subdued forever."

When I finish, Regina's face is rigid. I know I've gone too far. I bite the inside of my cheek, waiting for her reaction. Trying to figure out what I can say to make this better.

Her expression slowly softens, as does her voice when she answers, "Perhaps we can't. But we can try. We *will* try. It's not about control, Clementine; it's about their safety. I don't expect you to understand. But I would encourage you not to question our policies, lest we misconstrue your words as treason. We've pardoned you for your past crimes, but we won't pardon you if you commit more." There's a warning in her piercing green eyes.

I swallow hard. "I apologize. I meant no disrespect. I'm sure I don't understand leadership strategies the way you do."

Regina lets out a small, pealing laugh. "No, you don't. You've never had to lead a civilization, have you?"

I shake my head.

"Exactly. So leave your worries to me, my dear." Her tone is full of condescension, and she pats me on the head like I'm a small child.

Whatever she says, I'm sure she cares about her own power

more than the people's safety, just like Commander Charlie. They're both nothing but selfish monsters. Still, when she smiles at me, I force myself to smile back. The only thing helping me ignore the sick feeling in the pit of my stomach is I am already thinking of ways to overthrow the Developers. For now I will do what I have to.

The door to the other room opens, and Dr. Jeb and Charlie come back in. On the other side of the glass, the nurses are unhooking Dean and Skylar from the machines. There's feverish excitement in Dr. Jeb's face.

"It worked!" he says. "The subjects' symptoms are completely gone. We have a resistance serum."

This means we can go through with the plan I'd proposed; we don't have to detonate the Strykers. Relief overwhelms me.

"We owe this to you, Clementine," Commander Charlie says. He hands the vial he was holding to me. "Thank you for your service."

I turn the vial over in my hand. The liquid inside is silver with swirls of violet.

"How long will it take to have a batch ready?" Regina asks.

"Give me two hours," Dr. Jeb says, "and you'll have what you need."

"Wonderful," Charlie says. His eyes shine with anticipation. "We'll begin preparations so our troops can depart for the Surface city as soon as the batch is ready."

# 17

By the time I've changed back into normal clothes and returned to Restricted Division, word has gone out to all the soldiers shipping out today. There are a hundred things going on, what with the Developers going over their strategy with the military leaders, and transports in the flight ports being stocked with weapons and supplies. I'm allowed to sit in on the strategy meeting to hear the discussion of tactics, but I don't end up needing to chime in. Commander Charlie and the other Developers keep their word and order their leaders to carry out the plan I proposed.

There's a moment after the meeting when I'm suddenly struck with a pang of worry. I overhear one of the corporals talking about the lack of Mods he has in his squadron, requesting for soldiers with stronger modifications to be shipped to the Surface. The corporal's eyes dart to me, and Commander Charlie's eyes follow.

I'm terrified he's going to order me to go with the troops. I should've made it clear in my conditions that he couldn't ship me out in the first wave. I want to fight, but not until we're ready to target the Mardenite battle stations.

I'm too far away to hear Charlie's answer. After the corporal leaves, I hurry over to him. "I'm not going to the Surface," I say.

"Of course not," Commander Charlie says. "We can't afford to lose our most useful Mod subject at a time like this. No, you'll remain in the Core. I'm giving you a special apartment in Restricted Division, so you'll be closer to all the important happenings."

So he can keep a closer eye on me, he means. But I'll take it, if it means I'll remain far from the warfront a little longer.

Five squadrons depart for the Surface at eight o' clock. Thirty soldiers in each squadron. Five men in each battleship. They'll begin targeting raiders early tomorrow morning, hopefully before the Mardenites launch another attack against the city. Meanwhile, probes will be sent to investigate the battle stations, so we can rescue our prisoners as soon as possible and take out the power source of the fleet.

I watch the soldiers board their transports in the Core's biggest flight hangar. Men and women in uniform file into the ships one by one. A lot of these soldiers used to be stationed in the other lower sectors—Crust, Mantle, and Lower. But after the arrival of Marden's army, many were transferred to the Core for safety. Now they're the ones being shipped out, while soldiers and pilots like Lieutenant Dean and Skylar are staying behind. The Developers have faith in the mission, but not enough to risk sending their best officials.

I can only hope the resistance serum the soldiers will be given once they're aboard their ships will be enough to protect them from the Mardenite chemical weapons, should they end up on the ground in poison fog. But the serum won't save them from any other weapons they might come in contact with. Only the skill of their pilots and generals can do that.

A young woman in uniform walks past me, led by two soldiers. A prisoner. When I see her face, I nearly have a heart attack. She looks exactly like Fiona. But Fiona's dead. I left her body burning in the engine room of the hovercraft.

Immediately, I realize who she is—Paley, Fiona's twin. She's holding her head high, looking dignified even as she's being led with her wrists cuffed behind her back. Charlie must be sending her to the Surface.

I push through the crowd of soldiers to reach her, but there are too many people. And the guards are leading Paley farther and farther away. Soon she disappears inside one of the transports.

I turn back around. I need to find Charlie. He and the other Developers are up in a viewing room above the flight hangar, overseeing the whole operation. I can see their figures through a glass window.

On my way to the staircase that leads up to the viewing room, I nearly crash into Skylar. "Careful," she says.

"Did you know?" I ask.

Her brows furrow. "Did I know what?"

"The Developers are sending Alliance prisoners to the Surface. I just saw Paley boarding one of the transports."

"Oh," Skylar says. "Yes, I knew."

"Who else are they sending?" I ask.

"Lieutenant Malcolm's name was also on the dispatch list. And

Jensen. I don't know how many others, but I'd assume most of the people they captured in Crust and Mantle."

"How many more did they capture?"

"Everyone. All the rebels they had on their list."

This is Skylar's fault. Beechy only gave the Developers a partial list of the rebels who were working undercover in the lower sectors. Skylar gave up the rest of the names. I wish the Developers had sent her to the Surface too.

I push past her and continue toward the staircase, before my anger gets the best of me.

"Where are you going?" she asks.

I don't answer.

I find Commander Charlie in the viewing room, smiling down at the flight port. The other Developers have left to take care of business elsewhere. Only two guards remain, stationed by the door. They don't let me enter until Charlie gives me clearance.

"What can I do for you, Clementine?" he asks.

"You lied to me," I say.

"Excuse me?"

"You promised you'd pardon the other Alliance prisoners. Instead, you're sending them to the Surface and forcing them to fight."

"I promised they'd be pardoned *if* they cooperate with our war efforts," he says calmly. "That includes following any orders from their commanders. If your friends make it back to the Core and remain cooperative, I can assure you they will be forgiven for their crimes."

*If* they make it back to the Core. He knows he might've sent

Paley and Mal and all the others to their deaths. I bet he's hoping they won't come back. He doesn't want to pardon those of us who've fought against him; he wants to get rid of us one by one.

I'm sure he'll try to get rid of me too after he's gotten everything he needs from me.

"One of my guards will take you to your new apartment," Charlie says, signaling one of the men by the door.

"I want to visit Logan on the way," I say.

"You won't find him in his cell."

The warmth drains from my face. Charlie wasn't supposed to move him without my permission. "Where is he?"

"I've transferred him to your apartment."

It takes a moment for the words to sink in: Charlie released Logan from his prison cell. "Really?" I ask, hesitant to believe Charlie's telling the truth.

"Yes. I ordered his transfer an hour ago." Charlie chuckles at my disbelief. "You cooperated so well with the Mod tests, I thought you deserved something bigger in return. And I know how much you care about the boy. I know you see me as something of a monster, Clementine, but I assure you I can be a kind, reasonable man."

I return his fake smile with one of my own. I can play along with this game.

"Thank you so much, Commander." The gratitude in my voice is real. "I promise I'll keep cooperating."

"No, thank *you*," Charlie says, his smile deepening. "Thanks to your help creating our new serum, we have much more hope of winning the war."

✕

The apartment the guard takes me to is more luxurious than any I've seen before, even the other rooms I've had in the Core. The bed is huge, but there are also two lounge chairs and a sofa, positioned in front of a CorpoBot screen that's almost as big as the bed. A remote on one of the dressers switches on a simulation of a starscape, a peaceful ocean, or a forest on all four walls. If I wanted, I could fall asleep surrounded by starlight. The comforter on the bed is made of silk, and the sheets are the warmest cotton. There's a heater built into the bed that makes it even warmer. A screen on one of the walls spits out food and hot or cold drinks from a slot at the press of a button.

This apartment isn't built for someone like me; it's built for a Developer or a military leader. Clearly, Commander Charlie is trying to appease me. I'd be lying if I said it wasn't working a little bit.

The guard gives me a special wristband—a comm-band, he calls it—that I'm supposed to wear at all times. It will allow the Developers and their personnel to send messages to me, calling me for strategy meetings and the like.

A few minutes after the guard leaves, Logan comes out of the connecting bathroom, wearing only a towel wrapped around his lower half. His skin and hair are cleaner than they've ever been, finally rid of the dirt and grime from all the years he spent in the Surface work camp. He took showers in the Alliance compound, but nothing compares to the power of the steam-cleans here in the Core.

It's been so long since I've seen him like this, without the threat of someone coming to drag him away and never let me see him again. I can sense Logan realizing the same thing. Our eyes lock together in the silence, the weight of the horrible days we were apart crushing between us.

He hobbles toward me on his crutches, and I rush to him from where I'm standing in front of the CorpoBot screen. He kisses my face and wipes away the tears welling up in my eyes. I run my hands over his bare shoulders and chest, reveling in the warmth of his skin. This boy I almost lost time and time again. He's here and he's alive and he's not leaving. Emotion bubbles up and I realize I'm speaking nonsense. But no words are needed, not right now.

We cling to each other for a long time, until Logan can't take standing on his hurt leg anymore. Moving over to the bed, he leans his crutches against the wall. He sits down on the bed and pulls me to him, kisses my mouth tenderly. His heart is beating almost as fast as mine.

I lean back onto the bed, pulling Logan with me, and kiss him some more. His towel starts to come undone and my nervousness gets the best of me. Sure, I've thought about this before. But there's a difference between wanting something and being ready for it.

I pull away, blushing, and Logan realizes what's happening. He quickly fixes the towel and climbs off me. "I'll go change into some real clothes," he says.

"Okay," I say.

He disappears into the closet. While I wait for him to change, I switch on the starscape simulator. All the lights dim except for the lights on the walls and the ceiling, tiny pinpricks of stars glowing reds and purples and greens and oranges. I'm surrounded by a million of them, shimmering amid the darkness of space. They look so real, I might be able to step through the wall and float among them.

When Logan comes back out, he pauses for a moment, awed by the view. A comet shoots across the ceiling. "Commander Charlie has outdone himself," he says. "I didn't think he'd try so hard to win you over."

"Neither did I," I say. "It's not going to work, though. I won't forgive him, even if he helps us win the war."

"Good," Logan says, hobbling back over to the bed. He sits down again, putting his crutches back against the wall. "Because I have a feeling he'll stop playing nice soon. He's trying to distract us so we might not notice. We need to keep paying attention."

"I know."

Logan climbs under the covers, and I slip in beside him. He could've chosen silk pajamas from the closet, but he's wearing a simple set of trousers and a tunic like me. Clothes of the sort we used to wear in the camp. I'm glad; it would be strange seeing him in anything different.

Another comet shoots across the ceiling overhead.

"Remember when we used to sit outside the shack and watch the stars?" Logan asks. "On the roof, or on those boulders at the edge of the camp."

"Of course," I say.

I could never forget those precious moments when we were away from the officials and cam-bots. When it was just the two of us with our fingers intertwined, Logan and me and the stars shining through the acid shield. The world still seemed big, but it didn't seem so scary.

"I used to think about kissing you, then," Logan says, finding my hand under the sheets. "*Especially* then, I should say."

I laugh softly. "Really?"

He nods.

"When did you know?" I ask. "That you . . . wanted to kiss me."

"I think it was a year or two after I found you in that garbage bin," he says.

The day he and I first met, I'd been shoved into a Dumpster by some bullies from school. Boys who couldn't handle that I was better than them in every subject.

"So, when I was seven and you were eight?" I ask.

"Sounds about right."

I raise an eyebrow. "Yet you waited until I was sixteen?"

"I wasn't sure if you . . . wanted me to kiss you," Logan says. "You were my best friend. I didn't want to lose you over something stupid like that."

I grab the collar of his shirt to pull him closer to me. "It wasn't stupid. For the record, I would've kissed you back."

And with the stars surrounding us, that's what I do.

# 18

The next morning, I wake to warm sheets and Logan's arms wrapped around me. The starscape is still on; a galaxy drifts above us. I was going to turn it off before I fell asleep, but I must've knocked out too soon.

A wave of worry washes over me as I remember this is the second day of the Mardenite invasion. The dispatched troops must've reached the Surface city by now. I check my comm-band for messages, but there's nothing except for the standard daily schedule of mealtimes in the cafeteria.

I can only assume that means nothing terrible has happened to the soldiers yet. Things are going according to plan. I hope.

Logan wakes a few minutes after me. I kiss the sleepiness from his eyes, and he mumbles, "You're still here."

I laugh softly. "I am."

"I'm glad." He squeezes me in a tight hug. "I was afraid you'd run off again."

He's referring to the last time we spent the night together in

STEPHANIE DIAZ / 160

the Alliance compound. The night before our group left to invade the lower sectors. I was too anxious to sleep, so I left Logan hours before he woke up. He wasn't happy to find me gone in the morning, especially when he heard I'd been making plans with Beechy that would put me in danger of being captured.

"Didn't run, and I promise I won't," I say. "What do you want to do today?"

If any strategy meetings come up, I'll have to attend them. But in the meantime it seems best that I find something to distract myself with while I wait for news of the war happenings on the Surface. And Logan hasn't had a chance to see much of the Core yet. He's been stuck in a cell since we got here.

"I wouldn't mind exploring a bit," Logan says. "Seeing what everyone thinks is so great about this sector compared to the others."

"Do you feel well enough to walk around?" I ask.

To prove it, Logan rolls out of bed, grabs his crutches, and takes off around the room.

I laugh. "Good. Let's hurry to the cafeteria so we won't miss breakfast."

We get dressed and head for an elevator that will take us to the upper levels of the Core. I'm surprised Commander Charlie hasn't sent a guard to escort us everywhere. But then, Logan has to use crutches to walk and I have fractured ribs still healing. We aren't exactly huge threats to the infrastructure of his society at the moment. And he knows I understand there's no use trying to overthrow him until Marden's army has been defeated.

✳

The cafeteria is crowded with people. We take our trays from the ordering machines and sit down at one of the long tables. There are rows and rows of them, filling the oval shape of the room. On the domed ceiling overhead, there's a projection of the Core flag: a rectangle filled with blue-and-black stripes, and a silver circle at its center with words running along its bottom: *Invention. Peace. Prosperity.*

"*How* is this so good?" Logan says with a bite of a cheesy raerburger in his mouth. "It's even better than the food at the Alliance compound. And that was a hundred times better than camp grub."

I laugh. "I mean, they starved us in the camp, so I'm pretty sure anything is better than that."

"True." Logan wipes away the cheese dribbling down his chin with a napkin. "Still, I thought people might be exaggerating how good the food is here. I'm glad I was wrong."

When Logan and I were growing up in the work camp, all we heard from our teachers and guards were all the amazing things people had access to in the Core. It was described as a place of freedom and fun and extravagance, where the citizens had no fear of an early death. Those of us in the camps who performed well on our Extraction tests and were lucky enough to be transferred to the Core would be able to live with the same freedom.

But the reality is the only people with true freedom here are the Developers and their fiercest proponents. The people who display so much loyalty to the Developers' policies, they earn a pass on their monthly injections. Mostly colonels and lieutenants, from what I've seen. Military men who also hunger for power and violence. The only people who thrive in the system are the ones who adore it.

I swallow my bite of bansa stew. "The best place in the Core is Recreation Division. We can go there after this, if you want. I can show you the zero-gravity machine and the race pods. That's where we used to spend most of my time, when we weren't in training sessions."

"Who's 'we'?" Logan asks.

"Me, Ariadne, and Oliver," I say. My throat sticks on Oliver's name. "The friends I made during Extraction training."

Logan touches my knee under the table. There's anxiousness in his eyes. "Sorry, I didn't mean to bring him up."

"It's fine," I say.

Oliver has been gone a few weeks now. I still miss him, but thinking about him doesn't hurt the way it used to. It's not an overwhelming pain; it's just a slight ache in my chest.

There's a loud bout of obnoxious laughter from the young kids sitting at the table next to ours. Logan studies them, his expression turning serious, as he picks up his canteen.

"They don't know what's happening on the Surface, do they?" he asks.

All the people in the cafeteria seem too chipper and peaceful for a group of citizens whose planet is under invasion.

"No, they don't," I say. "The Developers think they'll be happier this way. And all they care about is keeping the public happy, you know." I roll my eyes.

"We could tell the people anyway," Logan says, setting his drink down. "We could stand up right now on one of the tables and shout out the truth before anyone could stop us."

"And then Commander Charlie would lock us up again."

"Maybe so. But at least we'd have done something to turn the people against them."

As I look around at the citizens at the other tables, I shake my head. It's no use; even Ariadne wouldn't listen to me. "They wouldn't believe us, not when they're all subdued. They aren't thinking for themselves. The Developers are thinking for them."

"You don't know that for sure," Logan says.

"You've never been subdued. You don't know what it's like." My voice cracks at the memory of the horrible feeling of suffocation, of being imprisoned in my own body with someone else pulling the strings. "Even if some part of them understood what was going on and wanted to rebel, most of them wouldn't be able to fight the serum."

"Well, maybe some of them are like you." A smile tugs at the edge of Logan's mouth. "You broke free, right? Why not others?"

I frown, considering. He's right; some of the people in this room must be like me. Citizens with genetic modifications similar to mine, who are secretly Unstable. Boys and girls who've figured out something's going on, but they don't know who to go to for help. Maybe there are even Alliance rebels here in the cafeteria, still in hiding.

"There are probably some," I say. "But not enough to make a big difference. Not enough to be worth the risk."

Most of them can't be like me, or they wouldn't be in the Core at all. Most of them are like Oliver or Ariadne—they'd need help from another injection to snap them out of their submission. It would take a thousand energy injections to make all of these people mindful again.

And even then, what would they do? They'd probably be lost and confused, not used to making decisions for themselves. It would take another leader to turn them against the Developers. Someone who could inspire people to follow him, but wouldn't abuse his power or try to control anyone. He'd let the people make the decision to fight or not fight, whichever they wanted.

Beechy, if he were here, could've been that kind of leader. But he isn't. I don't know if there's anyone else. I certainly don't think I could do it. My failed attempt to inspire rebellion in the Crust work camp proved that much.

"So you're saying you want to do nothing?" Logan asks.

"No. I'm saying if we're going to try to turn the people against the Developers, we need to be better prepared for it. We need more people on our side than the two of us."

"Who's going to help us?" Logan stabs his fork into his food. "Everyone who would is locked up somewhere, or still in hiding. We have no way to talk to them."

I sigh. "I don't know. But there has to be someone."

We can't be the only two people in the Core who want the Developers out of power. We just have to find the others without drawing attention to ourselves.

Logan and I are on our way to Recreation Division when my comm-band starts beeping. I quickly check the screen.

"What is it?" Logan asks.

"An urgent meeting," I say. "I'm sorry. I have to go."

"Does it say what the meeting's for?"

I shake my head. "Something must be going on with the troops on the Surface. Do you need me to take you back to the room?"

"No, I want to keep looking around." He kisses me on the cheek. "Be careful, okay? Let me know what happens."

"I'll come find you afterward. Where should we meet?"

"I'll wait for you in Recreation Division."

"Okay. See you in a little while." I drop Logan's hand and hurry to find an elevator.

Inside, I tap the button on the two-dimensional map of the Core for the main entrance to Restricted Division. My comm-band tells me the floor and room number for the meeting, but it's not accessible from this elevator. Security protocol and all that.

The elevator *whoosh*es across a horizontal shaft, then switches to a vertical shaft to take me down. I'm almost to the proper floor when it comes to an early stop at one of the floors for the health ward.

The door opens, and a man in a gray uniform walks inside. I'm surprised to see it's Lieutenant Dean, also in a hurry. But he stops abruptly when he sees me.

"Clementine," he says. "You're headed to the meeting?"

I nod. "Any idea what it's about?"

He shakes his head, closing the elevator door behind him. "I just got the message, same as you."

He looks a lot better than he did when I saw him last night, when he was still sick from the poison gas. There are dark circles under his eyes, but the fever sweat and the flush in his cheeks are gone. The antidote Dr. Jeb gave him seems to have completely cured him.

As the elevator continues going down, I ask, "What were you doing in the health ward?"

"Visiting Lieutenant Sam."

I bite my lip. I'd practically forgotten him in the chaos of everything. "How's he doing?"

"He's recovering at a very slow rate," Dean says. "He's starting to respond to his name, but he's still not making much sense."

"Have you . . . ?" I hesitate.

"Have I told anyone you were involved in the situation?" he finishes for me. "No, I haven't. I've told the commanders that the lieutenant became hostile and unfit for command on our mission, due to his inexperience in war situations and his fear of the Mardenites. I had to subdue him in order to save the mission. And the combination of the strong dosage of serum along with the poison gas made him have an averse reaction."

It's not so very far off from the truth. It certainly sounds believable.

"They didn't punish you, did they?"

"No, they agreed with my judgment call," Dean says stiffly. "It would take a lot for them to punish me after everything I've done for them."

The elevator comes to a stop with a *ding*.

"Restricted Division," a cool female voice says.

As the doors open, I remember: Dean brought me back to the Core for the Developers. He saved me for them, supposedly without knowing why they needed me kept alive. But after his reaction to my aversion to the poison gas, I don't think he was entirely honest with me.

I clench my hands into fists at my sides, but follow Dean out of the elevator. I wait until we've passed the first security checkpoint and entered an empty corridor before I speak. "You knew, didn't you? About the Mod Project. You knew I was their most promising test subject."

Dean nods, tight-lipped. "The Mod Project isn't a secret among people who are close to the commanders."

"Why couldn't you have just told me? You didn't have to lie to me."

"I had no idea how you would react," he says. "It was already difficult enough to get you to trust me. Anyway, there was no time to explain everything."

I remember the hushed conversation he and Beechy had in the infirmary, about making sure someone important made it off the Surface—me.

"Did Beechy know?" I ask, though I'm afraid to know the answer.

"No, he didn't," Dean says, and I exhale. "I only told him enough to make him believe it was important you returned to the Core, and that I would help you get there. I'm sure he suspected something, but he doesn't know everything. Not even Commander Charlie's daughter knew."

"Good," I say, though I'm not sure if it is. Beechy and Sandy should know about the Mod Project. Everyone needs to understand how deep the Developers' manipulation of humanity goes.

We turn a corner in the hallway, and I glance at the numbers on the doors. We're almost to the meeting room.

"I do apologize for lying to you," Dean says in a quieter voice, as stiff as ever. Almost as if he's afraid someone ahead of us in the hallway will overhear him. "I want you to understand I'm not proud of many of the things I've done."

"I get it," I say. "You were just doing your job."

We come to the door for the meeting room. Dean opens his mouth to say something else, but he hesitates.

"What?" I ask.

"Never mind," he says, and presses the button on the wall to open the door.

# 19

As soon as I step into the meeting room, I know something is wrong. There's a tense energy in the air, a wave of heat and anxiety much worse than when I met the Developers in the other strategy room last night. There are also a lot more people here: Cadet Waller and a number of other aids, a few scientists in lab coats, and at least ten army lieutenants and colonels. They fill most of the seats around an enormous round table, talking in hushed voices among themselves. We're still waiting for the Developers to arrive.

A holographic map of the Surface covers the back wall of the room. I study the map as I follow Dean to a pair of empty seats on the far side of the table. I easily locate the Surface settlement—it's the only actual city on the map, though there are other marked facilities, military outposts here and there. But there's nothing on the map that gives me any sign of the status of the war, or why this urgent meeting was called.

Sitting in the chair next to mine is Colonel Fred, the old scientist I met in Karum prison. The designer of the bomb that killed

Oliver and nearly destroyed the outer sectors. Fred is deep in conversation with one of the other scientists, wringing his hands. I interrupt the two of them.

"What's going on?" I ask.

"The Surface city," he says. The wrinkles are deep-set around his wide, worried eyes.

My chest tightens. "It was bombed." It's not a question.

Fred hesitates. "Well, not exactly."

"What happened?"

Before he can explain, the door at the front of the room opens. The Developers file in one at a time, Commander Charlie and Commander Regina at the front of the line. Two more military officers trail behind them.

"Thank you all for coming," Commander Charlie says. "Let's call the meeting to order."

A hush falls over the room as the commanders take their seats across the table. They all look flustered, not well kept. Regina has a smudge of lipstick at the corner of her mouth, and her bob is lying unevenly. Charlie touches a handkerchief to his forehead to wipe off the sweat.

"As some of you have already heard, we have a grave situation on the Surface," he says in a heavy voice. "Last night we sent five squadrons to defend the city against another attack. They were ordered to draw attention away from the settlement and the passage to the lower sectors by targeting raiders stationed a hundred miles away at six o' clock this morning, Core time. We received reports that their initial attack was successful. They took out two swarms of raiders—at least forty ships. They captured several Mardenites and were preparing to send them here for questioning. However, shortly after their report came through, all radio contact with the Surface—including video feeds from the cam-bots—went dark. We didn't recover contact until nearly an hour ago."

My blood courses with worry, but also with confusion. Why am I just hearing about this now, if it started hours ago?

"Based on preliminary reports," Commander Charlie continues, "we believe the Mardenites dropped an electrical pulse bomb on the Surface city, which effectively disabled all electricity within a fifty-mile or so radius of the settlement, including weapons, transports, and comm devices."

If this is true, the soldiers couldn't fire their weapons or fly their transports. They couldn't defend themselves. But any raiders who flew in from outside the radius of the damage still would've been armed for war.

"We don't know exactly what happened after the bomb went off." Charlie pauses to press his lips together. "But as of nine o' clock this morning, there appear to be no more humans on the Surface. The underground bunkers outside the settlement, which were occupied by Colonel Parker and his regiment, are empty. There's been no sign of them or any of the other squadrons. And the Mardenites have taken over the city."

Silence drenches the room as Charlie's words sink in.

It feels like someone's stuck a wrench through my chest. The city was our biggest defense on the Surface. All the child workers— Nellie, Hector, Grady, and Evie—are gone. And the 150 soldiers who were sent to the Surface last night are gone too, Paley and Mal among them. They were the last squadrons standing between the Mardenites and the entrance to the Pipeline, the passage to Crust, Mantle, Lower, and the Core.

Everyone around the table starts talking at once with a hundred questions.

"One at a time, please," Commander Marshall says loudly, holding up a hand for silence. "Yes, Lieutenant Brand?"

A young soldier with slick, shoulder-length hair asks, "How do we know for sure there weren't any survivors? Couldn't they be up there in hiding, unable to make contact with us? Their comms could be facing interference."

"You're right, there may well be survivors," Marshall says. "But as we've had no contact with anyone, we can't assume that's the case. All we know for certain is that many of our people have been captured and the city has been overrun. We've effectively lost control of the Surface. The lower sectors, including the Core, are at a much higher risk of facing an attack, should the Mardenites discover the Pipeline."

People raise their hands with more questions. On my left, Dean sits in silence with his lips pressed together. On my right, Fred's hands are still fidgeting in his lap.

I have questions I want to ask, but I'm not sure where to begin. This is all too much. I'm trying to picture what happened after the pulse bomb fell. Without power, our warships must've crashed. Soldiers were injured; some probably died. The child workers were suddenly trapped in dark buildings. And then the Mardenites landed and took all of them, one by one. Maybe they incapacitated them with poison gas first. The child workers weren't the ones who were going to be given the resistance serum, not right away.

Somehow, the aliens captured them all and overran the city. Some of them could be walking the streets of the work camp right now, looking for more humans they can drag aboard their raiders.

The scientist sitting on the other side of Fred is talking now: "Do you have a count of how many people were taken?"

"Roughly seven thousand child workers, along with the five

squadrons of Core soldiers we sent last night and the two that were stationed under Colonel Parker," Commander Regina says. "We can assume most of them are dead or beyond help."

"You don't know that," I cut in, my voice hard. "They were taken. You don't know what's happened to them."

"We know they are in the hands of the enemy," she says calmly. "So they aren't in good circumstances. They're facing tortures if they're still alive. If you care about them, you should hope they're dead instead of in that kind of pain."

She's almost smiling, as if she's amused by the idea of all those people in pain. I want to strangle her. She doesn't care about saving them. She just wants us to believe it's too late. Most of the people who were captured are worthless girls and boys to her, bred for labor and an early death and nothing more. Even the soldiers aren't anyone special.

But I'm not giving up on them. I refuse to believe they're already dead—and if they're not dead we can save them.

Dean clears his throat, finally speaking. His jaw is firm, his eyes serious. "Has there been any sign of Mardenites near the city's Pipeline entrance?"

In the Surface settlement, the Pipeline is accessible through the flight port. I'd never even seen it before the day I was picked for Extraction, when I boarded a transport for the Core. But then, I was mostly confined to the work camp. I was only allowed into the city for school and on the yearly days of the Extraction ceremony.

"Not yet," Regina says. "That entrance is currently blocked by rubble from the battle. Though if they knew what they were looking for, it wouldn't be difficult to access. So it's very likely they are—thankfully—still unaware of our underground cities."

"So maybe they'll leave now," Brand says. "As far as they know, they've captured everyone on the planet. Maybe they'll go home."

"That was our initial hope," Charlie says, pushing his chair back. "But it doesn't seem to be the reality." He stands up and walks over to the map. "The Mardenites are in the midst of building settlements around the Surface."

He presses a series of buttons on a screen to the right of the map, and the hologram changes. Giant black dots appear in seven places on the map, marking the location of the Mardenite settlements. One in the Surface city, one in the middle of the desert, three on the edges of the biggest oceans, two in the jungle to the east of the mountains.

"By the looks of it, they won't be leaving anytime soon," Charlie says. "And as long as they remain on the Surface, it's only a matter of time before they'll discover one of the entrances to the lower sectors. Any of our citizens in their custody could easily give up the information."

The Developers don't care about any of the people who were captured or killed in the bombing. The only reason they care about losing the Surface at all is because it makes their precious Core more vulnerable to discovery.

"We need to figure out how we can defend the lower sectors," Lieutenant Dean says. "And after we've put a strategy in motion, how we can regain control of the Surface."

"We should set off the Strykers," says Cadet Waller. She's sitting with the other aides, her back straight, her hands clasped on the table in front of her. "The aliens must've transported the child workers they captured to their battle stations. So, we can blow up their stations from the inside. Cripple their fleet."

There's a murmur of agreement around the room. I can't help

panicking. A move like that would kill everyone on board—Beechy, Sandy, Nellie, and all the other prisoners. We need to get them out before we destroy the battle stations.

Luckily, Commander Charlie is shaking his head, disagreeing with the plan.

"We've already tried," he says. "The electric pulse bomb seems to have damaged the devices. They're not responding to our long-range detonators."

"You already *tried*?" I repeat.

"Yes."

His daughter could've been killed. He doesn't even seem to care.

People have started talking over each other again. Dean raises his voice so he'll be heard: "What we need to do is set up an underground security barrier close to the city's Pipeline entrance. Place explosives there so that we can take out anyone who tries to get to Crust."

"What about the other entrance to the Pipeline?" Brand asks.

"We should also defend it, but we need to leave it open so we can get troops on the Surface. I'd say our best strategy at this point is to bombard their settlements while they're still building them up. Pick out the weaker ones first and work our way up to the city."

"If we raise an army out of the ground, the lower sectors won't be a secret anymore," Brand says. "Besides, all the aliens will have to do is drop another pulse bomb and our flight instruments and weapons will be useless. Even more of us will be captured. We'll lose our whole army."

"Do you have a better suggestion, lieutenant?" Dean asks through gritted teeth.

Brand looks disgruntled, but he says nothing. Dean's idea might not work, but it's still the best we've heard so far.

My mind is racing, trying to come up with something to say. But with every possibility I think of, there remains a way the Mardenites could overpower us again. They took the Surface less than forty-eight hours after their arrival. Even with the plan we put in motion and the soldiers we sent off armed with a resistance serum against their poisons, the Mardenites still captured everyone.

We underestimated the power of their forces and their weapons. We can stay holed up in the Core pretending we're safe here, but the reality is, as soon as they discover the Pipeline, I doubt they'll have any difficulty invading the Core. We'll all be captured or dead in the next forty-eight hours at this rate.

My heart is beating way too fast. I squeeze my eyes shut and try to calm down. *Inhale, exhale. Inhale, exhale.*

There's a solution for this, a way we can save ourselves. There has to be.

"Perhaps," Cadet Waller says, "we should consider a surrender. Try to negotiate terms for peace. We could offer to return their god we took prisoner."

I glance around the table, curious if everyone here knew about the Mardenite prisoner, since his existence isn't exactly common knowledge. But no one looks shocked or confused. All the aides and military leaders are privy to such information, it seems.

"We are not returning our prisoner," Commander Charlie says. "That creature has far too much power. He will be executed before he is released. The Mardenites are monsters that will stop at nothing to slaughter our people, until humankind is extinct. A surrender is not a solution."

"But sir," Waller says, "if their forces are too many for us to defeat—"

"We don't need to defeat them," Charlie says. "All we need to do is escape them."

Dean frowns. "What are you proposing?"

Charlie turns back to the screen on the wall and presses another series of buttons. The holographic map of the Surface disappears, replaced by a spinning hologram of the entire planet. "We return to a previous plan. We construct a new machine to separate the Core from the rest of Kiel, and then we fly away from the Mardenites and escape them forever."

A sick feeling settles in the pit of my stomach. Charlie doesn't really mean a machine—he means a bomb. A bomb that will destroy the outer sectors, allowing the Core to function as a battle station, the way it was designed. This is exactly what Charlie tried to do a few weeks ago, but the Alliance and I managed to stop him. I should've known he hadn't abandoned the idea.

There are intakes of breath around the table, and hushed voices. Not of dissent—of interest.

"Colonel Fred has been working on some updated designs for me," Charlie continues, gesturing to Fred in the seat beside me. He looks a bit nervous as everyone's eyes land on him.

I can't believe he's helping Charlie again. And this isn't something new—Fred must've started working on designs days ago, as soon as he was brought back to the Core from Karum prison. As soon as the last bomb was destroyed. He's known the Developers might put this plan into motion again, but he kept it a secret.

"With the colonel's weapon," Charlie says, "we'll be able to blast away the outer sectors in a simple wave, effectively wiping out any of the Mardenites still on the Surface. Their fleet will be pummeled by debris from the planet's ruins. They won't survive. The Core will be free to fly away, and with our battle station in working order, we'll have the fire power necessary to take down any of Marden's remaining forces, should they be foolish enough to follow us. But I doubt they will."

"Where will we go?" a scientist asks.

"We've been surveying local planets good for habitation, and there's a promising one in the next galaxy. We'll make our way there. But the Core has enough supplies and oxygen to allow us to thrive for centuries, until we find a suitable location for our new home."

Murmurs of agreement pick up around the room. Everyone likes this idea. And these aren't subdued, mindless citizens—these are the people who are allowed to think for themselves.

In theory, this plan could actually work. The force of the explosion should be enough to destroy all of the Mardenite forces on the Surface and on their battle stations. The Core could fly away to safety. All the citizens in this sector would survive the war. I would survive, and so would Logan.

But Beechy wouldn't. Neither would Sandy, Uma, Paley, or all the other thousands of people imprisoned on the battle stations. This plan would kill them, unless we rescued them before we set off the bomb.

"What about the prisoners aboard the battle stations?" I ask. "Can't we try to rescue them first?"

"It would be impractical," Charlie says. "It would require too big of a force, and we'd run the risk of losing more citizens. We've already lost too many. We need to keep everyone contained in the Core."

"So you don't care about rescuing your daughter or her baby girl?" I ask.

Charlie looks momentarily stricken, as I'd hoped he would. He can't have known Sandy was having a daughter, a little girl he surely would've doted upon. But he recovers quickly, wiping away the lines of guilt around his eyes with his handkerchief. "War requires sacrifices from all of us," he says in a solemn voice.

"Will you transfer people from the other sectors?" Dean asks. He's one of the only people at the table not smiling like everyone else.

"As many as we can," Regina says. "But the Core isn't big enough to contain Kiel's entire population. If we take too many civilians, we run the risk of depleting our resources too quickly."

I expected her answer. But it still makes me sick to my stomach. She and the other commanders will do what they've always done: Save the people with better modifications. Transfer the citizens with the highest obedience, intelligence, and strength, and abandon the rest. They're hardly people, anyway. They're just Mod subjects, bodies to be used and disposed of.

I look around the table at the other scientists and military leaders, urging them to speak up and propose another solution. But none of them do. They don't care if we leave thousands of people behind to die. All they care about is saving their own skin.

"How long until the bomb will be ready?" Dean asks. His voice is calm, agreeable, but there's a vein bulging in his neck.

"My construction team can begin as soon as the project is approved," Fred says. "Construction should be completed in about fifteen hours."

Fifteen hours. I have fifteen hours to find an alternative solution.

# 20

The problem is: I don't know where to begin.

After the meeting, I follow Lieutenant Dean out into the hallway. He has composed himself, but I can still sense his anger beneath his calm exterior. He's as annoyed with the plan as I am. But neither one of us says a word until we reach the elevator.

"There has to be something else we can do," I say as soon as the door closes. "I know the Developers don't care about saving the people who were captured, but I don't think we should abandon them. I *won't.*"

"I agree," Dean says. "But it's not just the prisoners I'm worried about. The Core was designed to function as a battle station apart from the rest of the planet. But we've never been able to test it out, for obvious reasons. The separation bomb could damage this sector too, which is why I was against the idea before. It's a dangerous plan, one we shouldn't go through with until we've exhausted all our other options."

"So what are we supposed to do?" I ask.

The Developers are in control of the army, the citizens, the weapons. How can we take all of that from them in the next fifteen hours?

Dean sighs. "I'm not sure there's anything we can do. But we'll see. You should stay put, okay? I know you might want to try something rash like last time, but you shouldn't. Not until we've found a real solution."

"Okay," I say.

But how can I stay put? If I come up with something to try, I'm not going to wait for Dean's approval. I'm going to do it.

Dean gets off on the next level, telling me he has to take care of something but he'll find me later if a solution presents itself. I stare at the buttons in the elevator, trying to figure out where to go. First, I guess I should find Logan and tell him what's going on. Maybe he'll have a better idea what to do.

I wander around the enormous, dark room of Recreation Division, between lit-up games stations where boys and girls fire fake weapons at simulated target screens, wrestle with one another, or float in zero gravity, making a general raucous of noise.

My eyes keep going back to the biggest object on this floor of the arena: the giant Phantom dome, looming over all the other game modules. Inside that dome is the room where Sam attacked me for the first time. I'd gotten an impossible score in one of Phantom's simulation games and wiped his name off the top of the high scoreboard. At the time, I thought he was ridiculous for caring so much about a score on a stupid game. But it wasn't just a game—it was another test of our intelligence and ability to react in war situations. And no one had ever beaten Sam before. It was the second time I'd challenged his score on an aptitude test, and he couldn't stand not being the best anymore.

Sam must not have had any idea I was Mod Subject 7, built to be the better soldier. If he'd known, he probably would've tried to kill me the minute he met me.

Tearing my eyes away from Phantom, I look up. The floors of the upper levels are made of glass; the people up there look like they're floating in the sky. A pod race is going on. The track weaves through open air lit by blue and green and red lights that look like stars or small planets. I've never been up there before; I only ever explored this lowest level. And I have a feeling Logan would've wanted to check out the pod races.

I take the staircase two steps at a time, checking the time on my comm-band. It's been fifteen minutes since the meeting ended. We have less than fifteen hours until Fred's bomb is finished. Already, the clock is ticking.

At the top of the stairs, people crowd around the entrance to the racecourse. Some of them are in line for the next race, while others are simply cheering on the racers. A giant screen looms over the entrance, showing a map of the track. Dots show where the seven pods are located. Pods two and five are neck and neck for the lead. There are forty-five seconds left until the race is over.

I push toward the left side of the entrance, one of the viewing spots for the course, looking for Logan everywhere in the crowd. He should be easy to spot with his crutches. But most of the people in the crowd are Core kids wearing skintight leather suits of vary-ing colors.

When I'm almost to the front of the crowd, I give up and decide to watch the race instead. The pods are making their way back toward the finish line by the entrance. They're racing so fast on the track, they're hardly more than blurs of light in the darkness.

I glance back up at the screen. Ten more seconds. Pods two and five are still on top of each other. I grab the railing in front of me, squinting to see them better in the darkness. They might crash if they get any closer.

Five seconds left in the race, and there's still no clear victor.

Four.

Three.

Two.

At the last second, pod five eases ahead enough to be the first across the finish line. People in the crowd behind me start screaming and cheering, "Yeah, Five! Go Matthew!" I can only assume Matthew is the name of the pilot.

From behind the railing, I watch the rest of the pods cross the finish line. They decelerate to a quick stop, and the pilots climb out one by one. I'm about to turn away and head back downstairs when I notice a worker handing one of the pilots a pair of crutches.

I push through the crowd, closer to the entrance, and wave to Logan as he crosses through the turnstile. I can't help worrying his leg is hurting him more after this, but he doesn't seem to be in any pain. His eyes are wild with excitement. His hair is a mess now that he's taken off his helmet.

"Did you see that?" he asks.

"Some of it. Which pod were you in?"

"Number two." He's smiling so wide, I can't help smiling too.

"You got second place?"

"Yeah!" He holds up a shiny silver coin. "Even got a medal. Wait, how long were you watching?"

"The last forty-five seconds of the race."

Logan groans in disappointment. "You missed it. I had a solid lead for the first two laps, until number five almost barreled into me."

"Well, you still looked pretty impressive, from what I saw."

"Thanks." He grins. He grabs my hand and sets the silver coin on my palm. "This is for you."

"But Logan, you won it. It's yours."

"I won it for you. No arguments."

I turn the shiny coin over in my hand. One side is etched with the figure of a small race pod with a half circle of stars around it. The other side has the words SECOND PLACE in bold letters, with smaller words and numbers around the edges of the coin stating the date and time of today's race.

"Thank you," I say, slipping the coin into my pocket. I touch Logan's shoulder as he starts to hobble past me. "Is your leg all right?"

"No worse than before. I only needed my hands to steer and power the engine." He takes my hand again. "Come on, we should get out of here."

The crowd is only growing bigger, so Logan leads the way through on his crutches. A few onlookers clap him on the back, congratulating him on his almost win. He grins and thanks them.

Though I'm happy for him, I can't help feeling a pinch of jealousy, and wishing I could've shown off my own flight skills in the race. But I shove the feeling aside. After all the times Logan's disability has kept him from being the one winning praise, he deserves this.

When we reach the edge of the crowd, we slow down a bit. Logan seems to remember what was going on before all this. His face turns serious. "What happened in the meeting?" he asks.

I hesitate, not sure where to begin. "Nothing good."

"Tell me everything."

I wait until we're well away from the crowd, and then I update him as quickly as I can. I tell him about the electric pulse-bomb dropping; the Mardenites capturing all the child workers and soldiers and taking over the Surface city; and the Developers' plan for how we're going to escape and simultaneously destroy the Mardenite fleet, along with all the people they've taken.

There are hard lines around Logan's mouth. "They feel the deaths of thousands of people are necessary casualties, I'm sure."

"They already sent them to the Surface knowing they could die. And if their deaths will save the rest of us, what does it matter, right?" I shake my head, clenching my hands in agitation. "We can't abandon all those people. We have to rescue them, some-how."

"How, though?" Logan asks, running his fingers through his hair. "The Mardenites took the Surface. If we send more troops up there to try to get it back or target the battle stations, chances are the Mardenites will drop another electric bomb and we'll lose even more people."

I hate that he's saying exactly what Commander Charlie and the other people in the strategy room said. I also hate that I don't disagree.

"I don't know, Logan. Maybe there isn't a better solution. But I don't think that means we should give up. Our friends were taken prisoner," I remind him. "Beechy, Sandy, Uma, Paley, Mal. All of them. After everything Beechy has done for me—for us—rescuing us from Karum, giving us a safe place with the Alliance, and help-ing me come from the Surface mission . . . I just can't leave him. Not without at least trying to bring him home."

Logan is silent, his lips pressed together hard. "So you want to work out a plan to rescue them, even if it means potentially screwing up Commander Charlie's current plan?"

"Yes," I say. "Will you help me?"

He closes his eyes briefly. When he opens them again, he looks at me with a steadier gaze. "I'm in. How long do we have until Fred finishes building the bomb?"

"A little less than fifteen hours."

Logan exhales. "Great. Should be plenty of time. Do you have any idea where to start?"

"I think we need to simplify our problems before we can start thinking of a solution."

We list the problems as the two of us head down the stairs to the lower level of Recreation Division.

Problem one: The Mardenites are in control of the Surface. Any troops we send up there could easily be shot down or crippled by another pulse bomb. Even more people could be captured.

Problem two: the battle stations. We don't know anything about their design or their weaknesses. We don't know where the prisoners are being kept, or how to get them out.

Problem three: time. We need more time to study the Mardenites and learn their weaknesses, to strengthen our army so we can attack their fleet. Unless we can convince the Developers to postpone detonating their bomb, we only have fifteen hours.

Which brings us to our biggest problem: the Developers. They're the ones in control of the citizens, the army, and the weapons. As long as they're in control, we can't send troops anywhere without their permission. Our hands are tied.

"But all we need to do is get the Mardenites to stop fighting, right?" Logan says. "Force them to surrender. Then we wouldn't need to set off any bomb. We wouldn't have to run."

I chew on my lip, considering. He's right. We don't necessarily need to rescue the prisoners; we just need to overpower their captors. But *how*? We've taken out forty of their raiders, but they have thousands of ships in their fleet.

There has to be a missing piece, something we're overlooking. A way to discover a weakness of the Mardenite army we could exploit.

It doesn't hit me until Logan and I are almost to the cafeteria for lunch. We've been silent for the last few minutes, both of us deep in thought, still not much closer to finding a solution.

"You know what I really want to know?" Logan says, his brows furrowing.

"What?" I ask.

"What the Mardenites want with us. We thought they came here to slaughter us, but they captured everyone instead. And they're setting up settlements. Why? I think there's something more going on with them we need to understand. If we knew what they wanted from us, we'd have a better idea how to deal with them."

I gasp. Just like that, I realize what I've been overlooking: We have one of the Mardenites in captivity. The leader we captured in a war long ago; the alien god. The Developers promised me a visit with him.

I'm sure they've already tried to extract information from him, but that doesn't mean I can't try. It's the best lead we've had so far, and I'm going to take it.

# 21

Since Logan can't come with me, we arrange to meet back in the cafeteria for dinner. Hopefully my meeting with the Mardenite will be over long before then.

I go alone to Restricted Division to find the Developers. It turns out they're overseeing the start of the bomb's construction. I have to talk to several security guards before someone grants me access to them, and even then I'm not allowed into the room. Someone carries my request to Commander Charlie and returns with the answer.

I expect to have to give an excuse for why I'm asking to see the Mardenite after today's events, but it turns out to be easy. Cadet Waller will escort me to see the prisoner. Apparently the Developers don't think letting me see the Mardenite will endanger their plans. I'm guessing they're also busy and they want me out of their hair.

Cadet Waller doesn't seem terribly pleased she's been assigned the task of escort. She purses her lips as she leads me down the hallway.

"Where is the prisoner being kept?" I ask.

"In a secure location," is all she says.

At the end of the hallway, Cadet Waller taps a code into the panel beside the door, and it zips open. She ducks her head to move through the door, and I follow. The corridor ahead of us is much narrower than the last. It makes me feel a bit claustrophobic.

We turn three corners—left, right, right—passing at least six unmarked doors before she stops in front of another. Waller's fingers fly across the keys on another security console, typing in a new code. All I'm able to catch is that the last number is two.

The door opens with a hiss. As we move into the room, a low sound of boiling liquid fills my ears. We've entered a laboratory. There are tubes of bubbling chemicals and stacks of glass vials and scales on the tables. A short set of steps at the back of the room leads to a glass door. The lights beyond the door are dark, so I can't see what's back there. But that must be where they're keeping the Mardenite.

A man with thick, dark hair stands in front of a giant microscope on the right side of the room, peering through the eyepieces. He doesn't seem to have heard us come in.

"Hello, Dr. Troy," Cadet Waller says.

The doctor startles and turns around. Clearing his throat, he switches off the microscope and sets the scalpel he was holding on the table. He walks toward us with a smile. "Afternoon, Ms. Waller. How may I help you?"

"We're here to see Prisoner V. I have orders from the commanders to allow this girl a short visit with him."

"I see," Dr. Troy says. He turns to me. "And your name is . . ."

"Clementine," I say.

"You would know her as Subject 7," Waller says.

Dr. Troy's eyes shift to me again, wider this time. "I see," he says in a softer voice.

There's a trickle of discomfort down the back of my neck. He's studying me like I'm a specimen in one of his jars, an experiment, instead of a person.

He clears his throat again, rolls up the sleeves of his lab coat, and offers a hand. "Allow me to introduce myself. I'm Dr. Troy, resident Mardenite expert, head of the department of evolutionary sciences."

"It's nice to meet you," I say, shaking his hand and giving him what I hope is a warm smile. His palm leaves a sticky residue of sweat on my skin.

"You'll take her from here?" Waller asks. "She'll need an escort out of the area when she's finished."

"Yes, I'll take care of it," Dr. Troy says.

The door zips shut after Waller's gone. With a sweeping motion of his arm, Dr. Troy gestures for me to follow him to the stairs. He seems twitchy. I can't tell if he's nervous or excited. He must not get visitors often.

"So, you want to see our Mardenite," he says. "Any particular reason why?"

*To find a way to end the war that doesn't involve killing thousands of innocent people.*

I shrug. "Not really. Just curiosity. I'd like to know what we're fighting."

"A very good reason. It's always a smart idea to try to understand our enemies." Instead of a security code, Dr. Troy uses his thumbprint to open the glass door at the top of the staircase. He flips a light switch on in the next room.

A blue glow fills the darkness, emitting from three glass tanks in the center of the room. Each is a cylindrical shape at least three times my size. The far left and right tanks are empty, but the one in the middle has something inside it.

The alien is curled up in the fetal position and tangled in tubes, floating in the water. It almost looks like it's dead; the alien's skin is shriveled up. I take careful steps toward it, my heartbeat thrumming in my fingertips. I've seen a Mardenite before, of course, on the hillside after the hovercraft crashed. But it was much farther away. This one is separated from me by glass, but I can't help worrying it will still be able to harm me.

A foot away from the tank, the alien opens its eyes. I freeze in my tracks. Two fiery red eyes stare at me, unable to blink because they are lidless.

I've seen those eyes before, this close.

Slowly, the alien unfolds its limbs and stretches out in the water. It has a humanoid body structure: two legs, two arms, two feet, two hands. But it has gills where it should have ears, and its hands and fingers are webbed. Its skin is clear, almost gelatinous, with thin blue blood vessels visible underneath.

*Vul.* That's what Beechy called this creature when he showed him to me in another tank in the Core, a tank far bigger than this room. He told me the vul had been discovered in the ocean on the Surface with others of its kind, but they attacked us and we had no choice but to wipe most of them out. Neither Beechy nor I had heard of Mardenites back then; all we knew is the lies we'd been taught.

"This is the Mardenite?" I ask.

"Among scientists, we refer to them as the *vul*, which is short for their scientific name, *vulyn sabius*," Dr. Troy says. "But yes, this is the Mardenite we captured in the last war. His people call him *Tessar* which, roughly translated, means 'savior.' They worship him because his birth brought forth a great flowering of life on their world. They believe he's a source of creation in the universe. He's been alive for centuries, his cells regenerating at an alarming rate. The genetic makeup of the vul is truly astounding. They're able to adapt and thrive in both saltwater conditions and on land."

The Tessar must've been transferred here recently, I bet soon after the Developers realized Marden's army was coming. They wanted to be able to keep a closer eye on him.

I walk slowly around the tank. The Tessar spins in the water to follow my movement, his unblinking eyes glued to my face. I wonder if he recognizes me at all.

"Can you communicate with him?" I ask Dr. Troy.

"Yes," Dr. Troy says. "I have a basic grasp of the vulyn language, but the Tessar hardly uses it. Mostly he doesn't vocalize at all. We communicate through gestures, or he responds to commands I give him in Kielan."

The vul inside the tank tilts his head, watching me curiously, slowly kicking his webbed feet to keep himself off the bottom of the tank. The tubes he's tangled in are connected to his stomach, some sort of catheter tube. Maybe to give him nutrients. Maybe because he could escape otherwise.

I take another step closer to the tank. Commander Charlie said the Tessar is much too powerful to be released from his prison, this creature the Mardenites believe is the source of life in the universe. Are the Developers afraid it's true?

"Would you say he's dangerous?" I ask.

"He won't be escaping anytime soon, if that's what you mean,"

Dr. Troy says. "The vul have exceptional strength, so we've had to take measures to keep the Tessar weaker than he normally would be."

They've been starving him. If I look closely, I can see bones poking through the vul's gelatinous skin.

"So, yes, in some ways he is very dangerous," Dr. Troy continues. "The vul are a genetically advanced race compared to humans; there is no denying it. But in all the years I've spent observing the Tessar, I can't say I've seen many signs of him having a particularly vicious nature. He's a curious creature, but mostly a docile one. At least, he is smart enough to know fighting won't get him anywhere. And he knows the Developers would order his execution if he caused any real damage."

"I'm surprised they've kept him alive this long," I say. "Especially knowing the Mardenites might come back for him."

"Well, the Mardenites don't know the Tessar is still alive. We spread word that he was executed after we captured him during the last war."

The vul in the tank swims closer to me, its lidless eyes piercing mine. He's so close I could touch him without moving my feet if there wasn't glass between us.

If the other vul don't know he's still alive, they didn't come to Kiel to rescue him. Unless they somehow discovered we lied about his execution. Either way, I still don't understand why they're capturing Kielans instead of killing us.

I need to somehow communicate with the Tessar and see if he can tell me anything more about the vul than what Dr. Troy learned from his observations and old war records. But I can't do it with Dr. Troy in the room, or he'll tell Commander Charlie everything.

"If you have any more questions, I'm happy to answer them," Dr. Troy says. There's eagerness in his eyes.

He's not going to leave me alone. Not without some prodding, at least.

"Do you believe the Tessar is really a god?" I ask.

Dr. Troy chuckles. "No, I can't say I do. I've spent most of my life observing the Tessar, and I've seen him do some . . . strange things. But not enough to believe he's a creator of the universe."

A memory tugs at me as the Tessar continues staring at me, his webbed feet still moving slowly in the water. He did something strange with his hands the last time I saw him. He pressed his fingertips together and they emitted a blue glow, and he let out a garbled noise that almost could've been speech. I had no idea what he was saying. But it seemed like he was trying to communicate.

"What sorts of things can he do?"

"Well . . ." Dr. Troy hesitates, seeming nervous. His cheeks are flushed red. "Yes, I think it'll be all right if I show you. Let me grab some samples—I'll be right back." He rushes out of the room, barely giving me another glance.

I smile, pleased at myself, and then quickly return my attention to the tank. The vul is still staring at my face. Maybe I'm crazy, but I swear he knows who I am.

"My name is Clementine," I say. "Do you remember me?"

The vul doesn't make any sort of response. He just keeps staring at me. It's eerie, the way they can't blink.

How will he be able to give me any sort of information, if he can only respond with gestures? I suppose I'd better try anyway. Dr. Troy said he responds to commands given in Kielan, so he should understand my language, at least. I don't know how much time I'll have until Dr. Troy returns with the samples; I need to talk fast.

I take a deep breath and move a step closer to the tank, lowering my voice in case there are any security cameras that could pick up sound. "Listen, the reason I came to see you is because I need your help. Our peoples are at war; your kind has taken over the Surface and captured many of us. But the people they took were innocent. Most of them were prisoners of our leaders before you came, bred to be slaves. They had no part in our past conflicts. Do you know what your kind want with them? Why did they come here for war? If it's revenge they want, the only people they should take it out on are the Developers, our leaders. They're the real enemy. Not us."

The Tessar continues staring at me. Frustration riles up inside me, but I force it back down. I have to stay calm, or there's no way he'll want to help me.

"Please, you have to tell me what you know," I say. "The Developers are planning something that's going to wipe out every last one of the vul in your army, as well as my friends you've taken prisoner. I want to stop them, but I don't know how. Maybe, together, we can find a solution. Maybe no one else has to die."

The vul looks over his shoulder in the direction Dr. Troy went. I can't see him through the door. I'm worried he's almost coming back.

Turning back to me, the vul opens his mouth and a string of noises comes out. Hisses and clicks that almost sound like actual words, but the water garbles them.

"I'm sorry, I can't understand you," I say.

He raises two fingers of his right hand and beckons me forward.

Running my teeth along my bottom lip, I do as he says. I stop a few inches in front of the tank.

Reaching his hand out, he presses his three fingers against the glass. He wants me to touch the glass too, but I hesitate.

What's the worst that can happen?

Holding my breath, I align my middle three fingers with his. A blue glow emits from his hand the moment our fingers connect. It grows brighter and brighter, a wave of light encapsulating the two of us in a bubble that drowns out everything else.

# 22

I'm inside a fighter ship, and a vul wearing silver armor sits in the pilot seat. A shudder runs through the ship; we've been hit. The pilot tries to slow us down as we speed toward the plains below, but not fast enough. I black out before we hit the ground.

I'm in a cell, strung to the ceiling by chains. Everything is hazy. A soldier yells at me and holds a gun to my head. He wants information. I want to know how many more of my people were taken. Neither of us gets what we want.

I'm alone in complete and utter darkness. I summon strength from somewhere deep inside me and press my fingers together to make light. A voice calls to me from far away, someone begging to know whether I'm alive. I've been too weak to send a message before now.

Yes, I'm alive, I tell the new Qassan of the vul, Hashima. She plans to lead her people to come and rescue me. I tell her the time is not right yet; the vul need to recover from the wreckage of the war and rebuild.

*I will wait. I will survive.*

*Time moves a lot slower when I'm alone. The years stretch longer and longer with every passing decade.*

*I watch old human commanders die and new ones be born. I watch them struggle to keep their control.*

*Sometimes I wish they would kill me, like they killed all the others they took when they attacked our home. But I am doomed to continue existing and feeling and knowing all things from inside my cell.*

*I feel my own people growing older. I feel their pain, their hunger, their sorrow. It is too much to bear when I can do nothing to heal them from so far away.*

*A new commander is born. I fear for those who will live and die under his rule.*

*Hashima tells me it is time. She has done all she can do to save her people and their home, but it is not enough. Help is needed. This time I don't tell her to wait.*

*I am moved to a new cell. I'm underwater, locked in a metal cage inside an enormous tank of ocean water. A girl in a diving suit, with an oxygen mask over her mouth and nose, peers closer to the bars of the cage. The girl's red-orange curls float around her head.*

*Clementine.*

The connection abruptly ends, and all the light disappears. I'm standing in the laboratory room again.

I pull back, startled, dropping my hand from the glass. There's a fierce throbbing in my head.

Those were memories; they had to be. I was inside the Tessar's past. I saw him captured in the last war, and I saw him imprisoned for three hundred years here on Kiel.

"You can share your memories," I say.

The Tessar stretches his lips, showing me his sharp yellow teeth. Smiling.

"What else can you show me?"

This time when our fingers connect, I'm ready. A weave of blue light surrounds me and I embrace the visions as they come. They feel different this time, like I'm seeing bits and pieces of memories from different vul, stitched together.

I see an unfamiliar world, where the light from the sun is golden instead of red and the sea is a greener blue. The thin, weblike grass of the plains weaves and tangles together, forming spiral shapes. I see an enormous silver city atop a cliff, a structure of interconnected, oval buildings that reminds me of an insect hive. Transports weave through the sky overhead. On the sea below, vul work on metal boats, fishing with spears that shoot lightning into the water. Other vul work in the fields on the other side of the city, flying hov-pods between perfect rows of strange-looking crops, climbing out of the pods to harvest the plants.

I'm flooded with peace, calm, and comfort. The vul are flourishing.

And then everything changes. A torrent of rain lashes down from the sky, flooding the crop fields. The storm rages on and on and on. The sea churns with waves so big, no rafts can go out onto the water. Lightning crackles through the sky above the city and hits one of the hive buildings. A shock of electricity shoots through the entire structure, making it glow bright red for a split second.

Again, the vision changes. I sense that many, many years have passed. Now the fields are barren of life, riddled with ash and dead grass. Wind howls across the emptiness. Fewer transports fly through the sky overhead. The sea remains the same, but the nets the vul haul in don't have any fish. Something has killed life in the ocean.

The vul plant seeds in the fields, but nothing grows. No rain falls. Inside the houses in the hive city, I see families huddled over bowls of liquefied food, and then over plates with nothing but crumbs. All of them look skinny, stricken with hunger. They're slowly starving to death.

I feel their terror. Their grief. Their fear.

This is why the vul came to Kiel. Not because they wanted to destroy us, but because our planet was their only hope. Their old home was dying, and they couldn't save it.

A voice comes into my head now, a hissing, clicking voice I somehow know belongs to the Tessar: *We must restore the balance.*

The image changes, showing me the planet before it was dying. The city on the cliff is gone. Instead, there are houses with dirt roads running between them. The fields are lusher than ever before, tended by humans. The vul work on wooden rafts on the sea, reaping fish in plenty.

A feeling of peace overwhelms me again. Harmony.

The planet was thriving before human and vul began fighting, before we stopped coexisting peacefully. Humans farmed the land, and the vul farmed the ocean. A balanced ecosystem. Only after the system fell apart did things go wrong.

Marden fades away, and I see a group of people huddled together in a dark hold. Hundreds and hundreds of people who look like refugees. Girls and boys from the work camps. The prisoners the vul captured in the Surface city. They look cold, hungry, scared.

Somehow, I know this isn't a memory—the vul is showing me where they are right now. They're still alive aboard the Mardenite battle stations. I was right; the vul didn't capture them to kill them.

*We need their help*, the Tessar's voice says inside my head.

The images evaporate, and I'm back in the laboratory room with the vul in the tank. The two of us are still surrounded in a bubble of blue light, which gives the world beyond the bubble a hazy quality. I feel strangely weightless, though my feet are still on the floor.

My eyes widen in awe and confusion. "What is this?" I ask. "How are you doing this?"

"We call it a *mayraan*," the Tessar says in his hissing, clicking speech. His voice sounds weaker than it did when it was only in my head, though clearer than it should when he's underwater. "It means our minds are connected, melded together. There is not time to explain how."

I stare at the blue glow emitting from his hand, pressed against mine with the glass of the water tank between our palms. The glow has drifted into my skin, making my hand look like it's on fire. But I don't feel any pain.

"Can you see my memories?" I ask.

"I cannot," the Tessar says. "Your mind is strong, and I am no longer strong enough to delve deep and see your thoughts. I have stretched out the moment to give us more time to speak before the doctor returns. But we do not have long. Do you understand what I showed you?"

"Your people want to bring the humans they captured back to Marden," I say. "They want to restore the balance to keep the planet from dying."

"This is right. We need your help, and I believe I am right in thinking you need ours."

This changes everything. The vul didn't come here to kill us; they need our help. But after all the wars of our past, they were sure we wouldn't help them except by force. And they were right; Commander Charlie and the other Developers wouldn't help them, or even believe their reason for coming. But the rest of the citizens? The boys and girls in the work camps who are controlled by ruthless leaders all their lives? If they knew the truth . . . I think they might.

Marden could be our new hope. It could be our escape, if we can help it grow again.

But there's still the problem of the Developers. Even if I could convince the vul most of the people on Kiel want peace, the Developers wouldn't give up their plan to detonate Fred's bomb. They don't want a ceasefire; they want to slaughter the vul. They've been working toward that goal for decades. Learning the vul are dying on Marden isn't going to change their minds. So how am I supposed to stop them?

It seems the Tessar is already two steps ahead of me. "The vul army in the sky must invade the Core," he says, his unblinking eyes piercing mine on the other side of the tank glass. "They can help you overpower the Developers and win freedom for your people."

We could somehow knock the citizens out of their mindless states, and then we could tell them the truth about everything. The control serums, the Mod Project, the war with the vul. All of it. We could let them decide if they want to return to Marden with the vul and try to save it, or if they want to remain here on Kiel and build a new, better society, one where the Developers wouldn't be in control.

But none of this can happen without the help of the vul army. I need to get a message to the vul commander as soon as possible.

"Can you still communicate with the other vul?" I ask the Tessar. "Can you talk to the commander of the army?"

The Tessar shakes his head. "I cannot communicate with them. I've grown too weak to make the *mayraan* from such a distance."

My stomach sinks, but the Tessar continues:

"But you can speak for me."

My heart beats fast in the silence. "How?"

The blue light consumes me again, and the laboratory room disappears. I see one of the Mardenite battle stations floating in space above Kiel's atmosphere. There's a flash, and I see a vul in silver robes walking over the roots of a giant tree. The tree seems to be growing inside an enormous room—a room aboard the battle station.

*Go to the sky and find Hashima, the Qassan of the vul*, the Tessar says in my head, as the vul in silver robes turns around. *She is our leader and the commander of the army. She is the one you must convince to help you. Tell her I sent you and she will listen.*

We return to the laboratory. The blue bubble still surrounds us in the lingering moment, but seems to be fading. The connection is breaking.

The quickest way aboard the battle station would be to go to the Surface and let the vul take me prisoner. It would require stealing a ship and escaping the Core, but I could do it. It wouldn't matter if anyone caught me leaving; I'd only need to get a head start to the Surface.

The real trouble will be convincing the Qassan, Hashima, to believe my warning, agree to my plan, and pull off an invasion of the Core in less than fourteen hours. If something went wrong, I wouldn't be in the Core when Fred's bomb went off. I'd die in the explosions.

"I don't know if there's enough time," I say.

"You must try," the Tessar says. His voice sounds weaker than ever. The blue glow between our hands is growing fainter.

Fear twists a knot in my stomach. Do I care so much about saving the vul and their prisoners to risk dying for them?

Beechy is one of the prisoners—Beechy, who has risked his life to protect me more than once. And his wife, Sandy, is pregnant with their baby girl. All of them will die if I don't stop the Developers. So will thousands of terrified child workers, and a thousand more vul, and none of them deserve it.

I'm not stupid enough to believe I'm safe in the Core, anyway. The Developers have sought to appease me in these last two days by giving me what I want, but it's just a ploy. They want me to cooperate until they've taken care of the vul, and then they'll assert their control again.

I'm the only one who can put an end to this war without a slaughter on both sides. No one else has seen what the Tessar showed me; no one else could convince the vul's Qassan to listen.

"I'll do it," I say.

"Saraashi," the Tessar clicks in vulyn, bowing his head in thanks, and then he drops his hand from the glass, severing the mayraan.

The blue light evaporates. The laboratory room returns to the way it was. The Tessar floats calmly in the water inside the tank, no longer kicking his webbed feet. I wonder if he feels as exhausted as I feel. My head is throbbing and my hands are shaking a little.

The door opens, and Dr. Troy walks back into the room. I quickly compose my expression.

"Here they are," he says. He's holding a tray of petri dishes with tiny plants inside them, flowers and the like.

It feels like I haven't seen him in a long time—hours, even—but he makes no mention of the passage of time. In reality, I bet he was only out of the room for a minute or two. He has no idea what went on while he was gone.

"These are some specimens I can show you," he says. "You see, the most fascinating thing I've seen the Tessar do is impact the growth of plants with the touch of his finger. The vul have very special nerve endings in their hands that allow them to, in a sense, communicate with certain species of plants. . . ."

I pretend to be interested in the specimens he's showing me, but really I'm hardly listening to him at all. My mind is focused on what I need to do to get to the Mardenite battle station as soon as possible, so I can set things on the track toward a peaceful resolution to the war, once the Developers are overthrown.

I'll leave for the Surface tonight. There isn't a second to waste.

# 23

I'll have the best chance of getting away with stealing a Core transport when there's hardly anyone in the flight ports, so I'll wait until late tonight. In the meantime, I need to gather food and other supplies I might need on the journey, in case something goes wrong.

There are also missing pieces of the plan to work out. Someone in the Core needs to know I'm seeking an audience with the Qassan of the vul—someone who could warn the citizens that the vul army isn't invading the Core to kill them, but to free them.

Logan would be the obvious choice. Only . . . I don't think I can tell him what I'm doing, not if I want to keep him safe. He insisted on being sent to the Crust work camp alongside me back when I'd agreed to go undercover for the Alliance, because he didn't want me sent into danger alone. He'd insist on coming with me to the Mardenite battle stations. He'd mean well, I know, but he'd be one more person I'd have to worry about losing when Fred's bomb detonated, one more person I'd need to protect. I can't afford to put him in danger for my sake. If my mission goes wrong, he'll have the best chance of survival here in the Core.

I can't tell Logan. But there's another person I can go to— Lieutenant Dean. I know he wants to find an alternative solution to end the war that doesn't involve setting off Fred's bomb, so he should listen to me. Hopefully he won't try to stop me from leaving.

The only problem is, I don't know where he is or how to find him. My comm-band won't let me send messages; it will only let me receive them.

So as Dr. Troy escorts me back to the main hallway of Restricted Division, I tell him I'm supposed to meet Dean at his apartment. I tell him Dean showed me where it was once before, but I'm not yet familiar enough with the division to remember where it is. Dr. Troy knows the general corridor where most of the lieutenants have apartments, so he takes me there. Then I'm on my own.

I walk slowly down the corridor, fidgeting with my hands, trying to guess which door leads to Dean's apartment. Wishing another lieutenant would come outside so I could ask. The longer I wander here, the more likely someone will notice me on a security camera and think I'm up to something.

I'm about to give up and find a staircase to get out of here when a door opens. Skylar walks out into the corridor. A second person follows behind her—Lieutenant Dean. There's tension in his jaw.

Skylar's in the middle of saying something, but she freezes as soon as she sees me. She frowns. "What are you doing here?"

"I was looking for Lieutenant Dean," I say.

"Why?"

"That's none of your business."

Skylar's lips purse slightly.

Dean clears his throat. "Clementine, you can come inside. I'll be right with you."

I push past Skylar and move into his apartment. I'm surprised to find it's smaller than the apartment Charlie gave Logan and me, but it has most of the same amenities. The same air of decadence.

I drop into one of the lounge chairs to wait for Dean. He's still talking to Skylar out in the corridor, though I can't hear what they're saying.

As soon as he comes back inside and shuts the door behind him, I cut right to the chase: "I'm leaving. Tonight."

Dean blinks at me, startled. "Excuse me?"

"I'm going to one of the battle stations, to talk to the commander of the Mardenite army. I spoke with the Mardenite we have in captivity. He told me . . . well, he *showed* me why the army came to Kiel. It wasn't to kill us—it was because they needed our help."

Dean stares at me, searching my expression for something. Trying to tell whether I'm making this up, maybe. But my anxiousness must be enough to convince him.

"Go on," he says. "What did he tell you?"

I tell him everything that happened. How I went and saw the vul in the tank and realized I'd seen him before. How he transferred what could only be memories to me when our fingers touched through the glass. How he showed me his own capture in the last war, and that Marden is dying. Dean listens with apt attention.

"We've been looking for a way to defeat them," I say. "But we need to help them. Negotiate peace and freedom for our prisoners, in exchange for some of us going back to Marden with them. I bet there are people who would go if they knew the whole story." I pause. "I would go."

"Even knowing the planet is dying?" Dean asks.

"Yes. Maybe it's crazy . . . but I think the Tessar is right. I think we could make crops grow on the planet again, if the vul and us worked together. Besides, I don't have a whole lot of fond memories here on Kiel. I want to start over somewhere else."

Dean starts pacing across the room. "You know the Developers don't really want peace with them. They want to slaughter all the Mardenites they can."

"That's why I'm going to the battle station," I say.

I take a deep breath. This is the tricky part. Dean isn't happy with the Developers' plans, but I don't know how deep his dissent goes. I don't know for sure that he'll want to see them robbed of their position of power.

But I tell him my plan anyway. I'm running out of people I can trust. At the moment, Dean is the closest thing I have to an ally.

When I finish, he looks thoughtful, not angry. Seems like a good sign.

After several moments, he says slowly, "I think I can help you free the citizens, if we can get the vul to the Core and take care of the Developers."

"So, you'll help me?"

Dean looks me in the eye. He's hesitating again. "You realize how dangerous this will be?" He glances at his comm-band. "We have less than fourteen hours."

"I've thought about the risks," I say. "I'm going to go through with this. There's no use trying to talk me out of it."

"Maybe I should go with you—"

"No. I don't need to put anyone else in danger. Besides, I need someone here in the Core to try to keep order once the vul invasion begins. You need to warn everyone the vul are coming to free them. The Developers are the only ones they plan on capturing."

"I'll do it," Dean says.

This time, I give in to the relief. "Thank you."

"Let's figure out how to get you aboard one of the battle stations," he says, taking a seat on the sofa across from me.

We figure everything out, to the best of our abilities. Tonight, he'll try to create some sort of distraction while I'm stealing a ship, so I'll have a head start before the Developers realize I've left the Core.

I realize there's a big thing I'm worried about—that Logan will be incriminated after I'm gone. I don't want him to be punished for my crimes. Dean assures me he'll do everything he can to convince Commander Charlie that Logan had nothing to do with what I am about to do, to keep Logan out of trouble.

There isn't a whole lot we can plan for when the vul invasion begins, except that Dean will do his best to get the citizens out of the way of the fighting, so they won't be harmed. We won't be able to do anything to knock them out of their submission until the Developers are overthrown, so that will be the primary goal.

Before I leave, I ask him one more question: "When did you change your mind about the Developers?"

Dean sighs. "I admit I didn't for a long time. I grew up here in the Core, so this was all I ever knew. I wasn't unaware of the horrible things they were doing, especially in the outer sectors . . . I just looked past them because it was easier. They'd given me a lot of opportunities, and they'd trusted me enough to let me live free of the control of their serums. I was grateful for that."

He pauses to take a breath. "But after I learned about their plans to destroy the outer sectors completely, I started to realize how deep their insanity for power and their desire for a stronger race of humans went. I heard about the Alliance, and I almost joined up with them. But I didn't know enough about their numbers or their plans. I was afraid the bomb would still go off and their uprising wouldn't amount to anything. So I stayed in my position for my own safety, pretending I remained loyal to the Developers. After you and the other rebels overturned the Developers' plans, I decided it was best for me to stay where I was and continue pretending, until blowing my cover could be of more help to your plans." He looks at me with guilt in his eyes. "I apologize for not telling you sooner, and for treating you poorly when we first met. I hope you understand; I needed to keep up a persona."

I press my lips together. I wish he'd told me the truth sooner instead of lying to me. But at the same time, I can understand why he wouldn't want anyone to know. And he has done a great deal to help me since the first time we met. I guess I can forgive him for the rest of it.

"I understand," I say. "Thank you for telling me now."

Dean nods. "Of course. I was going to soon; I was just waiting for the right moment."

There's an awkward moment where we're both standing there, unsure what to say. Then Dean pulls the gun out of his holster and hands it to me. "Take this," he says.

The last gun he gave me was taken when I changed clothes for the Mod Tests, and I never got it back. I take the new one from Dean and tuck it into the waistline of my pants. "Thanks."

"Good luck tonight and tomorrow," he says. "Promise me you'll be careful. All of us need you to make it back here."

"I will," I say. "Good luck to you too."

I leave his apartment and head down the hallway. Dinnertime is already over, so Logan probably isn't in the cafeteria anymore, but I still need to grab something to eat. I'll need to smuggle a few extra food things out so I can take them with me tonight.

Then the only thing left is to say good-bye to Logan.

Logan is pacing on his crutches when I finally get to our apartment. He stops and hobbles toward me as soon as I walk in. The lines of stress around his eyes make my stomach clench with guilt.

"Where've you been?" he asks. "I thought you were going to meet me for dinner."

I bite my lip. I wish I could tell him the truth; I'm just so tired of all the lies, even if they are to protect him. "I'm really sorry. I ran into Ariadne and we started talking and I sort of lost track of time. I was hoping you'd still be in the cafeteria when I got there, but I guess I was too late."

He exhales, calming down. "It's fine." He plants a kiss on my forehead.

Logan turns away, wincing as he puts weight on his injured leg, and goes over to the couch. I twist my hands nervously, watching him sit down.

How can I leave him, knowing I might not make it back? I'm breaking the promise I made to him.

But there's not any other way.

When he looks up at me again, I force a smile. "How did the meeting with the Mardenite prisoner go?" he asks.

"It was . . . interesting," I say, walking over to the couch. "It turns out I'd seen him before."

"What?" Logan's brows furrow. "When? How?"

Sitting down next to him, I tell him how Beechy showed Ariadne, Oliver, and me the giant tank of captured sea organisms during one of the first days of Extraction training. How he thought the humanoid creature inside one of the cages was the last member of a species that had nearly died out here on Kiel. But he was wrong.

"The proper term for their species is *vul*," I say. "Dr. Troy, the scientist I met today, told me the vul we have in captivity is called the Tessar. The vul worship him and believe he's a creator of life in the universe, basically their savior. Whether or not he's actually a deity, Dr. Troy has observed the Tessar do some extraordinary things. For example, he can help plants grow by touching them. It's something to do with nerve connections . . . Dr. Troy's description was complicated. The point is: We have reason to believe the Tessar is powerful. That's why the Developers refuse to even consider turning him back over to the vul in exchange for a peace treaty. They're afraid of him, and afraid of how much more damage the vul could do to us if they had his help again."

Logan is quiet, drinking in this new information. A short strand of his hair falls onto his forehead, and I have the urge to reach out and brush it out of his face. I used to do it without thinking, back in the days before I was picked for Extraction, when neither of us kept secrets from each other. Now, I'm afraid the simple gesture would make it too hard for me to keep my emotions in check.

"So the Mardenite army came here because they want to rescue this . . . Tessar?" he asks.

"That's the problem." The rock in my throat makes my voice sound a bit hoarse. "I still don't know. Dr. Troy told me the vul army believes the Tessar was executed centuries ago."

"If he's telling the truth, that would mean the army came here for revenge," Logan says.

"It would seem so," is all I manage to say. I don't want him to believe the vul are vicious warriors who came here to destroy us, but I don't know how to explain the real reason they came without giving everything away.

"Did you find out anything about weaknesses they might have?"

I shake my head. "Not anything substantial. I know the Developers have weakened the Tessar by starving him, but he's only one vul. That won't help us defeat the army. I wanted to speak with the Tessar himself and try to learn something more that could help us . . . but he could hardly communicate. And I was worried pressing Dr. Troy for more information would make him suspicious."

"So, pretty much, we're right back where we started, with no clue how to rescue the prisoners," Logan says.

"Yes," I say in a heavy voice.

I've told Dean to tell him the truth about everything after I'm gone, but Logan's still going to hate me. What if he never forgives me for this? What if Commander Charlie executes him after I'm gone?

My eyes start watering, and nothing I do can stop them. Luckily, Logan seems to mistake my tears for worry that we're not going to be able to rescue our friends. He puts his arms around me and pulls me closer to him on the couch. "We'll figure something out, okay? We still have time."

*No, we don't.*

"Okay," I say, clutching the bottom of his shirt with my hands. Wishing I could believe him.

"Maybe we should head to bed, so we can get some rest and get an early start tomorrow."

I take a deep, shaky breath, still trying to calm down. "Yeah. Good idea," I say, mostly because I need to be in the flight port within the next two hours. The sooner he falls asleep, the better. Though a big part of me also wants to keep him awake as long as possible.

Logan heads into the bathroom to change. I find a knapsack in the closet and put the food I'd stuffed into my pockets in the cafeteria inside it.

The coin Logan gave me after he won second place in the pod race earlier falls out of my pocket, and I pause, picking it up. I'd forgotten about it. I decide to take it with me to remind me of the person I'm fighting for. I stick it in the pocket of the pants I'm wearing tomorrow.

I also pack the gun Dean gave me, along with a change of clothes and a warm jacket. There should be a safety suit aboard whichever transport I take.

The sound of a door opening tells me Logan just came out of the bathroom. "Clementine?" he calls.

"Be right out," I say. I quickly shove the knapsack out of sight and change into clothes I can wear to bed.

Back in the bedroom, I slip beside him under the covers. It hits me suddenly that this is a future we could've had, if both of us had been picked for Extraction. Logan and I could've climbed into bed in a room like this every night and woken up beside each other every morning. Safe. Happy.

"I could get used to this," Logan says, pulling me closer under the covers.

The ache of sadness in my gut is unbearable. I blink fast so my eyes won't start watering again.

He kisses me and I kiss him back harder, putting all the words I can't say to him into the kiss. All the "sorry's" I can't tell him out loud. All the ache and worry I have that this could be the last night we'll ever spend together.

Logan must be able to sense my worry, because he pulls away. "Is everything okay?"

"Yeah," I say.

I don't want to waste this night worrying about what could happen tomorrow. I want to be with Logan in every way I can be, before it's too late.

I put a hand on his cheek and kiss him again, savoring the sweetness of his lips. I trail my fingers along the skin under the hem of his pants and feel a shiver run through his body. Getting a better grip on his shirt, I ease it over his head. His breath hitches and I pause, afraid I'm hurting him.

"Is your leg all right?" I ask.

"My leg is fine," he says, pulling me back down to kiss me again. I can feel the need in his lips.

I reach to undo his pant buttons, but he stops me with a hand. "Are you sure?" He sounds nervous, almost more nervous than I am.

"I'm sure." My heart's fluttering fast, but I've never been surer about anything. "I love you, Logan." It's the first time I've said those three words aloud to him, understanding how much they mean.

"I love you too," Logan says. "I always have."

Our kisses become desperate. His fingers tangle in my hair and trace lines down my back, inching their way everywhere. He gets my shirt over my head. His bare chest is warm against mine, solid, comforting. I've longed for this closeness, and I can tell he has too.

I undo his pant buttons, and he moves on top of me. There's nothing between us anymore, no secrets, no fears. Nothing matters but the feel of our bodies pressed close in the darkness of the apartment. We're clumsy and unsure, but we find our way together.

Afterward, we lie on top of the covers, his arms around me and my head against his chest, the way we always sleep together. I cling to him, pretending we can stay like this forever, the two of us apart from the rest of the world. Logan kisses my eyelids and tells me he loves me again in the moments before he falls asleep.

If everything goes wrong tomorrow, at least I'll have the memory of this last night with him to hold on to.

# 24

O nce I'm sure Logan is sound asleep, I slip out of the bed.
I plant a soft kiss on his forehead. "I love you," I whisper
again. No matter what happens, no one can take that from me.

I leave my comm-band on one of the dressers. Dean said there's
a tracking device inside it, so I'd better not take it with me. I change
into the clothes I'd set out earlier, grab the knapsack from the
closet, and slip out the door into the hallway. It's still early enough
in the night that no one should think anything strange of me leaving right now. But I have an excuse prepared in case I run into
anyone who asks questions.

Every step I take, I remind myself why I can't change my mind:
Beechy, Sandy, Uma, and thousands of other innocent people will
die if I don't do this. The vul army will be destroyed. Even Logan
could die. We don't know for sure if the bomb Fred's building will
truly allow the Core to escape unscathed.

And even if it did, we would all remain subject to the rule of
the Developers. The ruthless leaders who see us all as test subjects

and pawns for their agendas. They've slaughtered thousands of innocent people in their time, sending too many girls and boys to the kill chambers every year. If the bomb goes off and the Core becomes a battle station, I'm not sure we'll ever be able to overpower them.

This is my last chance to put an end to the war on my own terms, or die trying.

The flight port is quiet when I arrive. A faint echo of footsteps and voices comes from the far side. No one's shipping off to war tonight, so the only people in here are mechanics busy refueling ships and fixing engine parts.

I pause in the doorway, looking out over the spread of transports. I need to take a small ship, preferably a hovercraft, so it'll have some firing power.

There's a transport about twenty yards away that looks promising. All I have to do is slip aboard it without being spotted by anyone and use the clearance code Dean gave me to start the engine. If someone sees me and asks questions, I'll pretend I belong here. I'll shoot them if I have to. Whatever it takes to board one of the ships and get it in the air.

I pull out my gun, swing my knapsack over my shoulder, and move out of the doorway. I can glimpse the mechanics from here, walking between transports on the far side of the port. I duck behind a toolbox on wheels as one of them turns in my direction.

Once I'm sure they didn't see me, I continue walking, my hand glued to my gun. I pick up my pace. I'm almost to the transport. Just a few more steps.

I reach it and quickly search for the panel on the back of the hovercraft that'll lower the boarding ramp. It doesn't take long to find. The ramp lowers with a loud creak that makes me flinch. Luckily, the mechanics are drilling something on the other side of the port. I don't think they heard anything.

Inside the hovercraft, I set my gun on the flight dashboard. Now all I have to do is enter the clearance code, start the engine, and get out of here before those mechanics realize what I'm doing and raise the alarm.

I settle into the pilot chair and switch on the dashboard. The screen asking for a clearance code comes up right away. I enter the digits Dean gave me: 4-8-2-7-5-0.

The screen takes a moment to compute the code.

### CLEARANCE: GRANTED

I exhale in relief.

"There you are," a voice says behind me. "I was afraid you were gonna duck out of here without me."

I whip around, grabbing the gun from the dashboard. It's Skylar, out of breath and pressing a hand to her side like she was running to get here.

I lift my gun and click off the safety. "Get out or I'll shoot you."

"Whoa, steady there," Skylar says, freezing with her hands over her head. "I come in peace."

"Like hell. Get off my ship. I'm getting out of here whether or not you already alerted Charlie."

"I didn't alert anyone. I figured you could use some backup on the Mardenite battle station. Not to mention getting this piece of work in the air. You really had to pick the crappiest ship in the bay?"

I don't believe she didn't alert the Developers. She's still on their side, isn't she? Or has she suddenly decided to switch sides again?

"Who told you where I was going?" I ask.

"Who do you think?"

Dean is the only person I told. Clearly he trusted her enough to tell her what I'm planning on doing, but I don't trust her. She's the last person I would've asked to come with me.

"Get off my ship. I don't need your help."

"Listen, you don't have to forgive me for what I did," Skylar says.

"Wasn't planning on it."

"You have every right to be angry. But I can help you, if you let me. I want to help you."

"Why?" I demand. "You betrayed all of us to the Developers. Why would you want to help me kill them?"

"I know what I did," she says. "But I don't think their bomb is going to save us. I don't think they're going to give up, and if we let them keep making all the decisions, we're going to die. I think it's time for a change of leadership. That's why I came here. Okay?"

We're running out of time. I need to get the ship in the air before someone figures out I'm taking the transport. Otherwise there won't be time to escape the Core. All of this will be over before I've even had a chance to try.

Skylar could easily be lying to me again. But as much as I hate to admit it, I'm afraid I'm getting into something bigger than I can handle on my own.

Leastways, if something happens to her, she's one of the only people I wouldn't feel guilty about losing.

"I want you to know I have zero reservations about shooting you," I say, not lowering my gun. "If you try even the slightest thing to slow down my plans, I'll blast your brains open without a second's hesitation. Do you understand?"

"Yes," Skylar says.

"Then close the air-lock doors and buckle in."

She turns around to close the doors, and I sit back down in the pilot seat. I haven't flown a ship since Skylar and I copiloted a Davara jet back at the Alliance compound, but thankfully everything she taught me comes back to me. I do a quick pre-check of the flight systems. Everything looks good; fuel levels are high. We should have plenty to get us to the Surface, anyway. I'm not sure there'd be enough to get us back to the Core, but we can't return without the vul army anyway. The Developers would execute us for treason.

I start the engine as Skylar buckles into the copilot chair beside me. I wrap my fingers around the control clutch and ease it back, lifting the hovercraft off the ground.

Through the cockpit window, I see the exact moment the mechanics realize what's going on. They drop what they're doing and wave their hands in the air as they run toward our transport. It looks like they're shouting.

"Get us out of here," Skylar says.

I point our transport in the direction of a tunnel in the wall ahead, which will take us to the Pipeline. I accelerate a little, enough to get us to the Pipeline faster, but not too much. I don't want to crash the ship before we're even out of the Core.

The comm box on the dashboard starts beeping. A voice comes through the static: "Pilot, turn your ship around. You are not authorized to take your transport out of the Core hangar—"

Skylar presses a button to shut it off, rolling her eyes. "Yes, we know we don't have clearance."

STEPHANIE DIAZ / 222

We're coming up to the Pipeline. I tighten my grip on the control clutch, preparing to turn us in the right direction.

"Which way are we heading?" Skylar asks.

"To the mountains," I say. "Not the city. The entrance to the Surface is blocked on that side, not to mention the vul might assume we're part of another squadron of troops and blast us out of the sky. From the mountain side, we can plan a better approach to one of their settlements."

"Good plan."

We come to the Pipeline, and I turn the ship in the direction of the mountains on the Surface. Now it's safer to pick up speed, since it's a straight course ahead. Unless something slows us down, we should reach the Surface in an hour.

As if on cue, two dots of ships appear on our radar screen, emerging from another hangar in the Core, about a mile behind us. They're moving fast in our direction. They must've been dispatched to chase us down.

"You can lose them," Skylar says. "Jam the thruster forward and give us more speed."

I do as she says, but my hands are unsteady. Flying doesn't scare me on the Surface when we're out in the open, but in a tunnel like this, I'm terrified I'm going to lose control and veer into one of the walls. Especially when we're going so fast.

The transports are still gaining on us. One of them sends a stream of gunfire past our ship. It's far enough away that it's clear they weren't trying to hit us; they're trying to scare us into turning around. But it isn't going to work.

Skylar grips the clutches that control the firing weapons and sends a blast in the direction of the transport that fired. I watch through the rearview monitor: the fire nearly hits the hull, but the ship jumps aside at the last second.

Without a pause, Skylar sends a barrage of fire at the transports. One of them is hit this time, hard enough it is knocked off course and forces the second transport to veer too close to the Pipeline wall. I see a burst of flame and smoke through the rearview monitor. It grows smaller and smaller as we get farther away.

I feel a pinch of guilt for the pilots on board. But I'm sure they're okay; the crash didn't look deadly. And it was necessary. We can't have anything stopping us from reaching the Surface.

"Nice job," I tell Skylar.

"Same to you," she says, letting go of the firing controls. "We should be in the clear now. We're far enough away they wouldn't be able to catch us if they sent anyone else after us, so I doubt they'll try."

We've made it out of the Core. But there are still miles and miles ahead of us, and many more steps of the plan to be carried out before Fred finishes building the bomb and the Developers set it off.

I check the time on the dashboard. Twelve hours to go.

Skylar kicks up her feet on the dashboard, apparently less worried about the ticking clock than I am. "Please tell me you brought food."

"It's the middle of the night," I say. "Didn't you just have dinner a couple hours ago?"

"Of course. Doesn't mean I'm not hungry now."

I snort, but I toss her my knapsack. She digs through it and pulls out one of the meal bars I grabbed from the cafeteria.

I keep my hands on the control clutches, my mind wandering

back to Logan in the Core. The coin he won for me in the pod race burns a hole in my pocket. I am doing this for him, for everyone.

We need to survive, for Logan and for Kiel.

# 25

When we reach the Surface, the moon is dipping out of sight over the western mountains, beyond the shimmering acid shield. Time in the Core is kept according to the position of the sun in the city on the other side of the Surface, where it's just slipping toward midnight. But in this part of the world, the sun will soon be rising.

Skylar has taken over first pilot responsibilities. We've both changed into safety suits and helmets we found in the back of the transport. I examine the map on the dashboard, trying to pinpoint the exact location of the nearest vul settlement. I remember there was one on the edge of the Habus Sea to the east, beyond the plains that stretch for about fifty miles past the mountains. But it would be best if we had the actual coordinates. Something I should've tried to find out before we left.

"You remember the general area, yes?" Skylar asks.

"I'm pretty sure." The dot of the settlement Commander Charlie showed me on the map in the Core was on a promontory on the eastern edge of the Habus Sea. There were two more colonies in the jungle beyond, but those would be even harder to find without coordinates. The promontory should be relatively easy to spot.

"We'll search for the settlement along the ocean. They'll likely know we're coming before we see the colony. As soon as we pick up a raider signal, we'll put our ship down and send up a warning flare. Hopefully they'll realize we're surrendering instead of attacking them."

"Hopefully," I say.

We want them to capture us. What we don't want them to do is bomb us out of the sky, which is what could happen if we get caught in a swarm of raiders, or if we approach their settlement without giving any warning. I'm not sure we'd survive a crash landing in this small hovercraft as well as we survived the last.

Skylar types a set of possible coordinates into the navigational system to set us on a course. I grip my armrests with tight hands, keeping my eyes on the mountains out the window ahead of us. There's always a possibility we could run into raiders before we reach the vul colony. I search for black shapes on the horizon, where the first rays of sunlight pierce gray clouds. But there's no sign of any warships.

The vul don't know we're coming.

I've never been this far east of the Surface city. The snow-topped mountains turn into rolling hills, which become grassy plains leading to white shores on the edge of the Habus Sea. Thick gray clouds hang over the water, making the sky almost as dark as nighttime. The barometer on the dashboard shows the air pressure rapidly dropping. We're flying straight into a storm.

"Hang tight," Skylar says. "There might be some turbulence."

Sure enough, the bumpy weather starts soon after we make it over the water. Rain lashes on the glass of the cockpit. A bolt of lightning flashes in the clouds ahead of us, casting an eerie glow on the rocky sea. Skylar keeps us low, so we'll have more visibility, but it's still hard to see much ahead of us. There's only endless ocean and the storm.

A tremor runs through the hovercraft, jolting me in my seat. Pain shoots through my chest, and I press a hand to it, wincing. The pain medicine Dr. Jeb gave me must be wearing off. I should've taken another dosage before we left. I'll have to manage without the medicine, and hope my ribs won't take any more damage on this mission.

There's a beeping on the dashboard, a high-pitched whine. A message flashes on the control screen: LOW FUEL. My stomach clenches. The needle on the gauge is a few centimeters from empty.

Skylar curses under her breath. Her knuckles are white on the control clutch. "Well, that's just lovely."

"How much farther do we have to go?" I ask.

"A hundred miles or so. We should have enough to reach the coordinates I put into the system. The trouble is, that probably won't get us all the way to the colony."

We might end up stranded out here in the ocean, or on the shore miles from civilization. In this storm, who knows how long it will take for vul ships to find us? We could lose hours waiting for them to pick up our signal, or searching for them along the shore. And we don't have any time to spare.

"Can you do anything to conserve fuel?" I ask.

"I could power down some of the flight instruments," Skylar

says. "Rely on manual functions. But I don't think that's smart to do when we don't know where we're going and we can hardly see a thing in this storm. Don't worry, though. We'll make it." She doesn't sound all that confident.

Now I can't help wishing we'd run into a raider swarm. Even if they shot us down, at least we wouldn't waste any time waiting to be captured.

For a hundred miles, I remain tense in my seat, watching the fuel needle slowly move closer to empty. The storm doesn't let up. Ice forms on the cockpit window and the defroster works overtime to clear it up. The navigational system still seems to be guiding us toward the coordinates Skylar put in, but I can't help worrying we've flown off course. There's not yet any sign of land, and there should be.

"I think I'd better put us down," Skylar says.

"But we're not out of fuel yet." Wouldn't it be better to land on dry ground than in the middle of the sea?

"I know, but I think it'd be smarter to save our reserves until we have more visibility. We'll wait until the rain clears up and then we'll keep going." She eases off the thruster, slowing us down and lowering us over the water.

I hesitate, wanting to argue. But even if we kept going and made it to the shore, we'd be just as stranded and we'd have even less fuel. It does seem smarter to keep our reserves as long as possible. I just hope it won't take long for the storm to pass on.

Skylar puts us down on the sea with a bump. The ship has a special function that allows it to float on the water, but the waves still knock us this way and that.

I squint my eyes, peering out through the rain and heavy fog. We can't be that far from the shore, or even that far from the vul colony, unless our estimation of the coordinates was way, way off. "How many signal flares do we have?"

"There should be at least four or so on board," Skylar says, shutting off the engine.

"Maybe we should send one up. Just in case anyone out there can see it."

She frowns. "It's not likely they would. They'd have to be pretty close, and there's no sign of a ship on our radar."

"I know," I say. "But what if we're closer to the colony than we think? They wouldn't necessarily have raiders flying in a storm like this. And if there's even a chance they'd see us and come for us now instead of hours from now, we'd lose a lot less time."

The Core time on the dashboard tells me we're down to less than ten hours until the bomb's construction will be completed.

"Fine," Skylar says, unbuckling. "But we're only using one flare. If it doesn't work, that's it. We'll wait to use the rest until we're sure someone will see it."

"Works for me." I get out of my seat and follow her to the back of the hovercraft.

We find two flare guns inside the emergency compartment, along with a medi-kit and floatation devices. Each gun has two flares. There's an escape hatch in the ceiling of the hovercraft one of us can use to go outside and fire it.

"I'll do it," I say.

"Are you sure?" Skylar asks, raising an eyebrow. "It'll be dangerous in the storm."

"I'm sure I can handle it." Anyway, I want to get a better look outside, without the ice on the cockpit window blocking my view.

Skylar lowers the ladder from the ceiling. I take one of the floatation devices with me, just in case, and head up the ladder with the flare gun in my holster. Checking one last time to make sure everything is secure, I pull the lever to open the escape hatch. The storm rushes in, rain lashing against my helmet.

"Be careful," Skylar says.

I heave myself up the rest of the ladder and climb out onto the top of the transport. It's slick with ice; I can barely keep my footing. I hold on to the top of the hatch for support.

"Can you see anything?" Skylar yells from down below.

"Nothing!" I shout back.

But that's not entirely true. Even through the torrent, I can see the waves rolling all around us, crashing against our hovercraft.

Clenching my teeth, I pull the gun out of my holster and shoot the flare into the sky. It explodes in a burst of red fire that lights up the clouds overhead, almost as bright as a lightning bolt. I watch the fire streak into the ocean.

If there's anyone nearby, they couldn't have missed that.

As I peer out at the storm, searching for the black shapes of raiders, a fierce wave rolls beneath the hovercraft, knocking me off balance. I lose my grip on the hatch door.

I cry out, fumbling to get a hold on it again, but it's too late. My feet are already slipping, sliding down the icy top of the ship. There's nothing to grab on to. All I have time to do is take a gulp of air, and I'm underwater.

# 26

The force of the ocean presses against me on all sides. The flare gun has slipped out of my hand. The water is freezing; it feels like daggers are slicing through my safety suit. Waves pull me down and shove me back up to the surface. I suck my lungs full of air before I slip back down again.

I don't know how far the water has carried me. I can't tell which way the transport is.

The floatation device is still on my back, but I need to press a button to blow it up. I come up for air and struggle to get the device off my shoulder. But before I can manage, I'm dragged back under again.

Darkness engulfs me. The iciness is a burning hand, stabbing my chest. I kick my heavy legs, trying to get back to the surface, but I can't. Nor can I get the floatation device off my shoulder.

Panic grips me. My safety helmet's keeping the water out of my eyes and mouth, but I don't have an oxygen tank. I need to get to the surface for air or I'm going to drown.

I kick and kick with all my might, but I've lost all my sense of direction. The water is an icy tomb, caging me in darkness.

The ocean isn't anything like the tank I swam in once with Beechy, long ago, in the Core. It seems endless. I could sink far down into the black and no one would ever find my body.

Drowning . . . is this what it feels like? Slipping away from the light. Throat burning, wanting, needing air. The pain goes away, though, the farther you slip under. Like falling asleep. That's all it is.

Maybe it would be nice to never wake up.

The water shifts near me, and a hand closes around my wrist. Someone tugs on my arm. I glimpse a pair of red, lidless eyes. Then I'm surfacing, the roar of the storm filling my ears as I gasp for breath. Inhaling until my lungs are full. I'm light-headed.

But I know without a doubt the creature that rescued me is one of the vul.

The waves crash all around me, thrusting my body this way and that, as if they're trying to coerce me back under the water. But the vul doesn't loosen its grip on my arm. It floats easily in the water, paddling with one arm against the current.

A raider hovers overhead, lowering itself over the pair of us. A red light from its underbelly shines in my eyes, momentarily blinding me. The vul lets go of me and I panic, afraid I'm going to be dragged under the waves again. But something lifts me out of the ocean, some force working against gravity. It pulls me up through an open hatch in the underbelly of the raider.

The hatch closes underneath me, and I'm gently set on the floor. I lie there, blinking to clear my vision, shivering from the cold. My safety suit drips water everywhere.

A loud buzzing noise fills the air, reminding me of a hive of insects. I lift my head as much as I can, trying to see what's around me. The interior of the raider looks much like a cargo space in a Core hovercraft, except for one very different thing: There are yellow, tubelike plants growing on the walls. They move slowly in unison back and forth as if a breeze is pushing them around, but the air is still.

There's a clicking sound behind me, making me jump. Two vul have stepped into the doorway. They stare at me with their lidless red eyes. They're towering figures from this close to me, both of them probably seven feet tall.

I try to push myself to my feet, but the pain in my ribs is too much. "I need your help, and your people need mine," I say. "I need you to take me to the Qassan of the vul—"

A loud hissing noise cuts me off. White gas seeps into the room through a pipe in the wall. It quickly floods the air.

Poison gas.

It touches my skin, and I tense up, terrified it'll hurt me though I know it shouldn't be unbearable. But I don't feel anything. No needles, no pain. After last time, I've built up complete resistance to the poison, just like the Developers thought I would.

I breathe in normally, trying to stay calm. None of the Mardenite weapons can affect me. "I have a message from the Tessar," I say, steadier this time, pushing myself off the floor. The gas is so thick, I can hardly see the vul anymore. "We need to form an alliance. The people you've captured aren't the ones you should be fighting."

The vul make clicking and hissing noises, saying something in their language I can't understand. They must be amazed their poison hasn't knocked me unconscious.

"Please listen to me," I say, taking a step in their direction. A burst of pain ripples through my body, and I clench my teeth, trying to keep from crying out.

The poison is starting to burn my skin. There's too much of it; gas is still seeping into the room through the tube.

"Please," I say again, taking another shaky step. It feels like there are needles stabbing me everywhere, and my lungs can hardly get any air in, and my mind is growing hazy. "We"—I gasp for breath—"need—your—help."

When I try to move again, my legs give out and I fall to the ground, twitching from the pain. I'm vaguely aware of my vul captors stepping into the room and standing over my body, making more noises I can't understand.

My mind seeps into the darkness of the poison.

# 27

I wake to a steady buzzing. My ribs hurt and my head is pounding. I'm lying on something warm and squishy—a bed of moss, it feels like. But a foreign plant, something the vul brought over from Marden.

Panic rushes through me as I remember what happened. The poison gas knocked me out. How long have I been asleep?

I try to sit up, but my wrists are tied down. Not with rope or metal chains but with some kind of electric field. When my skin touches it, a light shock runs through my hands. My ribs hurt more when I move, anyway. So I remain lying still and look around the room.

It's barely bigger than a closet, and the plant bed takes up most of the space. This must be some sort of sleeping compartment or hold for a prisoner. There's a round porthole to my left, between the stringy tubelike plants on the wall. Through the glass, I can see we're soaring through the sky high above the Surface. We're approaching the shimmering pink acid shield at the edge of the atmosphere. One of the battle stations is visible from here, a massive hunk of metal floating in space. It looks just like it did when I glimpsed it in the *mayraan* with the Tessar.

*Thank goodness.* I don't know how much time I lost while I was unconscious, but at least the vul are taking me to the right place.

One by one, the other battle stations come into view. There are twelve in the fleet. They vary in size, some as big as the Surface city, some half that size. The black shapes of raiders soar between some of the stations.

We aim for the biggest station. A gaping hole in the side appears as we get closer, an entrance into the port.

The door to my sleeping compartment slides open, startling me. The vul who rescued me in the ocean steps into the room, but stops when he sees me looking at him. His gelatinous skin is bluer than the Tessar's, and he's wearing a thin layer of silver armor. Where the Tessar had gills, he has small pockets that look more similar to human ears. My guess is they expand when he submerges in water.

His forehead creases a little as he watches me. The veins running in thin strands beneath his skin seem to be popping.

"I need to speak with the Qassan," I say swiftly. "The Tessar sent me."

Silently, the vul moves to the side of my bed. It's strange seeing him—or any vul—move outside of the water. There's an unnatural sliminess to the way he walks.

He opens his mouth, and words emerge through the same hissing, clicking noises his kind make when speaking vulyn. But these words, I can understand: "Do not fight once you are free."

"I won't," I say. "I didn't come here to fight you."

The vul presses a button on the wall, and the electric current holding my arms down shuts off. I rub my sore wrists. "Stand," the vul instructs.

I sit up, wincing from the pain in my ribs. Carefully, I swing my legs over the side of the bed and stand up. The vul takes my arms behind my back. I can't see what he's doing, but I feel a pinch in my wrists. When I try to move them, an electric shock runs through my hands. He's cuffed my wrists again.

"I said I wouldn't fight you," I say.

"It is necessary," the vul says.

There's a soft bump in the floor. A glance at the porthole tells me we've landed in the station port.

"Now walk," the vul says.

He pushes me out of the compartment.

We've landed in the strangest flight port I've ever seen. If not for the other transports parked here and there, the room could be a greenhouse. The same yellow, tubelike plant that lived aboard the raider covers the walls in sheets. Maybe it's an organism they're growing for food?

My captor leads me toward a doorway on the right side of the port. Every time he prods me forward another step, I feel a flash of pain in my ribs. But I try not to let it show; I don't want him to know I'm wounded. I'm already weaponless and my wrists are stuck behind my back. I don't need to seem any weaker.

"Where are you taking me?" I ask.

"You will see," the vul says.

I notice two vul carrying a limp body down the boarding ramp of another raider. It's not a vul—it's a human girl, and she's wearing a safety suit. Skylar. She must've been found aboard the hovercraft after the poison gas knocked her out. The immunity she was supposed to have thanks to the antidote serum didn't save her either.

"That girl came here with me," I say quickly. "Please don't harm her."

"She will be put in with the others," the vul says. "You will join her soon. Do not worry."

"But you have to let me speak with the Qassan. It's urgent."

"Patience," is all the vul says.

I gnash my teeth together. I don't have time to be patient, and neither does he. Once he learns about the bomb Charlie is building, he'll regret moving so slowly.

I wish I hadn't left my comm-band in the Core. I have no way of telling how long it's been since I left, or how many of the fifteen hours have been used up. Here I am aboard a battle station run by the creatures that made Kiel's moon poisonous, who've captured thousands of people from my planet. I'm trusting the Tessar's word, but what if he was wrong? What if those images he showed me weren't even real memories? An itch of fear crawls down my spine. What if the Tessar lied to me, so I'd give his people the information they need to capture the Core?

The Mardenites could turn against me at any minute, and I'd have no way to stop them. All I have is my voice, and they could choose not to listen.

The vul leads me out of the port, down several corridors. These look similar to the hallways in the Core, only the ceiling is more square shaped than rounded. And there's a strange scent in the air; saltiness like ocean water.

We walk for so long, I start wondering if the vul is leading me in some sort of maze, so I won't have any idea how to get back to the flight port. But finally we come to a door where a guard is stationed. My captor says something to him in vulyn, and the guard replies in harsh tones. Their conversation carries on for a full minute. Then the guard steps aside to let us pass.

I'm in awe as soon as we step through the hatch combing. A wave of cool air rushes over my body. The room we've entered is a vast space filled with an enormous tree—the tree the Tessar showed me in the *mayraan*. I only glimpsed it before, and it's much more beautiful realized. Its branches are golden and spindly, and its roots stretch across the floor, which is covered in a thin layer of soil. Leaves that look like silver dust float in the air.

A group of vul stands beneath the lower branches, deep in conversation. The clicks and hisses of their speech echo through the room.

"Hashima," my captor says as we approach them, and one of the vul turns around. She's the only vul not wearing armor. Her limbs are long and sinuous, a yellowish color that reminds me of mucous, not clear like the Tessar's skin. Her lidless eyes are lilac instead of red, and thinner. Silver robes flow about her figure.

This is the Qassan of the vul, the commander of the army.

My captor bows his head to her, and then words in vulyn pass between the two of them. The only word I make out is *Tessar*. My captor must be telling Hashima that the Tessar is the one who sent me.

Hashima regards me with no emotion. She steps carefully over the roots of the tree, her silver robes rustling about her bare feet. "Who are you?" She spits the words in Kielan. "Why have you come?"

I swallow hard. I doubt she'll give me long to explain myself. I need to claim her attention. "My name is Clementine." I bow my head, the way my captor did. "I've come here to warn you."

"Warn us?" Hashima repeats, her eyes narrowing slightly.

"Your fleet is in danger," I say. "The rulers of Kiel are plotting a way to destroy all of your ships and everyone on board."

There's a murmur of clicks and hisses from the group of vul standing behind Hashima. She spits something at them in vulyn, and they fall silent. Turning back to me, she says, "Explain."

I hesitate. Part of me wonders if I should demand to see all the prisoners first, to make sure they're still alive. To confirm the Tessar told me the truth about what the vul army wants with us. But Hashima could easily decide to throw me in with them and not listen to me anymore. And then I'd have no way of stopping the Developers from setting off their bomb and blowing up this station, with me on board.

"I watched you invade us from the sky," I say. "I know you've captured thousands of Kielans. But there are thousands more still free out there, in cities underground. Including our rulers."

Hashima doesn't show even the slightest hint of surprise. Either she's exceptional at masking her emotions, or she'd already figured out there were more of us belowground.

"Our rulers are building a weapon that will destroy your fleet," I say. "It will kill you and all your people. But I have a plan that will put an end to the war and allow you to emerge victorious. I can get your army underground to where our rulers are hiding."

Hashima is silent, but the hushed noises made by the vul standing behind her tell me this is something they've been looking for, a way to the cities underground. They haven't found either of the Pipeline entrances on their own, not yet.

"Why would you want this?" Hashima asks.

"Because I want to save all the Kielans you captured. That's what I need in return, if you want my help. I need you to ensure they'll be freed."

Hashima's lip twitches in amusement. "What makes you so certain they're still alive?"

"I know they are," I say as forcefully as I can. "I know that slaughtering all of my people wasn't the only reason you came back to Kiel."

"Is that so?"

"Yes. You came because your home is dying, and you need our help to save it. You need to restore the balance that was lost. But here's our secret: You don't have to enslave us. We will come with you gladly."

Hashima studies my face, searching for the lie in my words. She won't find any. "Your lords say this?"

"The rulers of my people are not *lords*. They're cruel men and women who would see most of my race blown to extinction, so long as it would also take out yours. I came here without their permission, and I'm not speaking for them. I'm speaking for myself and those who want to see Kiel's rulers subjugated. Including the thousands of innocents you captured from the Surface city. We want the same thing. We want the Developers gone. The prisoners you took would fight on your side if you gave them the chance to listen."

"You and your kind would return to Marden and help us?" Hashima asks. She's looking me straight in the eye, challenging me. "I have your assurance of that?"

I take a deep breath. There's only one thing I can say, and hope it will turn out to be true. "Free the prisoners you've taken and tell them why you need their help. Offer them a place as free citizens with protected rights in your world, in exchange for their help restoring Marden's health, and I can assure you at least half of them will return with you." I pause, letting the promise settle in the air for a moment. "I will freely go with you and convince others to as well."

Again, the vul standing behind Hashima begin speaking in clicks and hisses. She turns around and spits vulyn at them. They seem to come to some decision, and Hashima turns around again.

"You speak lots of words," she says in a harsher tone. "But we do not make treaties with Kielan brutes. We've made that mistake before." She looks past me, at the vul who brought me here. "Zahesh, take her to the hold."

My captor, Zahesh, tightens his grip on my arms and starts to turn me around.

"You don't understand," I say. "You're all going to die if you don't overpower Kiel's rulers."

"We will find a way into the underground cities on our own," Hashima says.

"You don't have time!" I struggle against Zahesh as he tries to pull me toward the hatch comb. "The Tessar wants us to work together. He sent me here to help you, on his behalf, because he was too weak to make contact with you on his own."

Hashima says something to Zahesh in vulyn, and he stops struggling with me. The vul leader walks toward me, her robes flowing over the roots of the golden tree. "I can easily see if you are lying," she says.

I feel a pinch in my wrists; the electric force has been switched off, freeing my arms behind my back. When Hashima reaches me, she wrenches one of my arms up.

"What are you—" I start.

She touches her fingertips to mine, and a glow emanates from her hand. The light engulfs me, and there's nothing I can do to stop the connection; Hashima is too strong. It feels different this time, like heat is leaking out of my body.

*I'm running through the Surface work camp, my bare feet sloshing through the muddy street. Nine-year-old Logan limps behind me, trying to keep up. "Clem, slow down!" he says.*

*I'm watching officials drag Laila into the back of a hov-pod, along with the other twenty-year-olds being taken to quarantine. Logan grabs my arms to keep me from running after them. "No!" I scream. "You can't take her!" But they do anyway.*

*I'm leaving for the Core on the day of the Extraction test. Logan and I say good-bye in the lobby of the flight port. I cling to him when he holds me, not wanting to let go.*

*I'm shooting an Unstable my first day in the Core. I don't want to do it; I'm not a murderer. But I have to save myself, so I squeeze the trigger. The bullet misses the target.*

*I'm listening to the Developers make the announcement about their plan to separate the Core from the rest of Kiel. They're going to kill Logan and thousands of other citizens. I have to stop them.*

*I'm on a spaceship on my way to the moon, watching the bomb timer on the dashboard tick closer to zero. I try to take the escape pod out so Beechy and Oliver won't have to die, but Oliver gets in first. I can't save him.*

*I'm back in the Core. I've been captured working undercover for the Alliance. Commander Charlie forces me to inject myself with his control serum. I can't disobey any of his orders.*

*I'm on the Surface, watching the Mardenite army invade the sky. Raiders shoot down the hovercraft. My friends are captured.*

*I'm in a strategy meeting, listening to the Developers tell me their plan to build the bomb.*

*I'm in the laboratory talking to the Tessar. He shows me his memories. We realize we can form peace between our peoples and end the war.*

Just like that, the light disappears; the connection is broken. Hashima releases my hand with a gasp, her eyes widening. I'm blinking involuntary tears out of my eyes from the rush of emotion I felt in my memories.

Hashima saw all of my memories. She knows everything now.

Turning away, Hashima gives an order in vulyn to Zahesh. He grabs my shoulder and hauls me toward the door.

"Wait! What did you decide?" I ask. "Will you help us?"

Hashima says nothing, just watches as Zahesh drags me out of the room.

# 28

I pace inside the stuffy cell. It's like the sleeping room aboard the raider, except there isn't a porthole and there aren't any plants growing on the walls. All I have is the bed made of moss on the floor.

I'm not sure whether I should be relieved or worried Zahesh didn't put me in the hold with all the other prisoners. Was it because Hashima didn't want me spreading word of everything I've learned to them? Or because she's considering agreeing to my alliance, and she wanted to keep me close?

I'm afraid I might've screwed up by letting her read my memories. I've handed over every war plan, every secret I've learned from the Developers, and the vul don't need my help to overthrow them anymore. They know our weaknesses, and they could use them to destroy us.

But if the Tessar showed me the truth about the vul and their kind, and they aren't the monstrous aliens the Developers told me they'd be, what Hashima saw should've changed her mind. She saw how horrible the Developers have treated their citizens. She saw how most of us have been imprisoned all our lives, and we had nothing to do with the wars; we didn't even know about Marden's existence. She saw that her people are truly in danger. All I can do is hope she won't let age-old prejudices get in the way of peace.

I have no idea how long I wait in the cell. An hour? Two? Three? I almost fall asleep more than once, having been up all night. But I don't want to sleep through someone's arrival, so I do everything I can to stay awake. I shout and yell through the door, hoping someone will hear me.

After a long time, the door slides open. I'd given up and started dozing off, but now I startle awake and jump to my feet. Zahesh is in the doorway.

"Come," he says, putting the electric field around my wrists again.

"What did the Qassan decide?" I ask.

"You will see."

He takes me back to the chamber where the golden tree grows. Hashima walks over the roots to greet me. There's something slightly less harsh about her eyes this time, though her voice sounds the same when she speaks.

"Thank you for your warning of your commander's plans," Hashima says. "We will ally with you."

"You're going to help me overthrow the Developers?" I ask.

"We are," Hashima says. "My warriors have been informed. We will depart for your planet in three hours' time."

Sweet, beautiful relief washes over me.

"We must save both our peoples and rescue the Tessar," she says. "His survival is of the utmost importance. Balance cannot be restored on Marden without his guidance. I saw much of your invasion plan in the *mayraan*, but we will discuss more details shortly." Hashima gestures behind me, and I see another vul has walked into the room. A vul with lidless green eyes, a sheen of white hair, and silver armor. "Jehara will take you to your friends in the hold, so you can see that they have not been mistreated. We will announce the alliance immediately, but they will be freed after the invasion."

"What if any of them want to help you fight?" I ask, thinking of Beechy and the other Alliance rebels. I'm sure they'd want a hand in this final battle. "There are rebels like me among your prisoners who could be a great asset in planning out the invasion."

"If they are willing to give their help, we will gladly accept it," Hashima says. "Do remember, you are expected to uphold your end of the agreement and ensure at least half will return to Marden with us."

"I will," I say, forcing steadiness into my voice. I know the people in the work camp. Once they learn the truth about everything, I'm sure they'll agree.

"Good," Hashima says. She studies my face as Zahesh removes the electric field from my wrists. "You are a strange Kielan. Do you know this?"

"What do you mean?" I ask, rubbing my wrists.

"The *mayraan* has never been so strong with another," she says. "Nor has any Kielan before you ever been able to meld with the Tessar. I saw in your memory how the doctors modified your genes. They made your mind more like ours, in some way. Though I do not think they intended it."

I frown. What does that mean—my genetic modifications somehow made me more like the vul than any other Kielan?

I open my mouth to ask a hundred questions, but Hashima has turned away to return to the group of vul standing beneath the golden branches. She's no longer paying me any mind.

The vul with silver hair and armor, Jehara, beckons me to follow her out of the hatch comb, so I go to her. Her lips part in a smile that shows me her yellow teeth. "You are Clem-en-teen?" she asks.

"Clem-en-ty-ne." I correct her pronunciation of the word with a smile.

"I am Jehara," she says, leading me out into the corridor.

"Je-hair-a," I repeat, pronouncing her name slowly.

She nods and clicks her tongue encouragingly. "That is close. With practice you'll get better."

I examine her armor as she walks a step ahead of me. The material reminds me of silk, though it must be more protective than that. It clings tightly to her sinuous limbs, leaving only Jehara's hands exposed. "Are you one of the warriors?" I ask.

"I am the Qassan's aid," she says. Her voice is softer than Hashima's, though it has the same clicks and hisses. "I fight for her, yes, and also assist her in any way she needs. It has been said you met with the Tessar."

"I did. I wouldn't have come if not for him."

"How is he?"

"He's weak," I say. "But he is alive."

Jehara sucks in a shaky breath. "We must bring him home," she says, leading me through another hatch comb. I notice the ceiling is a few feet higher than in Core ships, probably because the vul are so much taller. "We must rescue him and help him grow strong again. The death of the Tessar before his time will hasten the death of many worlds. We feared he'd gone on to the next land already, but the Qassan had a vision. The Tessar spoke to us through her and told us he was still alive."

I remember hearing him speak to her in his memories, while he was locked in a cell in the Core. "Can you all communicate with each other from that far away?"

Jehara shakes her head. "Most cannot. But the Tessar is different. Special. When he was born, the ocean waters warmed and the fish stayed close to the surface. There was bountiful food to eat. That is why we call him *Tessar*. He has saved my people many times. It was a fearful day when he was stolen away."

"What happened?" I ask. "Why did my people attack your planet?"

I've heard the Developers' version of the story: My ancestors had left Marden to make a home for themselves, having been at odds with the vul on Marden. But they faced a horrible famine on Kiel, so they went back to Marden seeking a peaceful return, only to find themselves attacked by the vul. But I don't believe it was as peaceful a return as Commander Marshall said.

"Long ago we lived in harmony," Jehara says. "There is a pattern for all life, a rhythm in which the land and the sea must work in order to thrive together. Long ago, the humans lived according to this rhythm. All things were in balance. But they became greedy, wanting more than they needed. The Tessar warned the humans not to leave Marden, but they would not listen. They sought a new home, where they could grow more riches and build a vast empire. The humans no longer understood the balance. But they learned, yes they did, when the famine came. That is why they made war with us, to take back Marden. They made slaves of our people. We knew there would be no more harmony with them, so we could not let it happen. We fought back until they left, but they came back once more. That is when they stole the Tessar. We could not bear it. We feared there was no more hope for humans, so we sought to keep them from surviving anymore. Now it is clear we made a mistake. Marden will die if the balance is not restored."

We're walking down a hallway with the tubelike plants growing in the walls, so I ask Jehara about them.

"They are species from Marden," she says. "We wanted to save them from dying, so we transferred seeds from the soil and grew them here. We are hopeful we can make them grow again once we return home. We are also collecting samples of species from your planet to take back with us. We will cultivate them on the journey to Marden and see if they are likely to grow."

The vul must be collecting the samples in their settlements down on the Surface.

At the end of the next corridor, Jehara leads me through a hatch comb into an enormous room with one wall and ceiling made of glass. An observation deck. I slow my footsteps, staring out the window. The surface of Kiel looks eerily calm from so far away. There's no sign of the war. No sign of the danger brewing underneath, which could destroy the planet in less than a day's time.

From up here, there's only beauty. Rolling green fields, the sparse desert, and the bright blue of the great big ocean. My life was confined to such a small part of Kiel, and I wish I'd had the chance to explore more of it. To traverse the jungles and see more of the wildlife.

But the Developers took all that away from us, choosing to imprison us instead. It goes back long before they were born. My ancestors were the ones who started all of this, because they thought the vul were inferior beings that didn't deserve freedom. It's a poisonous way to think, and the poison has leeched through the centuries to the Developers who rule Kiel now. They've never gotten over the idea that some people are worth more than others, but it simply isn't true.

Jehara sees me looking down at Kiel and smiles. "Tell me about your life here."

"I grew up in a work camp," I say. I tell her about the fields where we labored, about the shacks with leaking roofs and the officials who would punish us if we made one bit of trouble. About the cam-bots that followed our every move, the force-field fence that kept us inside the settlement, and the gas chamber where we were sent when it was decided we weren't useful anymore and needed to be replaced. Jehara might not understand every word I say, but the look on her face tells me she understands the feelings behind my story.

"You will have a better life on Marden," Jehara says. "You will be free there. As long as everyone does his part, we can make it grow again."

"I'd like to help," I say.

I'd like to find a new home, a better one. One where we all can be free. I only hope we'll make it there, Logan and I. I can't go there without him. And I can't leave all of this behind until I know the rest of the people on Kiel are safe.

I tilt my head toward the window on the ceiling. The stars speckling the darkness of outer space are glossy and distant.

"How long did the journey here take?" I ask.

"Three months," Jehara says. "But the journey back will be

longer. The orbit of our planet has taken it farther in the expanse of space than it was when we left. Four or five months may pass before we reach it. But come, I must take you to your people."

She beckons me onward, and I follow.

The prisoners the vul captured from the Surface have been separated among four of the battle stations, but the largest group is aboard this station, which I learn is called the *Hessana*. The people are being held in different rooms in the hold of the ship, like I saw in the Tessar's visions. They've been fed and given blankets to keep them warm. Some of their worst wounded have been treated by the vul julas, trained healers. In most respects, they've been treated better than they would've been by the Developers, except they've had no idea why they were taken or what was going to happen to them. Most probably feared they'd soon be killed.

I ask to see the group of Alliance rebels and soldiers captured in the mountains in the first hours of the vul's invasion. Luckily they're aboard the *Hessana*.

By the time Jehara leads me to the part of the hold where they're being kept, the vul have made a ship-wide announcement of what's happening. They explain that they've received warning from a representative of the Core citizens that the battle stations are under threat of attack from the Developers, who don't want a peaceful solution to the war. If they're able to go through with their attack, all the Kielan prisoners will be destroyed. The Developers don't care about saving them. But the Core representative has proposed an alliance against the Developers, which the vul have accepted. The vul have received the information they need to access the

Core and overthrow the Developers, and in exchange all citizens and prisoners will be freed once the Developers have been taken.

The revelation about what's happening on Marden will have to come later, after the invasion is over. There's too much to explain, too many lies that will have to be unfurled.

Jehara leads me to one of the rooms in the hold. It's huge and crowded with people: girls and boys with dirt stains on their cheeks and mud in their hair, huddled with blankets on patches of mossy material. There's hardly room to walk between them. Four vul guards move into the crowd while Jehara and I wait in the doorway behind an electric barrier. The guards will find Beechy and the other Alliance rebels and bring them out to talk to me.

All the prisoners are awake, buzzing about the announcement.

"Do you think they were telling the truth?" a boy asks.

"Why did they capture us in the first place, if they were going to set us free?" a girl says.

"When are we getting out of here?"

As soon as they realize one of the vul is in the room, they turn their questions on Jehara. The guards hold up their electric sticks to keep the kids from hounding us.

"What's going on?"

"Are we going to die?"

"Are you really going to overthrow the Developers?"

Jehara answers them calmly. "Everything you heard in the announcement is true. We leave to invade the Core in an hour's time. You will be freed as soon as the invasion as over."

"Clementine?" someone in the crowd says. One of the prisoners staggers to her feet, wincing as the electric shock runs through her wrists. A girl my age with short black hair, whom I recognize from the Crust camp. But I knew her before then, on the Surface too.

"Nellie?"

She looks flabbergasted to see me. "How are you here? I thought you got away!"

"I did," I say. "I was taken to the Core. I came here on my own to speak with the Mardenite leader as soon as I found out what the Developers were planning. I've struck a bargain with them."

"So it's true what they're saying?" she asks.

"Yes, all of it is true. I don't have time to explain everything because I'm going with them on the invasion, but the Mardenites didn't come here to harm us." I look around the room at the other prisoners watching me, hoping they're listening. "Our ancestors once imprisoned them the same way the Developers imprisoned us. The Mardenites want to save us. They're giving us the opportunity to go back to their home planet, Marden, with them. We could make a new home for ourselves there. Free from the Developers, free from moonshine."

More voices start, people asking more questions. I want to answer all of them, but there isn't time. I can see the guards leading Beechy and the others through the crowd. So I assure Nellie and the other prisoners everything will be explained soon, and step out of the hold with Jehara.

I wring my hands, anxiously waiting for Beechy. So much has happened since we were separated, and I've been so worried he was being tortured or killed up here. I need to hear his voice and hug him and make sure he's all right.

As soon as he comes out of the hold, I run to him. His hair is matted with sweat, and his skin is dirtier than before. He's still wearing the safety suit he had on when I last saw him. I fling my arms around him, and he hugs me back with a tight grip.

"You're alive," I breathe.

"Yes, I am," he says. His voice is weak.

The other guards escort Uma out of the hold, but no one else is with them. The rest of the Alliance rebels—Paley and Mal and the others—must be in a different part of the hold, or on one of the other battle stations.

"Where's Sandy?" I ask, pulling away from Beechy.

"I don't know," Beechy says. "The Mardenites took her away, and I haven't seen her since."

"They probably took her to one of their healers," I say, looking to Jehara for confirmation.

She nods. "The woman prisoner is with a *jula*, who healed her wounds. She and baby are well. She is resting."

Beechy looks wary, uncertain.

"The Mardenites are going to help us invade the Core?" Uma asks.

"They are," I say. "I have a lot to tell you both."

"Start at the beginning," Beechy says.

So I do.

# 29

The rest of the Alliance rebels—the few who were sent to the Surface with the Core squadrons—are rounded up from the holds of the other battle stations. Paley, Mal, and Jensen will join us on the invasion.

Seeing Mal again is strange. The first time we met, I nearly killed him, mistaking his ship for an enemy transport. Even after I learned he was part of the Alliance, I continued to doubt his allegiance to the rebel cause, especially when I was in the Crust work camp and all I saw of Mal was him playing the highly convincing role of a soldier working for the Developers. I couldn't figure him out, so I wasn't sure whether I could trust him.

I feel like I owe him an apology after everything, but when he sees me he makes no sign that he wants one. He greets me with a smile and a handshake, and thanks me for saving him and the other prisoners. So I forget about what happened before, smile back, and thank him for blowing up the quarantine facility in Crust.

Skylar is sprung from the cell the vul had put her in earlier.

She's in a horrible mood, having been stuck in a tiny room for nearly five hours after being gassed, but she grows more cooperative as we're all thrust into helping with the preparations for the Core invasion. The vul have plenty of ships and warriors already armed for bombings and ground combat, but the rest of us have to be suited up in proper-fitting armor and given fighting gear. I'm given a handgun that's much sleeker and lighter than Core models. It hardly feels heavy enough to hold much ammunition, but when I shoot it at a practice target, the pulse blast rips the target into a billion pieces. There's also a "stun" setting. I'll probably stick with that one, until Commander Charlie is the person I'm aiming at.

With an hour left until we plan to depart, Beechy, Skylar, and I go into a room with Hashima, Jehara, and four vul who seem to be some sort of army generals—*kaarns*, the vul call them. The vul have worked out a preliminary strategy based on what Hashima saw of the Core's defenses in my memories. But Beechy is able to explain a lot more than I could show her.

The first step will be getting through the Pipeline. The plan is to bombard the tunnel from both sides of the Surface with as many raiders as we can, to make it impossible for the Core fighters to hold them off. Raiders will be sent through both Pipeline entrances on the Surface. Hashima has already made contact with her warriors in the Surface city so they can prepare.

By now, we have to assume the Developers have realized Skylar and I are the ones who stole the Core transport. They'll have remembered I met with the Tessar, put two and two together, and assumed we were heading to the vul battle stations to alert them about the attack. They'll be anticipating an invasion. They'll have put every possible defense in place.

"We're likely to run into security barriers they've set up in the Pipeline between the Surface and the Core," Beechy explains. "Bomb lines triggered when an object passes over them, or electric fields intended to cause equipment malfunctions. They'll be impossible to avoid."

I frown at Beechy. "Wouldn't the bomb lines damage the lower sectors?"

"Of course," Skylar answers for him. "But they're planning on blowing them up anyway, aren't they?"

Hashima and the army generals were talking in vulyn, but now she speaks for the rest of us to hear: "We'll send harmless probes ahead of us and trigger the weapons before we reach them. I'm sure there will still be casualties, but we are prepared for that. We'll make sure the raiders on the front lines carry fewer of our warriors than the rest."

Once the plan for the Pipeline is in place, we move on to arranging how the invasion will work once we reach the Core. The vul will storm the outer levels and capture anyone who fights them, using as little gunfire as possible. Uma, Paley, and Jensen will attempt to spread the word among the citizens that the vul are there to free them, not to harm them. They'll also try to make contact with Lieutenant Dean, who should be doing the same thing. Beechy, Skylar, Mal, and I will make for Restricted Division with a small squadron of vul. We will break out the Tessar, along with any other people in captivity, before going after the Developers.

We're down to five hours until the bomb's construction will be completed. It should take us two hours, minimum, to reach the outer limits of the Core. That should leave us with less than three left on the clock.

If the Developers are smart, they'll give up and surrender as soon as the vul warriors infiltrate their sector. Their bomb won't work the way they wanted it to if the Core is overrun with their enemy. But knowing them, they'll keep fighting as long as they're breathing. We need to be prepared to do the same.

The other Alliance rebels and I board a raider with seven vul warriors, including Jehara. Hashima is staying aboard the *Hessana* to oversee the invasion from afar. She is prepared to direct the battle stations to fly farther out of Kiel's range if everything goes wrong, to hopefully save all the people still aboard. If the clock ticks too close to zero without us overpowering the Developers, one of the vul kaarns will signal Hashima. But Hashima wants to do everything possible to conserve the fuel aboard the stations for the journey back to Marden, so it's only a last resort.

I strap into a seat next to Beechy, behind the cockpit. His face is a mask of emotion, but I know underneath he's worrying about what we've gotten ourselves into.

Before we left, he and I visited Sandy in the healing bay aboard the *Hessana*. She was lying on a mossy bed hooked up to monitors and an IV line. Her healer explained Sandy's gun wounds had been closed up, and she had no more internal bleeding. But she'd need to stay on bed rest for the remainder of her pregnancy.

Sandy's eyes fluttered open after a few moments, and Beechy's eyes filled with tears. He went and sat down beside her, and the two of them held hands, sharing kisses and quiet words. I felt like I was intruding on their privacy, so I left after a minute. But I was happy to see that she and her baby were going to be okay.

"Sandy told me the name," Beechy says, as our raider lifts off in the flight port.

"Of your baby girl?"

He nods. "We're going to call her Grace, after Sandy's mother. I think it's a good name. Don't you?"

I smile. "I do."

"Sandy's mother died giving birth to her, so she thought it would be nice to honor her that way," Beechy says. There's hoarseness in his voice. He's still afraid he's going to lose Sandy or Grace, before she's born.

I reach out and squeeze his hand. "Grace will be perfect. You and Sandy will make wonderful parents."

"I hope so," he says softly.

The ship rumbles beneath us as our raider departs from the *Hessana*. I watch all twelve of the battle stations grow smaller and smaller through the porthole as we leave them behind. My passage to freedom, if we can stop the Developers before they blow them to pieces when they destroy Kiel. Soon the acid shield blocks my view of the fleet, and then they fall out of sight in their orbit above the atmosphere.

I turn away from the porthole and look out the cockpit window instead. The black shapes of hundreds of raiders fill the sky ahead of us like a cloud of insects. We're approaching the range of snow-topped mountains. The same mountains where we were flying during the night the army of vul arrived. It seems a lifetime ago.

I fiddle with the pod-race coin I tucked into the pocket of my uniform, thinking of Logan when I saw him in the *mayraan*. Young Logan, the boy who was my first friend and my main comfort in the work camp. And older Logan, the boy who kissed away my tears last night and held me closer than ever before.

I'd give anything to hug him right now. I need to know he is safe. *Hang on a little longer.*

I look around the raider, at Jehara and the vul warriors sitting in their seats, poised and ready for battle. At Skylar, nervously chewing her lip in the chair on the other side of Beechy. At Uma and Jensen, talking in low voices. At Mal, unloading and reloading his gun, testing the weight of it.

At Paley, her eyes bloodshot and glazed with a mix of sadness and fury. She finally learned what happened to Fiona in the vul attack. I was afraid she'd be so angry with them—or me—that she wouldn't want to come with us on the mission. But she told me she only blames the Developers, since Fiona would've been safe inside the Alliance compound if not for their orders.

I see the ghosts of Fiona and the other friends we've lost in the empty spaces between our passenger seats: Oliver, Laila, Buck, Cady, and too many others I didn't know as well.

We can't let the Developers make ghosts of any more of us.

The first twenty minutes of the flight through the Pipeline are silent, save for the occasional hiss and click of the vul warriors talking among themselves.

Out of the silence, there's a faint booming sound that radiates through the tunnel outside. A bomb line must've been triggered.

I hold my breath, waiting for a message to pass through the comm system. It takes several minutes to come. Jehara translates it into Kielan for the rest of us.

"We've lost two raiders," she says. "Pilots have been ordered to fly with extra care, to avoid the wreckage."

"Did they not send the probes ahead to trigger the bombs?" Skylar asks.

"They did," Jehara says. "But the reach of the explosion was farther than anticipated."

Twice more, a faint booming sound reverberates through the Pipeline. Probes we sent ahead trigger two more bomb lines. Five more raiders are lost. With five vul aboard each ship, thirty-five vul warriors are dead before we've even reached the Core.

We're almost to the end of Mantle sector when we receive word the ships at the front of the swarm have made it to the Core's outer level. They fly into the first hangar they come to, as instructed.

"Our people are in," Jehara says. "They encountered no soldiers in the hangar."

I frown. The Developers know without a doubt the Core is under invasion now. Why wouldn't they have stationed soldiers to fight us as soon as we landed?

Beechy has the same worry in his eyes.

"You don't think they could've finished building the bomb already, do you?" I ask. My heart's racing fast.

We should still have three more hours. But maybe construction went faster than Fred expected. The bomb could go off at any second and ripple through the walls of the Pipeline, blasting our raider apart. We're not in the Core yet; we haven't made it to the zone where we'd be safe. And we haven't warned Hashima to move the battle stations away yet. They'd be destroyed, along with everyone on board and all the vul still on the Surface.

Sandy is still on board the battle station. Beechy's knuckles are white, gripping his armrests.

"I don't know," he says. "But we need to assume the timer is up and the bomb could go off at any second. We need to find Commander Charlie and the other Developers and capture them as soon as possible."

<figure>※</figure>

The vul pilot puts our raider down in the flight hangar closest to Restricted Division. The hangar is empty of people, like all the others. But in the upper levels, Core soldiers stormed the vul warriors in the nearby hallways. The soldiers had set up barricades and opened fire. It might just be my imagination, but I can almost hear the distant *BOOM!* of gunfire through the walls, and the pounding feet of the soldiers. I don't know how many vul we've lost so far, or how many Core soldiers they've killed or captured. But chances are, there will be soldiers waiting to attack us in a corridor close to here.

I unbuckle and move outside the ship with everyone else in our group. Two other raiders have also landed in this hangar, adding ten more vul warriors to our count. We're hoping the rest of the army can keep the fighting contained to the Core's upper levels, while we break into Restricted Division unnoticed and go after the Developers.

"We need to find a comm and use it to contact Lieutenant Dean," Skylar says, clicking off her gun's safety. "See what he's doing and whether he can help us. He might know where to find the Developers."

She's right. But we don't have any comms besides the one on the vul ship, which doesn't run on the right frequency.

"We know they'll be somewhere in Restricted Division," Beechy says. "The most likely place is the room where Colonel Fred is finishing his work on the bomb."

"They could've moved it to a different location," I say. In fact, I'm sure they would have.

"Where is the Tessar?" Jehara asks. "We should rescue him first and get him aboard our raider, in case the fighting turns bad. The savior must be returned to his people."

"He's in a laboratory on the way to the Core bridge," I say.

"Let's head there, then," Beechy says, leading the way to the hangar exit. At the doorway, he signals us to stop, and checks that the corridor outside is empty. "All clear."

I grip my gun tightly and follow the others around the corner. The hallway is quiet, save for the pounding of our boots on the linoleum. I tense as we come to the end of the corridor and another corner.

Again, Beechy stops us to check for soldiers. "All clear."

All the soldiers must be upstairs fighting the vul, or downstairs defending the Developers.

There's a staircase through the doorway ahead. Beechy leads the way inside. This is where we split up. Uma, Paley, and Jensen will go with five of the vul to the upper levels to deal with the Core citizens. The rest of us will go downstairs to Restricted Division.

"Good luck," Beechy says.

"You too," says Paley. There's fierceness in her eyes as she starts up the staircase.

When the stairs end, Beechy pauses, listening through the door for a sign of anyone waiting outside. But there's nothing but silence, and the faint echo of the others still climbing the stairwell.

Beechy carefully pushes through the door and steps out into the corridor.

We've made it ten feet when the blasters start firing.

# 30

The soldiers are shooting at us from the end of the hallway, where the corridor splits off into two perpendicular ones. They must've been waiting around the corner, listening for anyone coming through the staircase door.

"Get back!" Beechy yells, ducking at the front of our group.

There's nowhere to go, unless we retreat into the stairwell. But even as I stumble backward to avoid the fire—almost tripping over Skylar—Jehara and the other vul move forward, firing back at the soldiers. The vul at the very front of the group is hit square in the shoulder of his armor, but he doesn't even stagger. He just keeps shooting at the end of the hallway.

Smoke floods the air ahead of us, so I can hardly see the soldiers anymore. But I hear their grunts and thumps as their bodies hit the floor.

The gunfire stops after another minute. The vul are still moving toward where the soldiers fell.

"Come," Jehara says, beckoning for the rest of us to follow.

At the end of the hallway, there are seven bodies of soldiers on the floor amid the smoke. They aren't dead, just stunned. Who knows if they were subdued or not, but I can't help feeling relieved. We didn't come here to kill everyone in the Core; we came here to save them.

"Aren't you hurt?" Mal asks, looking at the vul warrior who was hit by the blaster.

The warrior has his hand covering his shoulder. When he pulls it away, there's blood seeping through the hole in his armor. "It will heal," is all he says.

"Thank you for saving us," I say.

His unblinking yellow eyes meet mine, and he nods at me.

"We'd better keep moving," Beechy says, stepping over the bodies on the floor. There's a door ahead that leads to the inner chambers of Restricted Division. It requires a security code to enter. Beechy tries four different codes, but none of them work.

"Here, let me try," Skylar says, pushing past me. She taps in two more codes. The third one unlocks the door. "Lieutenant Dean gave me a couple before we left that should get us through the security barriers," she explains when she catches me raising an eyebrow at her. "I'm just not sure which codes will open which doors."

I can't help feeling a pinch of annoyance that Dean gave Skylar the codes instead of me. But I'm glad he told one of us, at least.

Mal grabs a couple extra guns from the fallen Core soldiers before we move into the next hallway.

Another code Dean gave to Skylar gets us into the area where Cadet Waller took me to visit the Tessar. We encounter no more soldiers on the way to the laboratory. But there must be more of them here in Restricted Division; the Developers wouldn't leave the place unguarded. I wonder where they've all gone.

Jehara communicates with one of the vul kaarns in the upper Core level through the small comm she has in her helmet. "We've taken the two highest floors," she tells us. "There is still much fighting in the levels beneath them, though. The soldiers are not giving up."

"They won't give up until the Developers order them to quit," I say. "Most of them aren't in control of their bodies."

Just one more reason we need to reach the Developers and force them to surrender as soon as possible.

We come to the door to Dr. Troy's laboratory. It requires another passcode, but this time none of Skylar's codes work. Nor do Beechy's. All I can remember is that it included the number 2, but there are still four more digits that need to be figured out.

"There is a quicker way," Jehara says. "Stand back."

"What are you—?"

She fires a blast at the door, and I duck, gasping. The blast cracks the door down the middle, raining dust and bits of wall on all of us. The noise reverberates through the corridor.

"A little more warning next time, please," Skylar says through clenched teeth, slowly removing her hands from her ears.

"My apologies," Jehara says.

She and two of the other vul warriors kick through the door the rest of the way. Inside, the room looks exactly as I remember it. The same tables with stacks of vials and glass scales, the same giant microscope on the right side of the room. But Dr. Troy isn't here.

"Where is the Tessar?" Jehara asks, looking around the room.

"This way," I say, hurrying toward the stairs leading up to the second room.

As I reach the top, I freeze in my steps. I can see the blue glow of the water tanks through the glass door ahead of me.

All three tanks are empty.

"He's gone," I stutter.

Jehara pushes past me, touching the glass door and peering at the room beyond it. She bares her yellow teeth and hisses. "He cannot be gone."

"They must've moved him," I say. "They knew we'd try to rescue him."

"We must find him," Jehara says, spinning around. "They cannot harm him, or there is no knowing what worse destruction may fall upon the universe. There will be no saving Marden without him."

"I bet he's close to the Developers," Beechy says, heading back toward the door out of the room. "We find them, and we'll find him. We'll start at the first rooms we come to and work our way toward the Core bridge."

Jehara doesn't look entirely pacified, but there's nothing else we can do at this point. We all head back out into the corridor.

"What's the status on the fight upstairs?" Mal asks. "Maybe we could get some backup."

As if on cue, there's a crackle in the ceiling. A speaker turns on. "This is Commander Regina, a leader of the free people of Kiel. I am speaking to the Mardenites who've invaded our home, and also to those of you fighting on behalf of the Alliance, against your own people. I know you've all been fighting hard, but you are not going to win no matter how hard you try. I am giving you one opportunity to surrender. I urge you to take it. You have thirty minutes."

With a *click*, the speaker shuts off.

"What is she saying?" Jehara says, her eyes narrowing.

My heart's pounding in my chest, sending spikes of pain through my rib cage. "They finished building the bomb. They're going to set it off."

Jehara sends a stream of vulyn into her helmet comm, probably reiterating what I just said.

"What do we do?" Skylar asks.

"We keep going," Beechy says, his jaw hard. "We find them and we stop them."

"We're winning upstairs," Jehara says in a rush of air. "Almost all the upper levels have fallen. I've told the kaarns to send more warriors to this division to help us."

"Good. Tell them to hurry. Let's take the Developers and finish this."

We keep moving down the corridor, a new energy in everyone's step. We've almost taken over the Core; just a little bit farther.

But I'm worried a threat of force isn't going to make the Developers call off using the bomb. We could manage to take the Core from them, but they could still destroy the outer sectors if we don't reach them in time.

Thirty minutes from now, Lower, Mantle, Crust, and the Surface will be nothing but bits of dust floating in space. All the battle stations will be debris, and the people aboard—Sandy and Nellie and all the others—will be ghosts. Unless we can do something that will take away the bomb's power, make it useless, they're all going to die. And the rest of us will remain slaves to the Developers.

Suddenly it hits me. The Developers want to set off their bomb so the Core can operate as a battle station. But what if the Core couldn't fly?

We're not far from the engine room. I could wreck the hyperdrive systems and blow up the engine. Surely that would make the Developers give up the fight, if nothing else does. If I can't stop them from blowing up the rest of Kiel, at least I can keep them from having everything they wanted.

I need to go now, while the others keep trying to get to Commander Charlie. Telling them what I'm doing will only slow them down.

I wait until I'm sure they're all distracted, focused on the corridor ahead of us, and then I slip away. I keep a slow, steady pace, pausing at every corner to make sure I'm not about to run into any soldiers. These hallways look familiar; I'm close to where I need to be.

When I pass a door marked HALL OF COMMANDERS, I know I'm almost there. The engine room is only a few doors away.

The distant sound of footsteps slows my feet. Someone is nearby, but I can't tell whether they're coming in this direction. There's nowhere I can hide until I reach the engine room, anyway. So I keep moving.

There's no handle on the engine room door; it needs another passcode to open. I curse under my breath. Of course I'm the person who doesn't know any of the codes. Maybe I should've asked someone else to help me do this, after all.

There's nothing I can do but try combinations of numbers until they work. The footsteps are definitely growing louder. I don't have much time.

6-4-9-7

7-9-6-4

4-7-9-6

On my twentieth or so attempt, there's a *beep* and a soft *click*, and the door slides open. I laugh aloud and race into the room.

There are panels all over the walls, too many buttons and screens for me to count. An enormous cylindrical object that must be the engine sits on the left side of the room, behind a railing. I'm not sure it would be smart to blow it up while I'm in the room; I'd need explosives and a detonator. I'll dismantle the hyper-drive system first, and then I'll see what sort of damage I can do to the rest of the engine system.

There's an immediate, obvious problem: I have no idea what the hyper-drive system looks like. I assume it's close to the engine and all I'll need to do is destroy some wires, but there are all sorts of metal parts that could be the hyper-drive. I don't have time to dismantle all of them.

I'm going to have to hope my luck holds out again. I move toward a wide, rectangular object made of some sort of discolored metal, positioned to the right of the engine. Crouching, I set my gun on the floor. I'm prying open the object's cover with my fingertips when I hear footsteps behind me.

"Halt right there," a voice says.

Sam.

I freeze with my hands hovering over the hyper-drive system. He must've recovered from the control serum overdose. That's the only reason he would've been released from the health ward.

He has a gun pointed at my head.

Rage thrums through every part of my body. I reach for my weapon, but Sam snaps, "Don't touch it, or I'll shoot."

I grind my teeth together, but I don't have any choice. He'll shoot me before I've raised my gun. I let the weapon slide from my fingertips. I raise my hands over my head and turn slowly to face him.

Sam raises a hand to switch on his ear-comm. "I have her, Commander. She's in the engine room."

I hear a muffled voice—Commander Charlie—say something in response.

Sam lowers his hand and smiles at me, a cruel smile. "He's on his way."

"You know, I could've killed you on the Surface," I say, scowling at him. "I had another syringe of serum I could've given you. A quick pinch, and you would've been dead."

Sam laughs. "But you didn't because you were weak. I'm sorry, but you won't be getting another opportunity."

"No, I didn't kill you because I felt sorry for you."

The slightest crease crinkles Sam's forehead.

"Commander Charlie has controlled you all your life," I say. "I realize that now. It wasn't your fault you trusted him. Did he ever tell you why he cared about saving me so much? It was because he made me special, Sam. I'm Mod Subject 7, genetically modified to be the perfect soldier. Has he told you about the Mod Project, or did he keep that a secret from you too?"

"You don't know what you're talking about," Sam snaps. But the look in his eyes, that slight confusion again, tells me I was right; he knows nothing about the Mod Project.

There are footsteps behind him.

Commander Charlie walks into the room with three guards. He must've been close by to get here so quickly. Instead of his usual slick blue suit, he's wearing the full body armor of his army generals, minus the helmet. He smiles at me, his lips stretching wide and showing me his wrinkles. He is an old man, and he won't get much older if I can help it.

He signals to his guards, and they come toward me and force

my arms behind my back. "Let go of me," I say, struggling against them.

"I'm glad you came back," Commander Charlie says, almost kindly. "I heard you brought some special friends with you. I can't imagine what went through your head when you decided to strike a deal with them. But I hope it has paid off."

"It will," I say forcefully. "The Mardenites are taking over the Core as we speak. They're on their way here, to find you and the other Developers."

"They may find us," Charlie says. "But it will be too late."

He is acting far too calm about this. Worry churns in the pit of my stomach. "Even if you set off the bomb, there are enough vul in the Core to overpower you. Your soldiers are losing; they've taken the upper levels. This will all be over soon, and you'll have lost."

"That is where you are mistaken. You see, we can easily take care of the upper levels."

My heartbeat stutters. "What do you mean?"

Charlie walks slowly past me, farther into the room. He clasps his hands behind his back as if he's going for an afternoon stroll. "May I ask what you were planning on doing in this particular room?"

There's no point in keeping it a secret; I failed anyway. "Destroying the engine and the hyper-drive systems so you wouldn't be able to fly the Core away even if you wanted to."

"You didn't really believe we'd make the mistake of having only one engine, did you?" Charlie says with a chuckle. "Even if you'd destroyed this one, the ship still would've been able to function. And our engineers could've easily built another."

"It doesn't matter," I say. "The Mardenites are taking the Core. You've lost, Charlie."

"Unfortunately for you and your friends, you are incorrect."

Charlie pulls something out of his pocket, a small device that looks like a clicker. His thumb hovers over the plunger.

"What is that?"

"A Stryker detonator," he says.

I'm frowning again, trying to figure out how the detonator's going to help him. All the child workers aboard the battle stations still have Strykers inside their bodies, but they no longer work, thanks to the pulse bomb the Mardenites dropped on the Surface.

"You already tried to detonate the Strykers," I remind him. "They didn't go off. They were damaged by the electric pulse bomb."

"We lied." When he smiles this time, it's a wicked one. "We never tried to detonate the Strykers. We always intended for them to end up aboard the battle stations, so we could set them off at the proper moment."

A few feet to the right of Charlie, Sam is smirking at me, still aiming his gun at my head.

My heartbeat has stalled. This is why he changed his mind about detonating the Strykers when I put forth another plan.

"You wanted the child workers to be captured and taken aboard the battle stations. That's why you put them in the Surface city."

"That is correct."

Anger sets my body trembling. "So agreeing to send more squadrons to the Surface, making the resistance serum with my blood, giving Logan freedom . . . all of those things were lies?"

"Not all of them," Commander Charlie says. "If you'd continued to cooperate with me, you would've been saved, along with your friend, Logan. But you made the mistake of fighting me again." He shakes his head, disappointed.

He's a liar if he says he believed I wouldn't fight him once I found out he planned on destroying the battle stations with my friends aboard. No, all of his promises were false, meant to keep me from getting in the way so I wouldn't screw up his plans. He's been planning this all along—to lower my defenses and make me think I'd won, only to strike from a different angle.

"Oh, and there's one more thing you should know," Charlie says, a spark of cruel amusement in his eyes. "I didn't just implant Strykers in the child workers in the camps. Fifty young citizens here in the Core were specially handpicked to receive the implant too. I've made sure they're all in the upper levels of the Core, where most of the vul—and your friends in the Alliance—have been fighting my men."

Fear slices through my chest. Uma, Paley, and Jensen are all upstairs. What if Logan is up there? Knowing him, he wouldn't have stayed put once he found out what was going on. If the Developers hadn't locked him up again because of the escape I pulled, he would've gone upstairs and tried to help us. I should've done something more to ensure he'd stay out of danger.

"You would damage the Core and kill its citizens to destroy the vul?" I ask, a tremor in my voice. I can't let Charlie go through with this.

"The most important weapons, machinery, and citizens remain here in Restricted Division, and they will not be harmed," Charlie says. "The rest of the Core can be fixed. It would be a setback, yes, but this is war. I will do everything necessary to win, to save the human race."

"You won't be saving humanity," I spit. "You'll be killing thousands of people. You'll be decimating more than half of our race."

"Those who will die are not of our race, not anymore. They don't have as many modifications. They are lesser beings, the dredges of humanity. We, you and I and all the others who've been transferred to the Core before you, are the new, evolved race. The superior humans our ancestors always wanted to create. It's time for the future to begin." His thumb moves over the clicker.

"No!" I cry, wrenching against the guards holding me back.

But it's too late. Charlie has pressed the detonator.

# 31

I don't hear any of the explosions, but a ripple of energy permeates through the walls, making the whole room tremble like there's been an earthquake. The battle stations are far, far away, but I can picture their hulls being ripped apart, the child workers inside screaming as the Strykers buried in their digestive tracts split their chests open and silence them forever.

Four of the battle stations had prisoners in their holds. It's likely everyone aboard—Sandy, her baby, Hashima, Nellie . . . they're all dead.

My heart thuds in my chest like a sledgehammer. There's a loud beeping sound on the wall behind me. Turning my head, I see warnings flashing on several of the screens. Dots on a cross-sectional map of the Core show there's been serious damage to the five uppermost levels. Who knows how many citizens and soldiers—both vul and human—were up there when it happened.

Logan could be dead.

Commander Charlie speaks a command into his ear-comm: "I need a disaster squad sent to the upper decks immediately."

I can't believe he did it. He really killed them.

Charlie smiles as he slips the detonator back into his pocket. "Now that that's done," he says calmly, "we'd best get back to everyone. Colonel Fred's contraption is on its way to the detonation site as we speak. The Core will soon be a fully functional battle station, free from the restrictions of the rest of Kiel. You wouldn't want to miss such an important event in history."

My whole body is trembling with fury. I can't comprehend how he could care so little about human lives. How does he live with himself?

"It might interest you to know your daughter didn't come here with us," I say. "She stayed aboard one of the battle stations. But you just killed her. Her and her baby, Grace."

The slightest flicker of emotion crosses Charlie's face. It's hardly a crease in his forehead, really. But enough for me to know he almost, almost cares. "That is unfortunate," he says. "But a necessary casualty. Guards, take her to the bridge."

The guards haul me forward, shoving me past Sam toward where Charlie is standing beside the doorway. As I pass him, I want to reach out and blind him with my fingernails. But my arms are being held behind my back by one of the guards. So instead, I turn my head and spit full on in Charlie's face. "You disgust me," I say.

Charlie carefully wipes my saliva from his cheeks. "It's nice to know you feel that way."

⋇

The guards take me to the Core bridge, the room at the heart of Restricted Division where a pilot could control the flight functions of the Core, if it were useable as a battle station. Soon it *will* be, if the Developers get what they want.

There's a massive blockade of soldiers outside the entrance to the bridge, ready to defend it if the vul make it this far down.

*They're coming,* I want to tell the soldiers. *Be ready.*

Beechy and the others should've made it here by now, but they haven't. They must've been held up on the way. After seeing how much damage was done upstairs, I'm worried the vul's numbers have diminished considerably. There might not be enough of them left to take on all these soldiers waiting for them, if they get here in time at all.

I'm worried all the power is back in the Developers' hands, and we won't be able to seize it from them.

Every important Core official is inside the bridge, beyond the blockade. The army generals. The governors who were transferred here to safety from the outer sectors, so they'd survive the destruction of Kiel. Commander Regina and the other four Developers stand on the far side of the room, beyond the monitors lining the walls and a short set of stairs, before a screen of a night sky speckled with stars. The screen Charlie used to show me Marden's fleet was on its way to our planet, days ago.

The Tessar is bound and gagged in the corner of the room. I'm surprised the Developers haven't executed him yet, to anger the vul army, but maybe some part of them is still afraid to kill him. Or maybe they're just waiting for the perfect moment.

Out of his cage, the Tessar looks unbelievably thin and weak. He seems like he's barely clinging to life on his own, and his eyes are devoid of hope. I wonder if he felt the trauma of his people when the battle stations were destroyed. If I could get close enough to him to touch him, perhaps he could find the strength to form a *mayraan* with me again, and we could figure out a way to stop the Developers.

But my guards don't take me anywhere close to the Tessar. They shove me up the steps toward the wide, rectangular table with a spinning hologram of Kiel. They turn me around to face the room. Almost everyone is watching me.

"Well, well, well," Regina says, stepping around the table. Amusement stabs the coldness in her eyes. "Subject 7 found her way back to us and brought an army of savages with her."

I don't say anything to her in reply; I don't need to give her any satisfaction. I look at all the people around the room, trying to see who else is here. Hoping beyond all hope Logan is somewhere nearby, not upstairs amid the wreckage of the Stryker destruction.

"How close is Colonel Fred's machine to the detonation site?" Charlie asks, his boots clunking up the short set of steps. Sam follows close behind him.

"Twenty minutes away, sir," Cadet Waller says, standing with her tablet in hand to the right of Regina.

"Wonderful." Charlie claps his hands together. "In the meantime, we have some business to attend to. Bring forth the prisoner."

My gaze automatically goes to the Tessar, the only other prisoner in the room. I can't let Charlie kill him.

I open my mouth to protest, but stop when I realize no one's making any move to bring the Tessar closer to Charlie. Charlie's eyes are focused on the door on the right side of the room.

One of the army generals opens the door. I glimpse computers and technicians sitting in front of monitors—it must be one of the security control rooms—but as soon as the prisoner steps through the door, everything else falls away.

Logan has a gag between his teeth, a rag that makes it impossible for him to speak. But I can see the panic in his eyes. There are streaks of blood on his shirt, and there's a fresh bruise around his eye. He's stumbling with every step, barely able to walk without his crutches.

The guard leading him onto the bridge is Lieutenant Dean. His expression is stony, impossible to read. He doesn't meet my eyes.

He couldn't convince the Developers to leave Logan out of this. I wonder if he even tried. Is this all part of his plan to keep his cover until the last possible second, or did he lie to me about everything? Was he ever really on my side?

He hauls Logan to the foot of the stairs. Commander Charlie moves down one of the steps to stand in front of him, almost blocking him from my view. I struggle against my guard, trying to get closer to Logan, but the soldier's grip on my arms is too strong.

The bridge door abruptly opens, and soldiers bring five more prisoners into the room. Beechy, Skylar, Jehara, Mal, and the vul warrior who was injured earlier. They're all in rough shape, bruised and bloodied from another gunfight, one they clearly didn't win. There's a big gash in Skylar's shoulder. Mal is almost on the ground from a wound in his knee. Beechy is the only person who seems relatively unscathed.

"We intercepted these rebels out in the hallway," the lead guard says.

"Thank you for bringing them," Charlie says. "Put the savages in the other room."

Jehara and the other vul are hauled through the door into the security control room. Beechy, Skylar, and Mal are kept where they are. Their hands aren't bound, but they're held in place by five burly soldiers and they have no weapons.

"You're just in time for the fun," Charlie says.

"The vul army is on their way," Beechy says in a hoarse voice. "You're going to lose." But the fear in his eyes tells me he doesn't entirely believe what he's saying.

All Charlie says is, "We'll see," and smiles. He focuses on Logan again. "Citizen Z13729, you are charged with treason against the Core, for collaborating with the Alliance rebels and helping the Mardenite army break into this sector. You are hereby sentenced to death."

Panic. Anger. Both of them rush through me at once.

Logan makes a noise through his gag, a wordless response. He can't even defend himself against the allegations.

"Lieutenant Dean, if you'll do the honors," Charlie says.

Dean pushes Logan onto his knees, hard. He shoves his head forward with one hand, and with his other he removes the gun from his holster. There's still no emotion in his eyes; the hazel is filled with a haziness I couldn't see when he was farther away.

Charlie subdued him—he must've caught a whiff of Dean's involvement in my escape.

"You can't shoot him!" I yell, struggling against the grip of my guard. "Logan had nothing to do with the army breaking in—I didn't even tell him I was going to them for help. He's innocent."

"Perhaps he didn't know you'd gone to the Mardenites," Charlie says, turning to me. "But we know he was collaborating with you against us. Earlier this morning, we caught him breaking into the health ward attempting to steal a supply of energy injections. It seems he was trying to break the citizens free of their submission. You can thank your friend, Ariadne, for reporting his crime."

This is insanity. Charlie would never kill a person for a crime like this before; he'd subdue them, or throw them in Karum if that didn't work. But this isn't the real reason he's killing Logan, anyway. He's killing him because he knows it will ruin me. Ever since Charlie discovered how important Logan was to me, he's been trying to use him to break me. And it's working.

"What do you want me to do?" I ask through clenched teeth. My eyes are watering. "How can I make you change your mind?"

"My dear, you won't change my mind," Charlie says, almost sadly. "But that reminds me, there is something you can do for me."

Charlie snaps his fingers in Sam's direction, and Sam walks toward me, smirking. He pulls something out of his pocket. It's a long, rectangular metal box. Opening the lid, he removes an enormous syringe filled with orange liquid. Orange like control serum.

"Thanks to your cooperation with our most recent Mod tests," Charlie explains, "Dr. Jeb was able to examine your blood and DNA in a more thorough manner than before. After he developed the serum that would make our people more resistant to the Mardenite poisons, I put him to work attempting to create a stronger control serum for you, one you and others who share the same level of resistance wouldn't be able to escape. Dr. Jeb believes he found the missing element he needed. A way to make our serums long-lasting, so they only need to be administered once and the subject will be controlled for life."

"What was the missing element?" I ask. My heart's pounding so fast, it feels like the beats are tripping over one another. The pain in my ribs is unreal.

"A resistance gene in Logan's blood, in fact."

"Logan?" I startle. "When did you test his blood?"

"We took samples while he was in the hospital, the night you shot him. Logan was never one of our most promising mods, due to his physical condition. But it seems we were wrong to overlook him entirely."

"So then why are you executing him? You might need him for something else."

Charlie waves my question away with a hand. "We took what we needed from him for the serum. That's the most important thing. We've already tested it in simulations, but I believe it's fitting that you'll be the first human test subject."

# 32

Across the room, Beechy looks as panicked as I feel, desperate to find a way out of this. I've got nothing.

Cadet Waller speaks up, abruptly. She has a hand to her ear-comm; she's relaying a message from someone else. "Commander, sir, security says the Mardenites are massing toward the main entrance to the bridge. There are at least fifty of them. It looks like they're trying to storm us."

Commander Charlie and the other Developers give quick instructions to some of the soldiers in the room, sending a few of them out to help guard the entryway. The rest will remain here in case the vul break through the blockade.

"We won't need to hold them off long," Regina says. "Colonel Fred's machine is almost to the detonation sight. Once we set it off, we'll announce that the rest of the vul army has been demolished, and they'll have no choice but to surrender."

Charlie turns back to Logan and me. "We'd better get the

tests and executions over with. Clementine, we'll have you go first, shall we?"

He'll subdue me before he kills Logan, he means. So Logan can watch me slip away from him forever, and then I can watch Logan die without being able to do a thing to stop it.

Sam sets the metal box down on the table and holds up the syringe.

I can't let him give me the shot. I try to slide my wrists out of the grip of my guard, but he's holding my arms too tightly.

Sam moves beside me and pushes the edge of my armor aside, exposing part of the skin of my neck. I subdued him before, and now he'll get me back for it. I should've killed him when I had the chance.

As he lowers the needle over my neck, there's a tremor through the walls. Distant shouting. The vul are here; the fight has begun outside.

"Sam, you don't have to do this," I say quietly, so only Sam can hear me. "Do you really think you're so special Charlie wouldn't kill you, like he's killed so many other people today? You don't have to fight for him. You can be free from him. We all can, if you help us."

His lips thin slightly, but he doesn't say anything in response. He slowly lowers the needle over my neck.

I'm not going to be able to stop him. The water in my eyes spills over as I find Logan's bent-over figure at the bottom of the steps. I lock eyes with him.

"Logan," I say, not caring who else hears me. "I love you, and I'm sorry I couldn't save you. I'm sorry I left you again without saying good-bye. But this isn't good-bye, okay? We'll see each other again."

I don't know what world lies on the other side of death, but I have to believe it's kinder. I have to believe it will bring us together again.

Logan makes a noise through his gag. His eyes are overflowing with tears too.

I feel the needle pinch my neck, and a sob breaks in my throat. I'm not ready for this. I'm not ready to lose control again.

There's another, louder tremor through the walls, like a bomb went off close by. Commander Charlie and the other Developers turn swiftly in the direction of the door leading out of the bridge. Almost everyone else's attention shifts that way too. Including Sam's, and my guard's.

"Now!" Beechy shouts.

I don't know what his plan is. But I wrench my arm out of the grip of my guard and knock Sam's hand away from my neck. The syringe drops on the floor, but it's made of plastic, so it doesn't break. Sam goes to pick it up, and I reach and grab the gun he has in his back holster.

Out of the corner of my eye, Beechy and Mal and Skylar are moving too. All three of them break away from their guards and grab guns from the soldiers' holsters. We're all armed before anyone has even given an order.

And three of us are pointing our guns at the Developers. I turned my weapon on Sam, to keep him from picking up the syringe. He scowls at me.

"Don't draw weapons, or we'll shoot," Beechy says.

Most of the soldiers around the room were halfway to drawing their guns, but they halt, awaiting orders from the Developers. My eyes flit to Logan, still on his knees with Dean holding a gun to his head. I need to get to him and free him. But I can't take my gun off Sam, or he'll subdue me.

"You don't want to shoot us," Charlie says. He should not sound so calm.

Beechy laughs. "Oh, and why is that?"

"Because Colonel Fred has been ordered to detonate the contraption as soon as it's ready. The only thing that will stop him from destroying the outer sectors is a direct order from one of his commanders." Now Charlie is the one laughing. His voice echoes through the room, over the noise of the battle going on outside.

Fury fills every part of me, knotting my veins and making my rib cage feel like it's about to explode. What he's saying is that this fight has been hopeless from the beginning. The Developers have stacked up all the cards in their favor. Even if we kill them, we're going to lose too much. The humans left on Kiel won't be enough to sustain a population.

"We'll shoot the other people in this room unless you call off the detonation," Skylar snaps. "The people you wanted to save."

"There won't be anyone left who is loyal to you," Beechy says.

"You can shoot everyone in this room, if you wish," Regina says with a slick smile. "We will still destroy the outer sectors."

Silence hovers over the room as her challenge sinks in.

"Fine," Skylar says, and shifts her weapon and shoots Cadet Waller through the head.

I gasp aloud, and there are cries around the room. Waller slumps to the ground. Blood seeps through the hole in her head and pools around her body.

Regina and Charlie barely flinch.

"Keep going," Charlie says.

I'm still aiming my gun at Sam. I meet his eyes and see the realization churning through them: I could shoot Sam and Charlie wouldn't stop me. Charlie doesn't care whether Sam lives or dies.

"I told you he wouldn't protect you," I say.

There's a flicker of fear in Sam's eyes. He thinks I'm really going to shoot him.

My finger hovers over the trigger, but I hesitate. Sam isn't my real enemy. His death won't save the people I care about.

Out of the corner of my eye, I notice something lying on the ground. My eyes dart to it—it's the syringe full of orange control serum.

When I look back at Sam, he's noticing the syringe. Anger courses through his face, popping the veins in his neck. His eyes flit to Commander Charlie.

Charlie gives the command so quickly, I almost miss it: "Shoot the rebels."

All around the room, the Core lieutenants and generals draw their weapons. Sam doesn't; he grabs the syringe from the floor.

The shooting starts before he can move toward Charlie. Laser fire fills the bridge. My guard lifts his gun, and I shoot his arm before he can get a shot in. The vul weapon has no trouble blasting through his armor at this close range. The soldier lets out a mangled scream.

I scramble to take cover under the hologram table, barely avoiding another blast near my head. At the corner of my vision, I see Logan fighting Dean at the bottom of the stairs. He broke free of Dean's grip, and he's struggling to knock the gun out of his hand. Screw taking cover—I need to help him.

But as I move to crawl out from under the table, a blast hits the wall behind me. I turn my head away, raising an arm to block my neck. Fragments of glass and metal impact my armor, and I cry out. I'm not hurt badly, but my ribs are on fire again. It doesn't help that I'm stuck crouching under the table.

When I look back at Logan, he's gone. The body of a soldier who must be Dean is limp on the floor. I hope that means Logan took cover, but I can hardly see through the smoke to tell where he went. Nor can I tell who's firing at whom anymore. I'm pretty sure some of the Core soldiers aren't shooting at us rebels; they're shooting at each other. They've turned against the Developers, like Sam.

*Sam.* I've lost track of him and Commander Charlie in the madness of everything. I crawl toward the other end of the table, looking for them between the laser blasts.

There's a body on the floor at the end of the table, a few feet from Cadet Waller. Commander Regina's eyes are closed, and blood pools from her temple. She's dead.

Where did the rest of the Developers go? I don't have a good enough view from under the table. I crawl out of my hiding spot, raising my gun in case I need to fire.

That's when I see Sam catch up to Charlie. He's fleeing toward the door on the right-hand side of the room, the one leading to the security control room. Two lieutenants defend Charlie from gunfire on his left, but they don't notice Sam coming behind them, or they don't realize he's a threat until it's too late.

Sam lunges at Charlie, stabbing the syringe's needle at the exposed skin of Charlie's neck. The lieutenant to the left of Sam turns to stop him, but I take him out with a blast to his side.

Charlie punches his elbow back and knocks Sam's arm away. The syringe drops on the floor and rolls several feet. It's far away from me, but I can still see it's empty. The serum has entered Charlie's bloodstream.

He staggers, his face contorting with pain. I need to reach him and command him to call off the bomb's detonation. I hurry toward him, ducking as a laser flies in my direction.

The other lieutenant who was protecting Charlie shoots Sam in the leg, knocking him to the ground. The lieutenant looks up and I see who it is—Brand, from the strategy meeting. I aim at him and shoot, but Brand ducks and it hits a monitor on the wall instead, sending metal fragments flying everywhere.

"Clementine, get down!" someone yells. Beechy. He runs at Brand from behind, lifting his gun to fire.

But Brand turns around too soon. He fires his own weapon.

The lasers and dust and smoke around me become a blur. The only thing in focus is Beechy.

He falls onto his knees with a choking sound, blood gurgling out of his mouth. His gun slips from his fingers, clattering on the floor. His eyes meet mine across the room, wide and flooded with disbelief. And fear. For what seems like an infinite moment, he stares at me, still breathing, still fighting. Then his eyes roll back into his head.

Beechy falls face-first onto the ground, limp. He can't be dead. He can't be.

"No!" I scream.

The rest of the room comes back into focus. A laser flies at me, coming from Brand, and I barely duck in time to avoid it. Clenching my teeth, I raise my gun and aim at him. This time I don't miss.

I keep running until I reach Beechy. I drop to my knees beside him, feeling his wrist for a pulse. There's nothing.

Around the room, the fighting is letting up. Mal and one of the Core soldiers hold the other three Developers—Marshall,

Talbin, and William—at gunpoint. There are a lot of bodies amid the smoke. I look frantically for Logan and find him in the corner of the room with Skylar. They're both crouching over the Tessar, who seems to have been wounded. There's a gun in Logan's hand he must've stolen from someone. He's alive, and that's all that matters.

Beechy is dead. But I can't think about that right now. Not until this is over.

I grip my gun as tightly as I can and get back on my feet, turning toward Commander Charlie. He's leaning against a table with his back to me, looking as if he's struggling to breathe. The serum is still taking hold.

"Charlie," I say, and he turns around without hesitation. His eyes are becoming murky, hazy.

The sounds coming through the door leading out of the bridge tell me the war is still going on outside. Vul and humans are decimating one another. And for what? For old, ruthless tyrants who don't care about any of them.

"Call off the detonation and tell everyone to stop fighting," I say. "You've lost. It's time to surrender."

I hope Fred hasn't set off the bomb yet. I hope we're not too late.

For a moment Charlie seems to be struggling with himself, fighting against the serum's hold. But it's too much for him. His hand moves to his ear-comm and he switches it on, and swiftly gives the command: "Colonel Fred, abandon your previous orders. Do not detonate the device. I repeat, do not detonate the device. We have lost and we are surrendering to the Mardenites."

I wait until I hear the buzz of a reply through his comm. "Does he copy?" I ask.

"He copies." Charlie's voice is monotone, lifeless. "He will return to the Core."

"Now, tell the rest of your people to surrender."

Like a bot, Charlie moves to the wall to the left of the hologram table and flips a switch on one of the control panels. His voice spills out of a speaker in the ceiling. Everyone still alive in the Core will be able to hear him.

"Core soldiers, surrender your weapons," he says. "The war is over."

He flips the switch again and turns back to me. The color in his eyes is almost completely gone, replaced by the serum he created with my help and Logan's. This is what he would've turned me into, if he'd had his way.

I could let him live like this, trapped in his own body. An endless torture. But I'd always worry he'd find a way to escape from it. And I've lived too long in a world where I feared him.

No longer.

"Commander Charlie, you are charged with treason," I say, and squeeze the trigger.

# 33

Most of the Core soldiers surrender immediately, as instructed, but it takes a long time for all the fighting to completely die down. Some of the soldiers in the uppermost levels, where the Strykers destroyed the wall speakers, didn't hear the announcement.

I stay in the bridge with Logan while Mal, Skylar, and Jehara lead vul troops through the other divisions of the Core to assess the damage and round up all the surviving citizens and soldiers. A jula who was among the vul army also remains in the bridge, to tend to the Tessar's wound from the battle. It is only a flesh wound; he will recover with time, and he will gain back his strength aboard one of the battle stations.

I leave Commander Charlie's body where it lies on the floor and kneel beside Beechy, carefully rolling him over. The warmth is already leaving his skin. I take his hand in my own, trying to squeeze the life back into it. But it's useless. He won't wake up.

Sobs shake my body and tears spill from my eyes. Logan wraps his arms around me from behind, and I press my head into his chest.

"He saved you," Logan says softly. "You know that?"

Beechy distracted Brand so he wouldn't shoot me. But that doesn't make it any better. He's still gone, and I want him back.

I cry for a long time in Logan's arms, until my sobs become dry ones. Eventually I become aware that more vul have come into the room. Jehara and Skylar are back from going through the upper levels. They're joined by the other Alliance survivors—Paley, Uma, and Jensen—who luckily survived the fighting upstairs.

By their initial assessment, the vul army lost almost a quarter of their warriors here in the Core when the Strykers were detonated. We don't yet know the extent of the damage to their battle stations.

At least four hundred Core civilians and soldiers are dead, and the rest of the population remains subdued, not understanding what's going on. Fearing the vul have taken control to enslave or slaughter them.

It's time for us to explain the truth to all of Kiel's people and start rebuilding our broken world. I need to stay strong in the face of all this, as Beechy would've done if he'd survived.

I wipe my eyes and get to my feet.

It takes several days for all the citizens to be freed from the control serum. The vul administer energy injections to the people in batches, first to the Core nurses and the military men who'd been subdued, including Ariadne and Lieutenant Dean. The injections help speed the process along, making the people more aware and alert, but it takes some longer than others to wake up completely.

I visit Lieutenant Dean in the health ward when I hear he's awake. He's in a recovery room with ten other survivors, most of them soldiers who were wounded in the fight on the Core bridge. There are so many injured being treated in the ward that extra beds have been brought into many of the rooms.

Dean is sitting up in his bed, sipping broth from a bowl. There's a bandage around his shoulder, where Logan shot him with his own gun in order to escape him. Dean looks up when he sees me and smiles, but there's a pang of guilt in it.

"You did it," he says. "I'm sorry I couldn't be of more help. And I'm sorry I almost executed Logan."

"It wasn't your fault," I say. The same thing I told Ariadne when she came crying to me earlier today, apologizing for the things she did and said to me while under the serum. Of course I forgave her. "You were subdued."

Logan explained what happened after I left for the Surface. Dean found him, as we'd arranged, and filled him in on everything I'd learned and what I was doing. The two of them decided to try to get their hands on energy injections to start freeing some of the civilians, but they were both caught in the act. Charlie didn't believe their cover story, since he'd already learned I'd escaped from the Core with Skylar. So he took Logan into custody and administered control serum to Dean.

"What's happening now?" Dean asks. "I haven't heard a whole lot."

"We're in the process of waking up all the civilians. Everyone's being told what happened to the Developers, and how they were responsible for the bombs in the upper levels. Explaining the situation with the vul has proved a bit trickier. People have a lot of questions, of course, but it helps that most of them had some idea the Developers were controlling them while they were subdued, and they're grateful to be free even if they don't trust the vul. Tomorrow, Lieutenant Mal and a representative of the vul will make a formal announcement of peace. Then an election will be held for the civilians to choose new government officials."

The bodies of Commander Charlie and Commander Regina have been burned, and their ashes were buried in the Hall of Commanders. The three surviving Developers and their military leaders were taken into custody. They'll be put on trial for their crimes, and the people will decide what happens to them. In the new government, a tribunal council made up of elected officials will make all the decisions. There will be trials held for crimes. No one will be shot or dragged away to a kill chamber by dictators.

"What happened on the battle stations?" Dean asks. "I heard the Strykers went off."

I nod, my lips thinning. "They did. The four stations with prisoners in their holds were seriously damaged. But we were somewhat lucky. Only about a fourth of the Strykers went off." We don't know if it was because the long-range detonation signal didn't reach them, or if they'd been disarmed when the vul dropped their electric pulse weapon, like the Developers claimed before. Either way, it was a small victory.

"How many prisoners survived?" Dean asks.

"About four thousand."

There were seven thousand to begin with; we lost three thousand people. It's a staggering number to picture. How many of them were only three or four years old, little boys and girls who barely understood what was happening to them? It's even worse because they were so close to freedom, a few days away from being able to leave Kiel forever.

I haven't been up to the battle stations to check for all the people I knew among the survivors. The only person I know for sure survived is Sandy, along with her unborn baby, Grace. I started crying from relief when Jehara told me she was alive and her baby was well. But I can't imagine how Sandy feels, knowing her husband is gone.

I don't know yet if Nellie, Grady, Hector, or any of the other child workers I knew are alive or among the dead.

"I should go," I tell Dean. "But I'll come visit you again later."

"Hopefully I'll see you before then," he says. "They should be releasing me in the next hour or so."

On my way out of the room, one of the curtains around the beds moves aside. Sam steps into view. He came to the ward to receive treatment for the wound Lieutenant Brand gave him in the battle, but by the look of it, he's just been released.

Sam stops walking when he sees me. There's stiffness in his body, though the coldness in his eyes doesn't seem as heavy as usual. Awkward, wary silence stretches between us. We haven't spoken since what happened on the Core bridge.

"Thank you for helping me kill Commander Charlie," I say stiffly.

Sam scoffs, answering in his usual cruel tone, "As if I was doing it for you."

"Whatever. I just wanted to say thank you." I stride past him, heading for the door.

"Wait," he says.

I stop walking and turn back around, crossing my arms. "What?"

I can sense Sam struggling to force the words he wants to say out of his mouth. Finally, he gets them out. "Thank you for not shooting me, twice now. I owe you."

"You're welcome," I say.

He hesitates, then offers his hand. I grasp it and Sam gives it a quick shake, grimacing like the gesture's causing him pain.

"You know, there's a place for you on the vul fleet, if you want it," I say. "You could come with us when we go with them to Marden."

A formal announcement of the vul's proposition hasn't been made yet, but the word has been getting around, so I know Sam has heard some of us are leaving.

"I'll think about it," Sam says, and walks out of the room ahead of me.

The next day, Logan and I walk hand in hand down a hallway in the Core, on our way to the Pavilion for the official announcement of peace with the vul. Logan decided it was time to abandon his crutches, so we're moving slowly to make sure he can handle walking on his leg.

The Stryker explosions didn't harm the Pavilion, so it looks almost exactly as it did the first night I came to the Core, after I was picked for Extraction. People crowd the stands in the viewing pods. Lieutenant Mal and Jehara, who will speak as the representative of the Qassan, stand on the balcony, with an array of vul and human officials behind them. Skylar is up there with them. She's already told me she wants to remain on Kiel to help rebuild the society.

Peace between the nations of Kiel and Marden is declared. Jehara and Mal shake hands to confirm it.

"As many of you have already heard," Mal says, "the Mardenites have requested our help in renewing their homeland, which faces crop shortages due to harsh weather conditions. We are sending them back to Marden with samples of our own vegetation from the Surface to help them rebuild. But what they really need is people to help them farm the land. Anyone who wishes to leave Kiel and make a new home on Marden with them will have passage aboard their fleet. Those who go will be allowed their own government and leaders, so long as they honor the peace treaty. You may go with them, or you may stay behind. Neither decision will affect your freedom. The fleet will depart for Marden in fourteen days' time."

A wave of chatter fills the crowds. Some of the people sitting closest to us look interested by the offer, but most seem hesitant. I have a feeling most of the Core citizens won't accept the offer. They aren't used to open land and farming like those of us who lived on the Surface and in the work camps. They're more comfortable here in their underground home, though it also needs rebuilding.

Once we're back out in the hallway, Logan turns to me. "What are you going to do?"

In the frenzy of everything that's been going on, I haven't told him yet that I already promised the vul I'd go with them.

"I'm going to Marden," I say. "I had to promise the vul I would go in order to get them to agree to the alliance. I can't go back on my word without breaking their trust. But I want to go, anyway. I'm sick of this place; I want to see what's out there." I take a deep breath. "But if you wanted to stay here, I wouldn't stop you."

Logan shakes his head and laughs.

"Don't laugh," I say. "This is a serious decision. There's no guarantee you'd be able to come back to Kiel for a long time. If you left, you'd likely be stuck on Marden for a while."

"Stuck on an exciting new planet with the girl I'm in love with?"

Logan groans with obvious sarcasm. "You're right. I do need to think this through."

I punch him lightly in the arm, but I can't help smiling. "It won't be all fun and games, you know. We'll have to do hard labor. And there's no guarantee the weather won't turn horrible again and keep all the new crops from growing. And—"

Logan gives me a light peck on the lips to shut me up. "I know. I'm still coming with you."

He's not the only one who decides to come. Ariadne, Dean, Paley, and Sam will join us aboard the fleet, along with all the child workers already on the ships. A couple hundred civilians from Crust, Mantle, and Lower also decide to come, but only fifty Core civilians do. One of them is Dr. Troy, who has been staying close to the vul since their arrival. I'm not completely convinced he's switched over his allegiance from the Developers to us, but the Tessar trusts him, and he's the one who's seen the most of Dr. Troy out of all of us. So I decide not to argue about it.

As I expected, most of the other Core civilians want to stay where they're comfortable, even if this place holds memories of living under the controlling hand of dictators. But there are those who want something different, and they'll have a place on the battle stations.

Mal will stay here on Kiel, along with Darren and Uma. Mal has already been elected as a peoples' representative, so he'll have plenty of work to keep him busy.

Part of me wishes I could stay on Kiel awhile longer and see how it all turns out. But if I stayed, the bad memories from my life here would be impossible to forget. Now that I know there's at least one other world beyond the reaches of Kiel, I have to see it for myself. I'm ready for a new hope.

✳

We leave for Marden on a morning two weeks after the peace treaty is signed. Logan and I are aboard the *Tuliare*, one of the smaller ships in the fleet. We stand on an observation deck, watching the blue-golden planet of Kiel grow smaller through the window. It's still encased in the shimmering acid shield. The shield won't be taken down until the scientists are sure the Surface is free of acid and there's no more threat to the planet.

The vul have assigned rooms to all of us on board. They gave us real beds instead of mossy ones, to help us be more comfortable. Ariadne is just down the hallway from Logan and me, and so is Nellie. She was the only child worker friend of mine who survived the Stryker explosions aboard the battle stations. Grady, Hector, and the others I knew on the Surface and in Crust are all dead.

Sandy was also transferred here from aboard the *Hessana*. It takes me several days to work up the courage to see her. I feel partially responsible for Beechy's death, since he died saving me. And I'm the person who shot her father, Commander Charlie. I know she hated him, but I'm sure part of her loved him. He was her family, after all.

"Come in," she says when I knock on her door.

I hesitate, and move inside the room. She's lying on a simple mattress and pillow like the bed in my room. She's still hooked up to the monitors that keep an eye on her vital signs. Her cheeks have more color in them than they did the last time I saw her. But the redness in her eyes tells me she's been crying.

"How are you feeling?" I ask.

"Good," she says brightly. "You can come closer. I won't bite."

I've been lingering near the doorway. I bite my lip, but walk closer to the side of her bed.

"How far are we from Kiel?" she asks. "They wouldn't let me watch the departure."

"About sixty million miles away now. You can barely pick it out among the stars."

"They said it'll be months before we reach Marden. That means Grace will be born there, as long as she doesn't pop out ahead of schedule. Can you imagine?"

I hadn't even thought about it. I smile. "No, I can't." Silence lingers for several moments. I need to tell her what I came here to say. "Listen, I want you to know how sorry I am about what happened to Beechy."

"Oh, sweetie." Sandy shakes her head. "I don't blame you at all. I know you did everything you could. And I want to thank you for putting an end to my father. You saved a lot of people's lives that day. I'm very grateful, and Beechy would be too."

Her eyes are watering, and so are mine.

Sandy gasps suddenly and places a hand over her belly. "That was a big one."

My brows furrow. "What was?"

"Grace just started kicking. I have a feeling she's gonna be a real fighter. Would you like to feel?"

"Erm . . ."

She grabs my hand anyway and places it on her belly over her shirt. For a moment, I don't feel anything at all. Then the baby's foot thrusts against Sandy's stomach. I gasp loudly.

"Crazy, isn't it?" Sandy says, smiling.

"It is."

Quiet falls between Sandy and me. We're both thinking

about Beechy and how he missed out on this. He's going to miss out on too many things.

I quickly let go of Sandy and stand up. I need to leave before we both start crying. "I'll visit you again soon, okay?"

"You'd better," Sandy says.

The days pass slowly aboard the *Tuliare*.

A week in, one of the julas learns I'm still suffering minor hearing loss in my left ear and offers to do a procedure to repair my eardrum. I'd gotten used to hearing everything muffled, and I can't believe how much clearer things sound after it's over. I wish I weren't going to be confined to a spaceship for the next six months, so I could experience the sounds of nature I miss—wind and rain—again in all their clarity. But it'll be worth it once we reach Marden.

I spend a lot of time with Jehara, learning as much as I can about the place I'll soon call home. We both watch the vul working with the human scientists who came with us, led by Dr. Troy. They study the samples of species they collected from Kiel and try growing them in the soil rooms aboard the battle stations. On occasion, the Tessar emerges from his chamber, where he is slowly healing and recovering his strength under a jula's watch, to oversee the work, smiling at the way we are cooperating together. By the time we reach Marden, we should know which of the species would be likely to thrive.

"Balance will soon be restored," the Tessar assures the vul, and they cry tears of relief and joy.

I defeated Commander Charlie, but he still haunts my dreams many nights. He wraps his fingers around my neck and strangles me. He sticks my body full of needles, pumping my veins with serums I won't be able to escape. He gives me the same cruel smile he always has.

Every time I wake thrashing in my sheets, covered in sweat, Logan is there to comfort me. To kiss me. To remind me we are safe.

It will take time to believe. But I will get there.

# EPILOGUE

## FIVE MONTHS LATER

We first glimpse the planet at 0700 hours.

On the observation deck of the *Tuliare*, Logan and I stand hand in hand before the window with a group of people, including Nellie, Ariadne, and Sam, blinking at the bright yellow Zanda star floating out in the otherwise empty darkness. The tinted windows protect our eyes, so we can stare directly at the light beaming from the star's surface. As our battle station slowly circles the sun, the planet Marden comes into view for the first time.

It's a murky reddish-brown color from far away, but as we move closer I make out the blue-green of the oceans. The world looks even more beautiful than I imagined it. It is a harsh one, and we will face trial and error helping the vegetation to thrive again. But with vul and humans working together, we will save it.

Two moons hang in the sky beyond Marden, both smaller than the moon orbiting Kiel. They are round, one dark gray and the other icy silver. Neither is poisonous, because moons aren't meant to be.

This isn't just a new world, a new place to call home. It's a promise of a life I once believed impossible. A chance to live many more years, and have children of my own that could grow up without fearing kill chambers or an acid sky. If I decide I want children. It's a choice now, not a requirement like in the work camp.

Our lives will evolve into something different here. I don't know what they will be like, but I hope they'll be better.

"It certainly looks promising," Logan says with a wry smile.

I laugh and intertwine my fingers with his. "I guess we'll find out."

"Together?"

"Together."

# ACKNOWLEDGMENTS

Four years ago, the idea for this series fell into my head: two planets and a cast of characters I wasn't sure anyone else would ever care about. Some very special people played a role in the process of these books becoming real, and I owe each and every one of them my gratitude.

Thank you to my wise agent, Alison Fargis, and my brilliant editor, Eileen Rothschild, for rooting for Clementine all the way to the end. Thank you to Kathy Huck for saying "yes" and helping guide *Extraction* into the world.

To the awesome publicity, marketing, and sales crew at St. Martin's, especially to Michelle Cashman and Karen Masnica, thank you for pushing to get these books in front of readers. To James Iacobelli, thank you for designing the incredibly gorgeous covers.

To my parents, thank you for your continued support of my crazy career endeavors. Elisabeth, thank you for reading and loving the series before it was polished. Julianne, thank you for being my bestie and twinsie, and for not hating me for all the times I don't hang out with you because I'm writing.

To Jennifer, you poetic and noble land mermaid, thank you for your constant friendship, for your late-night phone calls, and for talking me through plot twists in books and real life. No matter how far apart we are, you'll always be my favorite Galentine.

To Matthew, thank you for listening to me ramble about made-up characters, for driving me to bookstores, for making me laugh on my worst days, and for pushing me to keep writing when I'm afraid I have nothing interesting to say. You're pretty awesome-sauce, Halpert—and yes, you're usually right.

To the Class of 2k14, Binders, Riley, John, and all my writing buddies, thank you for reminding me I'm not going through this alone.

And finally, to the readers who boarded a ship to Kiel and stuck with Clementine through every battle of her war, thank you. This world in my head comes alive through you. *Saraashi.*